CHAPTER ONE

AS THE CREAKING ceiling fan whooshed rhythmically high above the bed, Reid Holmes tried his hardest to fight its hypnotic affect. He couldn't allow himself to be lulled back to sleep, no matter how much his body craved another two hours in this bed. With a groan, Reid cracked one eye open.

And found himself nose-to-tip with a pert, dusky brown nipple.

He blinked hard and opened his eyes again.

Yup. Still there.

As far as nipples went this was a nice one. Pebbled and standing at attention, looking like a sweet, chocolate Milk Dud. And now he wanted Milk Duds.

His stomach growled.

Ignoring the hunger pangs, Reid focused on the more pressing matter of the morning, trying to recall who the erect nipple belonged to. He drew a blank. As gingerly as possible, he lifted his head from the pillow and scrutinized the face of the woman laying supine on his bed, searching his cloudy memory for a name. *Any* name.

He had nothing. Not one clue.

She shifted, and those perfect breasts thrust higher, his navy blue bed sheets falling even farther down her smooth, light brown skin. Reid did his best to remain quiet as he braced his hands on the mattress and began to lift himself up.

Until he looked over at the alarm clock on his night-stand and noticed the time.

"Shit!" He sprang from the bed.

He'd promise Alex he'd be at the construction site early to receive the shipment of electrical wiring arriving this morning. He should have been out of here by now.

Reid pushed at the sleeping woman's leg.

"Hey...uh." *Fuck! What is her name?* "Uh, ma'am, you need to wake up." He caught her big toe and wiggled it. "Hey!" She turned onto her side and he saw the name Vivian intertwined with a rose tattooed on her arm. "Hey, Vivian, you need to wake up."

She stirred, then she sat up and leisurely stretched her arms above her head, the sheet pooling at her waist.

Damn, she was fine. Too bad he was having such a hard time remembering what they did last night. He recalled snippets, like seeing those fire engine red nails clutching his back in his mirror as he held her up against the dresser and buried himself deep inside her. And he faintly remembered those flawless breasts bouncing as she rode him like a mechanical bull. And he was pretty sure some kind of strawberry-flavored lubricant had made an appearance during the course of the evening.

Hmm. Guess he remembered more about last night than he'd first thought. Just not her name.

She looked up at him, a sleepy smile lifting the corners of her mouth.

Oh, yeah. He definitely remembered that mouth. It had

tasted like strawberry after she'd used some of that oil on a certain part of his anatomy.

"Good morning," she said, lifting her arms in another stretch. She patted the mattress. "Get back in."

Reid shook his head. "Umm, no, sorry. I can't." He glanced at the clock. "Look, I'm really sorry about this, Vivian, but I need to get going. I'm late for work."

Her forehead furrowed with her puzzled frown. "Why are you calling me by my dead grandmother's name?"

Oh, shit.

"I—" Reid started, but how in the hell was he supposed to answer? His fatal mistake was glancing in the vicinity of her tattoo.

She looked at her arm, then back up at him, her eyes spitting fire.

"Seriously!" She threw the sheet to the side and shot up from the bed, planting her hands on her bare hips. "You don't even remember my name, do you, David?"

He'd given her his middle name, which told Reid he hadn't been one hundred percent comfortable with her vibe last night, but not so uncomfortable as to pass up the chance to sleep with her.

"Look, I'm sorry, but, no, I don't remember your name. That doesn't mean I didn't have a good time last night. I did. But I need to get to work, so..." *Shit.* "What's your name again?"

"Fuck you! That's my name!" She slammed her palms against his chest, pushing him out of the way. Then she strode her fine, naked ass into the adjoining bathroom. She was in there for less than two minutes before she walked out, picked her dress and underwear up from the floor, and quickly put them on.

She snatched her cellphone and a tiny purse that was

no bigger than a deck of cards from his dresser and stomped out of his bedroom.

Following her into the living room, Reid said, "I'd really like to know your name." That wasn't entirely true, but it seemed like the right thing to say.

"You're an asshole," she shot back as she rapidly tapped on her phone.

"Yeah, I know," he muttered. He blew out a weary breath. "Do you need a ride home?"

She extended her middle finger in the air as she continued toward the front door.

"What's the address here?" she barked, then stopped at the door and picked up the mail he had on the table right next to the entrance to his apartment. She turned to him. "Who is Reid?"

Damn. This just wasn't his morning.

"You gave me a fake name? God, you really *are* an asshole." She looked down at the mail while typing into her phone—probably to get his address—then looked up at him again. "I would tell you to forget my number but I'm sure you already have." She yanked his front door open. "Don't follow me," she shot at him.

For a half second Reid considered heeding her order, but he'd been enough of a bastard this morning. He followed her outside, making sure he kept a good three feet behind. She seemed like one who wouldn't think twice about taking a swing at him. Not as if he didn't deserve it.

A moment later, a car with a black Uber sticker in the window pulled up to the curb.

"I'm sorry," Reid said. "Can I at least pay for your ride?"

She ignored him and told the woman behind the wheel to drive.

Reid waited until the car turned at the first stop sign

before heading back inside. He closed the front door and thumped his head against it, closing his eyes tight.

This shit was getting old.

There'd been a time in his life when waking up to a random woman in his bed was something he would brag about to his friends, but that time had passed. He didn't want anyone knowing about what had just taken place in this apartment.

"You gotta stop this," Reid whispered as he pushed away from the door.

He'd forgo a shower if he could, but the scent of whatever perfume Vivian's granddaughter had been wearing clung to his skin. If he arrived on the construction site smelling like a field of spring flowers Reid knew he'd never hear the end of it.

He jumped into the shower and was out in less than three minutes. He quickly pulled on his jeans and grabbed a Holmes Construction T-shirt from the dozen folded neatly in his top dresser drawer. It would be nice if he could sit at the kitchen bar and drink a cup of coffee, but enjoying a leisurely cup of coffee before work was reserved for people who didn't send random women storming out of their apartment after treating them like shit.

Reid stuffed his feet into his steel toe boots, slipped his wallet in his back pocket and locked up the apartment. Maybe, if he managed not to hit too many streetlights, he wouldn't be too late.

He hit every single streetlight. Karma.

As he drove along Paris Avenue, Reid made an effort to block out the rough start to his morning. There was nothing he could do about it now, except maybe try to treat the next one better. Or, maybe he could make sure there *wasn't* a next one. Going home with a stranger he met in a bar was something he'd done more often over the past decade than he cared to admit, but now that he was knocking on thirty's door, it was time he grew up.

Reid parked his Chevy crew cab alongside the temporary fencing that cordoned off the Holmes Construction worksite. Two months ago, the charred, hollowed out remnants of an old strip mall stood here. Today, they were preparing to erect the interior walls of the second wing of a new urgent care clinic that was scheduled to open the week before Halloween. Whether or not they hit their target remained to be seen.

Last week, a tropical storm formed in the Gulf of Mexico and quickly made landfall on the Louisiana Coast, halting their work for several days. To make matters worse, half the crew had suffered flood damage. His cousin, Alex, who owned Holmes Construction, gave everyone three days off so they could take care of their homes. He'd provided them supplies at cost and even allowed them to use some of Holmes Construction's heavy duty equipment for free.

It was just one of the reasons why those who worked here at Holmes Construction were so loyal. Alex had earned their loyalty. He *deserved* their loyalty.

He deserves your *loyalty too, asshole.*

He *was* loyal. He'd been loyal to Alex for years. Just because he and his buddy Anthony were considering starting up their own handyman business, that didn't mean Reid was no longer loyal to his cousin. Just because he wanted to see if he had what it took to make it on his own, without having to rely on his family for help, that didn't mean he was ungrateful for everything Alex had done for him over the years.

Reid pushed those thoughts out of his head. Guilt over the way he'd treated Vivian's granddaughter had already staked claim on his psyche today. He didn't have room for his guilt over possibly leaving Holmes Construction.

He entered the gate and went straight to the temporary trailer that served as Alex's office on the site. He caught a whiff of freshly brewed coffee the moment he opened the door and his mouth started to water.

Alex looked up from his desk, then looked pointedly at the clock on the wall.

"I know, I know," Reid said. "I'm sorry I wasn't here for the delivery. Did everything go okay?"

"It's in the back. Lloyd and his crew will start wiring the lobby area this afternoon."

"Good," Reid said. He tipped his head toward the coffee pot. "Can I bum a cup of coffee off you?"

Alex nodded. "You look like you had a rough weekend."

"You can say that," Reid muttered.

"Shepard called out sick this morning too. Said he has a stomach flu. Should I believe him?" his cousin asked.

Reid shrugged. He had no doubt that Myron Shepard was suffering from *something* this morning, but it probably wasn't the stomach flu. More like the hangover to end all hangovers. The guy had kicked back at least six shots last night. They'd been celebrating his engagement, after all. His longtime girlfriend had finally agreed to get married after years of Myron pleading with her. Reid personally didn't consider getting hitched a reason to get shit-faced, but Myron was happier than a pig in slop. Who was he to judge?

One thing he and his friends could probably all agree on this morning was that they should have saved the celebration for their usual Friday night get-togethers, instead of partying on a Sunday night.

"Trust me, you don't want Myron on the site today," Reid said.

"Do I want *you* on the site today?"

"I'm straight." Reid held up his coffee cup. "Once I get a little of this in me, I'll be even better."

Alex shook his head. "It's a good thing you're a damn good plumber."

Some would take those words as a slightly veiled threat, but Reid knew he didn't mean anything by it. The eldest of the six Holmes boys, Alex had hired Reid to work for him straight out of high school, back when they mainly took on residential jobs and when Reid didn't know jack shit about anything other than running his mouth. These days, Holmes Construction was strictly commercial, contracting for both the state and private companies. It had taken Alex just over a dozen years to build his business into one of the only black owned construction companies in the south, with Reid as one of his senior plumbers.

Of course, he still ran his mouth more than he should, but at least he had the skills to back up his talk.

"Don't worry about Myron," Reid said. "I'll make sure he puts in the extra hours to make up for today."

Alex waved that off. "We're behind, but not by that much. You know I always pad the schedule, especially for jobs we take on during hurricane season." Alex tipped his head toward the door. "But I can't spare too much more wasted time, so get your ass out there."

Reid chuckled. "Alright, man. I'm outta here."

"Oh, one more thing," Alex called. "The new site coordinator starts today. She'll be here at ten. I want you to show her around this week, help her learn the ropes."

Reid halted in the middle of turning the knob, his brightening mood instantly turning dark again.

When the previous site coordinator left a few weeks ago, Reid had practically guaranteed the job to Donte Fischer. Donte deserved that job. He'd been with Holmes Construction long enough and had proven himself.

Going outside the company to find someone to fill the vacated position had been a shitty move on Alex's part. It also made Reid look like an ass who didn't have the kind of pull with the boss that everyone thought he did.

What was even shittier? Alex now expected Reid to hold this new person's hand when his cousin knew damn well how Reid felt about the situation.

But apparently his feelings didn't matter. Alex was the boss. It was his call.

He knew it was useless, but Reid decided to make one last argument on Donte's behalf anyway. Folding his arms across his chest, he walked back to Alex's desk.

"You want to explain to me again why you think someone who doesn't even work here would be better for this job than Donte?" Reid asked.

Alex took off the reading glasses he'd started wearing a few months ago and looked up at Reid. "No, I don't want to explain it," he answered.

"He knows the system and the workers," Reid argued. "He's stepped in more than once when your foreman got sick. And whatever Donte can't do, I'm here to pick up the slack."

Alex sat back in his chair and folded his hands over his stomach. "Can you or Donte handle scheduling for both my guys and the subcontractors? Can you monitor project expenditures so we don't go over budget, and file all the compliance paperwork with OSHA?"

Reid didn't bother responding. They both knew the answer to those questions.

"Well?" Alex asked. "Can either of you do any of that stuff? And keep in mind that these are the things I've had to do on the weekends, when I should be spending time with my family." He picked up the squishy stress ball shaped like a construction helmet and squeezed it once before tossing it on the desk. "Look, Reid, now that we're branching out into multiple areas, it's even more important that I find someone who can work as my surrogate for the times I'm not here."

"So this new person you hired, is she supposed to be the second coming of Alex Holmes or something?"

"Close enough," Alex said. "Brooklyn LeBlanc knows her way around a construction site. She's Warren LeBlanc's daughter."

"From LeBlanc & Sons?" Reid asked. "Why isn't she working for them?"

"Because after forty years in the business, Warren has decided to retire. I don't have to remind you that I got my start with LeBlanc & Sons. Anyone who's ever worked for them is welcome to work for Holmes Construction. In fact, I'm hoping to bring on their head electrician, Eddie Nunez. He's one of the best out there."

"What about the daughter?"

"She's worked as the bookkeeper, site coordinator, HR and everything else outside of the field at LeBlanc & Sons. She'll be a good addition to the team, Reid. Trust me on this. However," Alex said, sitting up from his reclined position and bringing his elbows up on his desk, "now that you've brought this up, it reminds me of something else I wanted to talk to you about."

Reid raised his brow.

"I owe Warren LeBlanc a lot. I doubt Holmes Construction would exist if not for him teaching me in those early years."

"Okay," Reid said, unsure where his cousin was going with this.

"I don't want to bring his daughter here and have something happen to her," Alex said.

"What do you think will happen to her?"

"It's been a while since I've been out in the field, but it hasn't been *that* long," Alex said. "I know what happens out there. And as much as I try to keep this place on the up and up, I also know I can't police everything that goes on. I'd feel better knowing you were watching out for Brooklyn."

"So I'm a babysitter now?" Reid asked incredulously.

"Think of it more as a big brother watching out for his kid sister. You've always been the baby of the family. Now you get to see what it's been like for us older Holmeses all these years."

How he refrained from rolling his eyes, Reid would never know.

"Are we done here?" he asked Alex.

"Do you need me to justify any more of my hiring decisions?"

"Nope." Reid shook his head, and then headed for the door. Alex stopped him just as he reached for the door handle.

"Before you start your work, I need you to do a round for me," Alex said. "The HVAC team is installing the duct work in the front area today. Let me know how it looks."

Reid lifted his fingers to his forehead in a salute before opening the door.

Alex stopped him. Again.

"Hey, Reid," he called.

He turned.

"I thought long and hard about this before giving Brooklyn the job," Alex said. "I know Donte's a good worker, but she's a better fit. I don't want you to think I went into this lightly."

"I know you didn't," Reid said. "You never do."

It wasn't as if Alex owed him an explanation at all. And if anyone else were standing here, they wouldn't have gotten one. But his cousin respected his opinion, and always took what Reid said into consideration. The fact that he'd chosen this new person over Donte told him just how much Alex believed in Brooklyn LeBlanc's abilities.

That didn't mean Reid wanted to babysit her.

He left the trailer and headed for the other side of the worksite so that he could do the cursory walk-around.

When his cousin first hired him, Reid had been the runt of the construction site, lending a hand wherever one was needed. It had been the best on-the-job training he could have asked for. He'd learned everything, from bricklaying to drywalling, but he'd settled on plumbing, because the plumbers made the most money. It was as simple as that.

He was also damn good at his job. And he made a good living at it. In a family with one cousin who was a doctor, an older brother who was a lawyer, and everyone but him with a college degree, it would be easy to feel intimidated. But Reid had no reason to feel anything but pride over what he'd been able to accomplish.

Yet...

In these last few months, he'd started to feel as if something was missing. As if there should be more. He just wasn't sure exactly what that *more* was yet.

He blamed his rapidly approaching thirtieth birthday. For some reason, the milestone had him thinking about his life in ways he never had before.

A thunderous clang rang out from the area where the cement mixer and backhoe stood. He turned to find a bunch of workers trying to lift the machine's front loader bucket out of the cement mixer's cylindrical drum.

What the hell?

Reid took off, heading toward the commotion. He didn't have time to stand around contemplating life. He had work to do.

———

HIS ARMS CROSSED over his chest, Reid stood next to the orange cement mixer, whose drum now sported two six-inch gashes courtesy of the teeth on the backhoe's front loader. He directed his attention to the three men staring at the dripping cement, as if it would give them the answer to the meaning of life.

"What happened?" Reid asked again.

LeVar Daniels, who'd started with Holmes Construction just a few months ago, lifted his shoulders. "I was just trying to roll the cement over there." He pointed to where the masonry crew would be working today. "I didn't realize the backhoe was so close."

"We have safety protocols in place for a reason," Reid reminded the three of them. "Any idea the kind of shit we'd be in if one of you got hurt and OSHA was called out to the site?" He gestured to the globs of cement collecting on the ground. "Get this cleaned up. I'll see about getting a new mixer in here." He looked over at LeVar. "Next time follow the correct procedure for moving heavy equipment from one area to another."

They all just stood there staring at him.

"What're you looking at? Get moving," he barked, and the three quickly got to work cleaning up the mess. Reid turned to find Alex observing him from a few feet away. His cousin lifted a brow.

"We need to get another cement mixer out here asap," Reid said.

Alex held up his phone. "Already on the way." He tipped his head toward where the mishap with the backhoe had just happened. "That was impressive. I thought I'd have to step in, but you handled it pretty well."

Reid shrugged. "I know what a pain in the ass it would be if someone got hurt. I was here for the last major accident, remember?" Reid looked pointedly at Alex's shoulder.

"Yeah, me too." His cousin huffed, rolling said shoulder.

Six years ago, Alex had fallen victim to an on-the-job injury that had required surgery and months of rehabilitation. It had been devastating at the time, but in the end Alex had come out on top. During those months while his body healed, he'd started volunteering in his daughter, Jasmine's, kindergarten class. It was there that he met his wife, Renee, who taught at the school.

It was also during those months while Alex recovered that Reid had stepped up here at Holmes Construction. He'd just completed his apprenticeship and hadn't even earned his plumber's license yet, but that hadn't stopped him from taking command, along with Holmes Construction's longtime head foreman, Jason Deering. Alex had a team of loyal employees who believed in the work they were doing, but they didn't have the same family connection. For Reid, it was personal. This company was his cousin's life work. Its success meant almost as much to him as it did to Alex.

Yet another reason for the inner battle his mind continued to wage over joining Anthony in this new venture. After all these years—after all Alex had done for him—how could he just up and leave Holmes Construction?

But could he see himself staying here forever? Was this really *it* for him?

Reid shut his eyes in an attempt to block out the intruding thoughts that continued to prod at his conscience.

"You okay?" Alex asked. "You don't have whatever flu Myron has, do you?"

"No, I'm good," Reid said. "I didn't have enough beers last night to catch Myron's flu."

Alex grunted. "I knew it," he said. Just then, his cousin's phone blasted Rihanna's latest song.

Reid raised a skeptical brow.

"Jasmine had my phone this weekend," Alex explained. He glanced at the screen, declared he had to go, and headed back for the trailer, giving Reid the chance to finally get started on today's work. He made his way to the area that would eventually house several exam rooms. The plumbing job on this particular worksite was more involved than most, seeing as nearly every room in the urgent care clinic would require access to water.

Not even twenty minutes after he'd settled in to work, Anthony Hernandez sidled up alongside him. Anthony had started as a general laborer at Holmes Construction around the same time Reid had. They'd become quick friends, and other than his brothers and cousins, Reid couldn't think of anyone else he was closer to.

"Hey," Anthony said in a voice that was just loud enough to be heard over the noise around the site. "You talk to your guy yet?"

Reid looked over his shoulder, even though he knew Alex had gone back to the trailer. "Not yet," he answered.

Anthony let out an impatient groan. "What's the hold up? We gotta get going on this, Reid."

"I told you, Jonathan's a busy man. He and my brother just took on a huge case. They're working around the clock."

"I'm sure he'd spare ten minutes to answer a couple of questions," Anthony said. "We've wasted too much time already. If we're going to do this, we need to get the ball rolling before someone else swoops in with this idea."

"I know," he said. "Just...give me a couple of days."

"You said that two weeks ago. Look, Reid—" Anthony started, but stopped when Jarvis Collins, one of the welders, came up to them.

"Hey, have y'all seen the new hire?" Jarvis asked.

Reid and Anthony both shook their heads.

"She's pretty cute. The bossman said he wants to introduce—"

A loud whistle cut off Jarvis's words.

"Gather 'round," called Alex's booming voice.

Before Reid could move, Anthony stopped him, catching him by the forearm. "We need to talk about the project. What are you doing after we clock off?"

Reid considered coming up with an excuse, but he knew he wouldn't be able to dodge Anthony forever.

"I'm free," Reid said. "Let's grab a beer at Pal's."

Anthony nodded and they both started for the front of the worksite where most of the workers had gathered. Alex stood on the short dais made of scaffolding that surrounded the temporary trailer, dwarfing the woman standing next to him.

Reid stopped short.

This is who Alex hired to be his surrogate on the job site?

The woman, who couldn't be more than a few years out

of high school, barely reached Alex's shoulder. She stood with her hands in the back pockets of her worn blue jeans. He recognized the symbol on her T-shirt to be that of the Green Lantern, only because his nephew, Athens, was really into DC Comics these days and roped Reid into watching the movie a few weeks ago.

The Green Lantern's signature emblem stretched across what Reid had to admit was a fine set of breasts, possibly even nicer than the set he'd woken up to this morning. She wore her mess of thick, curly hair in an untamed style. A tiny streak of green that perfectly matched her shirt ran through it.

Okay, so Jarvis wasn't lying, she *was* pretty cute. She was more than just pretty cute. Those high cheekbones and full lips teetered along the edge of gorgeous territory. And as his perusal shifted downward, Reid couldn't deny that the combination of a slim waist and curvy hips were having a definite affect on him.

But having a cute face and a fine ass meant nothing when it came to the site coordinator position at Holmes Construction. From where he stood, this girl looked *way* too young to handle the job she'd been hired for. And she was tiny. Reid doubted she reached five feet. What was Alex thinking, bringing in this little pixie to work on a construction site?

"I won't keep you long," Alex started. "But I want everyone to meet Holmes Construction's new site coordinator, Brooklyn LeBlanc. Although she's filling the position Claude Morris vacated, Brooklyn's duties will be slightly different from what Claude did."

The moment Alex began his explanation of what their newest employee's role would be, Reid's phone trilled with a text message. It was from his sister, Indina.

Working late. Will have 2 push mtg 4 the party 2 Thurs.

Reid frowned. He had no idea what Indina was talking about. No one had mentioned anything about a meeting to him.

He replied to Indina's text: *???*

Almost immediately Indina replied: *sorry wrong group text*

Wrong group text? What the hell?

Reid tapped on his screen. *WTF? Y'all got a secret group text I'm not included in? And what meeting?*

Me, H, and E are taking care of it. Don't worry about it.

Like hell, Reid texted back. *Is this for Mama's foundation? Y'all planning the kickoff party without me?*

FCOL, don't be so dramatic! Gotta go.

Where's the meeting? Reid texted. *Harrison's?*

Yes, Indina replied, followed by the rolling eyes emoji.

I'm coming to the meeting.

Fine. Whatever. Bye.

He typed his own flippant reply, but erased it before hitting SEND. He wasn't about to get into a texting war with Indina. Instead, Reid stuffed the phone in his pocket and tried his best to curb his irritation. He was damn tired of being left out of the loop by his older siblings, especially when it came to his mom's foundation.

He, his brothers, Harrison and Ezra, and his sister, Indina, had come up with the idea to start the foundation in their mother's honor after losing her to heart disease earlier this year. As usual, the two oldest had taken the lead, which is how things usually operated in his family. But both Harrison and Indina had agreed to include Ezra and Reid in all aspects of the foundation.

Last week it had been apparent to Reid that his older siblings were just paying him lip service after they'd shot down an idea he'd suggested regarding the scholarship they planned to offer through the foundation. Not even twenty minutes after Harrison disregarded the idea Reid had put forth, Ezra was lauded for suggesting the same thing. It was in that moment that Reid realized no one in his family took him seriously.

The fault didn't lie entirely with his siblings. Over the years, Reid had been more than happy to play the role of the charming slacker who shrugged off responsibility. But he didn't want to be that guy anymore. He wanted his family's respect, especially when it came to this foundation. This would be his mother's legacy. Even if his ideas *were* shot down, Reid at least wanted them to be heard.

He would be at Harrison's for their secret meeting on Thursday. He would not allow them to cut him out.

Reid returned his attention to the dais, where Alex was still speaking to the workers.

"We're breaking ground on the new library annex this week, so I'll be back and forth between this site and the one on the Westbank," Alex continued. "Brooklyn will handle everything, from scheduling to inventory, so if you're running late, you call her. And if we're running low on something, get word to her as soon as possible so she can put in an order. Let her know if you have any questions or concerns. She's basically me when I'm not here. Except she has a better personality," Alex said, tacking on a rare dose of humor.

"And a better ass," someone called out.

A second asshole, just over Reid's shoulder, let out a loud whistle.

Alex's face turned to stone. He leaned over and said something to Brooklyn, who had visibly stiffened at the whistle. She nodded at whatever Alex had just said, gave a slight wave to the crowd, then went into the trailer.

When his cousin turned his attention back to the workers assembled before him, Reid knew what followed would not be pretty.

CHAPTER TWO

BROOKLYN LEBLANC STOOD JUST inside the door of the trailer that, as of today, served as her new place of employment. She eased closer, straining to hear Alexander Holmes's deep voice as he chewed out whichever poor soul had made the mistake of commenting about her nice ass after he'd introduced her as the company's new site coordinator. Of course, she *did* have a nice ass, but the workplace was not the appropriate venue for anyone to comment on said niceness, especially someone who didn't even know her.

Relief and admiration mingled within Brooklyn's chest as Alex continued his tirade, reminding his workers that Holmes Construction did not tolerate harassment of any kind. She immediately felt safer. She was sure the handful of women she'd noticed out there in hardhats also felt reassured, hearing those words from their boss.

Given that she'd worked on construction sites since the age of fifteen, one would expect having lewd comments tossed her way was a common occurrence. One would be wrong. Brooklyn had been afforded the added protection of being the boss's daughter at her previous job. She couldn't think of a single worker who would have dared get caught commenting on any part of her anatomy on a LeBlanc & Sons site. Not having that security shield had been just one of the unsettling realizations she'd faced once she'd finally accepted that she would have to find work outside of the family business.

Brooklyn allowed herself a moment to pretend she was back in the little corrugated trailer that her dad hitched to the back of his quad cab and drove around to different work-sites. It was a shanty compared to the structure she currently stood in, but that didn't matter. She'd loved that rickety old trailer. She would sell her soul and her pristine copy of *Justice League Apokolips Now* to be sitting within the familiar confines of its warped paneled walls.

Okay, maybe just her soul. Selling one of her most prized comics would just be stupid. But there was not much Brooklyn wouldn't give to have her family's business operational again.

Stop it.

She would *not* allow herself to get caught up in nostalgia. LeBlanc & Sons Construction no longer existed. It was an achingly difficult fact to face, but one she needed to come to terms with. Instead of waxing nostalgic, she should be thanking God or kismet or whatever force had brought Alexander Holmes to the granite yard the same day Leroy "Smitty" Keller, who'd worked as a bricklayer for LeBlanc & Sons for years, had been there.

Smitty, who'd decided to retire right along with her dad, had told Alex about LeBlanc & Sons having to close up shop, and explained what Brooklyn's role had been for her family's company. A few days later, she'd received a call from Alex, asking if she would consider joining the team at

Holmes Construction. Brooklyn had accepted the job offer without hesitation, because when it came to earning a living, this was pretty much all she knew.

No matter how much she wished that wasn't the case.

Aaaaannd she would stop that kind of thinking too. She was good at her job. No, she was freaking *amazing* at her job. She'd been told time and again that LeBlanc & Sons would not have survived as long as it had had she not taken over the managerial side of things once her grandma—LeBlanc & Sons original Jane-of-all-trades—retired. Her entire family had sacrificed for the sake of that business. And they'd instilled a work ethic in her that Brooklyn held steadfast to.

She could hear her dad's voice in her head right now.

Find what you're good at and give one hundred and ten percent.

She lived her life by that motto.

As for what she would be doing if she wasn't such an ace at managing construction jobs? Well, that's what hobbies were for. The world was filled with people who'd had to choose between what they *wanted* to do and what they *should* do.

Her one foolish attempt to reject her role—to prove she wasn't as good at working for LeBlanc & Sons as everyone lauded her to be—had ended in disaster. And it had cost her family everything.

Alex Holmes didn't know it, but he'd given her a chance to make things right. With this job, she could help her parents get out of the debt she'd inadvertently plunged them into, and make up for all the hardship her stupid mistake had cost them. And that's why Holmes Construction would get 110% out of her.

What she wanted didn't matter. She would give everything to the job that paid the bills.

Brooklyn heard footsteps coming toward her and quickly scampered to the desk closest to the door. She perched her backside against it, picked up a random sheet of paper and pretended she'd been reading it all this time. She realized she'd picked up a grocery list and quickly tossed it back on the desk. She would rather get caught eavesdropping than reading her new boss's personal shopping list.

A second later, Alex entered the trailer. Accompanying him was a guy who, astonishingly, stood an inch or two taller than Alex, and whose shoulders were as broad as any Brooklyn had ever seen. And that was saying a lot, given how many broad shoulders she'd encountered on construction sites over the years.

They walked over to her and Alex made the introductions.

"Brooklyn, this is Reid Holmes." Her brows lifted upon hearing the last name, and Alex answered her unvoiced question with a nod. "Reid and I are first cousins."

He was much younger than Alex, probably only a couple of years older than her own twenty-six years. Of course, she still got carded whenever she tried to buy wine coolers, so she knew better than most that looks could be deceiving when it came to telling one's age.

His rich, dark skin glistened with perspiration courtesy of the summer heat, reminding Brooklyn to thank the good Lord that she was lucky enough to work in an air-conditioned trailer. The temperatures had been brutal this year, and that stifling heat didn't seem to be letting up anytime soon.

Reid removed his work glove and stuck his hand out to

her. "Nice to meet you," he said, though his unenthused tone belied his words.

"You too," Brooklyn said. His hand was rough and calloused, despite his use of gloves. Not surprising. Rough hands went with construction sites the way red beans went with rice.

"Reid is one of HCC's senior plumbers," Alex continued. "He's also the person I trust the most when it comes to keeping me informed about what's going on around the worksite."

Brooklyn nodded. Having worked in a small family business all her life, she understood those dynamics.

"If you need anything and I'm not around, Reid here is who you should call. He's going to help you get acquainted with how we operate around here. I thought it best you have someone show you the ropes, particularly this first week on the job," Alex finished.

Brooklyn was pretty sure if she Googled "apathetic" right now, Reid Holmes's face would pop up. He wasn't just apathetic; the stony set to his jaw suggested that he was downright averse to the thought of showing her around.

What the heck? She'd just started this job an hour ago. How had she managed to offend him already?

Alex's phone chirped. "Dammit," he said as he read the text message.

"What's wrong?" Reid asked.

"I need to get down to the job in the Quarter. I told Jason I'd be there later this morning, but later this morning came quicker than I thought it would."

"Weren't they supposed to finish the building on Royal Street yesterday?" Reid asked. "What happened?"

"The crew found a bunch of faulty wiring when they went into the walls."

As he and Alex talked about the renovations a small Holmes Construction crew was working on at an antiques store in the French Quarter, Brooklyn took the time to study Reid.

He was hot. No use denying that. It was his cheekbones, she decided. They were pronounced without being *too* pronounced. A sharply trimmed goatee covered the bottom half of his face, but it was those warm brown eyes the color of the whiskey her Grandpa Joseph used to drink that commanded the most attention.

Yep, Reid Holmes was hot. If a bit standoffish.

As surreptitiously as possible, she allowed her eyes to travel from his firm jaw downward. Even if she'd randomly encountered him on the street, Brooklyn would have known he was a construction worker. She'd been around worksites long enough to tell the difference between muscles honed from hours of heavy labor and those that came from working on a machine at a gym. He stood with his legs spread apart, which caused his jeans to stretch taut across his solid thighs and tapered hips. The well-worn cotton of his Holmes Construction T-shirt molded to his sculpted shoulders and chest.

And just like that, Brooklyn felt a crush coming on.

Well, shit.

This was so not the time for an instacrush. Why on earth would her brain go there now, and with a guy who apparently didn't like her even though they'd only met a few minutes ago? Maybe she should tell the butterflies in her stomach to chill until she'd had the chance to peek at some of the other guys on the worksite. Crushing on Mr. I'd Rather Be Anywhere But In This Trailer wasn't the wisest course of action.

Then again, maybe he *was* the smartest crush. This

way, she wouldn't be tempted to treat it as more than just a harmless little infatuation.

Brooklyn held no illusions when it came to the Reid Holmeses of the world. Guys like him didn't go for girls like her. That wasn't to say there was anything wrong with her. She was cute. She was *damn* cute.

Okay, fine. She was kinda cute.

Being kinda cute had always served her well. Someone had just commented on her ass not even twenty minutes ago, for crying out loud! She wasn't starving for attention from the opposite sex.

But she was also a realist. Certain people fit with certain people. And people like Reid, who with a crook of his finger could easily have a dozen salivating women at his side, tended to go for the tall, cover model divas of the world. Not petite and curvy comic book nerds.

And that was just fine with her. She knew her lane and she stayed firmly within the lines. Reid Holmes was *not* in her lane.

That's why she would welcome this admittedly swiftly-formed crush. He'd give her something nice to look at while at the job. There was absolutely nothing wrong with that.

"So, are we good here?" Alex asked. "I need to get going."

Brooklyn nodded and looked at Reid. "We're good," she said.

He hitched a shoulder. "Yeah, I guess."

"Reid, why don't you take Brooklyn on a tour of the worksite so she can get a feel for the place," Alex suggested.

She noted the reluctance in the way Reid's mouth pulled tight at the edges.

"Actually," Brooklyn said. "If it's all the same, I'd rather spend today getting used to my workspace here in the trailer. I also need to familiarize myself with the scheduling system Holmes Construction uses. It's a lot more involved than what I'm used to."

"Right, right," Alex said. "That's good. Why don't you two meet here in the morning? You can take her on your initial morning rounds," he said to Reid. "And try to be on time tomorrow."

The crease in Reid's forehead deepened. "You know this morning wasn't typical," he said.

"Yeah, I know. Just thought I'd remind you," Alex said as he rolled up several 24x36 CAD drawings and stuffed them into cylindrical containers. "I'm going straight to the Westbank worksite in the morning. I should get here in the early afternoon." He turned to Brooklyn. "If you need something, go to him," he said, tipping his head toward Reid. "If he can't help you, you have my number."

"I'll be fine," Brooklyn reassured him.

Alex's eyes crinkled at the corners. "I have to remind myself that you've been working on construction sites longer than half the guys out there in the field."

His warm smile broadened and Brooklyn felt another crush coming on. It didn't matter that Alex was probably old enough to be her dad. He had his own brand of hotness going on.

A few minutes later, both men left the trailer and Brooklyn set about familiarizing herself with her surroundings. This would be her home for a large portion of the day. She needed to feel comfortable. After adjusting the temperature to something other than frozen tundra, she spent the rest of the afternoon watching every YouTube tutorial she could find on the scheduling system Holmes Construction employed. It would take some getting used to, but she felt confident she'd have this conquered by the end of the week, possibly sooner.

She considered moving on to the inventory system, but her brain revolted at the mere thought. Rome wasn't built in a day; her knowledge of how things worked at Holmes Construction wouldn't be either.

Just as Brooklyn powered down her computer for the night, the trailer door opened and Reid walked in. He removed his hardhat and her soul released a satisfied sigh.

Goodness, but he was nice to look at.

He frowned when he spotted her behind the desk. Apparently, she wasn't so nice to look at.

"I thought I was running late," he said. He walked over to Alex's desk, which was separated from hers by about seven feet. "Why aren't you packed up and ready to leave? Didn't Alex mention that the workday ends at five around here?"

"He did, but I'm not used to working by the clock," Brooklyn answered. "At LeBlanc & Sons, daylight is what dictated whether or not we left the jobsite."

"Yeah, well, Alex is usually pretty strict about sticking to an eight-hour workday. He's big on the work/life balance thing—at least for his workers. We only work overtime when we absolutely have to."

Oh, look. He could speak to her without frowning. Who knew?

"So what are *you* still doing here when it's..." She pointed to the time on her computer screen. "Five-eighteen?"

The barest grin tipped up one corner of his mouth. It made him even *more* gorgeous, because, of course.

"I'm one of the exceptions to the rule," he answered, that hint of a smile lingering.

God, she wished he would go back to frowning. She was smitten enough as it was.

He tossed his work gloves onto Alex's desk, then turned and started for hers. His relaxed gait summoned thoughts of every movie Brooklyn had ever watched where the hunky hero strolled with a confident, sexy swagger. If she were writing this particular movie, he would come around her desk, brace his hands on either side of her chair, lean down and whisper inappropriate things in her ear.

He stopped a couple of feet from her desk and asked, "So are you ready for me to walk you to your car?"

That wasn't the line she would have written.

"Why would I need you to do that?" Brooklyn asked. But then she answered her own question. "Alex told you to, didn't he?"

Reid put his hands up. "I'm just doing what the boss asked me to do."

Great. That's exactly how she wanted her crush to view her, as someone in need of a babysitter.

Brooklyn sighed. A big, deep, dramatic sigh. "I know Alex promised my dad that he would look out for me, which apparently means that *you* have to look out for me when Alex isn't here, but it isn't necessary. I've been around construction sites my entire life. I know how to take care of myself."

"If you think that matters to Alex, you don't know who you're dealing with. He's got it in his head that you need a bodyguard." He lifted one of those broad shoulders in an insouciant shrug. "I'm just doing my job."

In her movie, she would happily pay for Reid Holmes to willingly guard her body? *Willingly* being the keyword. If he had even *tried* to hide just how much he didn't want to do this, Brooklyn could have pretended that he was onboard with playing the role of protector. But she'd seen the expression on his face earlier when Alex had first introduced them. This was about following the boss's orders, and nothing more.

For some reason Reid didn't want her here. And her pride was just a little too stubborn to allow her to accept any kind of help from him.

"You may feel obligated to watch over me because Alex asked you to do it, but I'm letting you off the hook," Brooklyn said. She locked the top drawer on her desk, where she'd stored the backup flash drives holding the personnel files, and stood. Drawing the strap of her battered Comic Con San Diego canvas bag over her shoulder, she said, "I'm a big girl, despite being vertically challenged. I can take care of myself."

He looked on the verge of refuting her statement, but then Reid held his hands up in surrender. "It's your call. Just know that Alex won't like it."

"He seems like a reasonable guy. He'll get over it," Brooklyn said.

Reid's sharp crack of laughter reverberated around the trailer. "Now I know for sure that you have no idea who you're dealing with when it comes to your new boss."

"I guess I'll find out soon enough," Brooklyn said with her own nonchalant shrug. She headed for the door, but turned when she noticed Reid following her. "What are you doing?"

"Going home," he said. The *duh* was silent. He gestured for her to keep walking. "Go on. I'll lock up the trailer."

Brooklyn exited the trailer and continued down the steps and through the gate of the chain-link fence that surrounded the worksite. She'd walked only a couple of yards along the sidewalk before Reid appeared at her side. She glanced over at him.

"Still going home?" she asked.

He nodded.

Brooklyn pointed toward her car, which was parked underneath a large oak tree in the next block. "I'm pretty sure you're not driving that bright yellow Volkswagen Hatchback," she said. She hooked her thumb over her shoulder. "That Silverado back there looks more your speed."

A grin tipped up the corner of his mouth, but he didn't say anything, just continued walking.

"So?" Brooklyn prompted.

"So what?" he asked as they reached her car.

"I told you I didn't need you playing bodyguard?"

He shrugged again. "Doesn't matter. Alex wants me to look out for you."

"But you said it was my call."

"I lied." He reached over, took her keys from her hand, unlocked the car door and opened it. "I'll see you in the morning." Then he tossed the keys to her and pivoted, heading back in the direction of his truck.

Brooklyn slid behind the wheel and slumped in her seat. She didn't know what to make of the last ten minutes. This movie was one she hadn't seen before.

———

AN ARGUMENT over a call in the baseball game currently playing on the flat screen above the dozens of liquor bottles that lined the bar's mirrored wall greeted Reid as he entered the doors to Pal's Lounge. He spotted Anthony sitting at the far end of the scarred wooden bar, raising a longneck to his lips.

"Hey," Reid said. "Sorry I'm late. I had to make sure the new site coordinator got to her car safely."

"Uh-oh. The bossman tapped you to play babysitter, huh?"

Reid let out a derisive snort as he straddled the stool next to Anthony's and signaled for the bartender. "Alex claims I'm not her babysitter, but how many other workers do I have to escort to their car at the end of the day?"

Of course, Brooklyn LeBlanc had insisted she didn't need him to walk her to her car, but if something did happened to her Reid knew he wouldn't be able to handle the guilt. Not that he expected any of Holmes Construction's workers to physically attack her or anything, but he'd seen them catcall a woman walking down the street a time or two. He would make sure they all knew that shit would not fly where Brooklyn was concerned. Hell, they shouldn't do it at all. He would demand that women be treated with the utmost respect by everyone working for Holmes Construction. Period.

Says the guy who woke up to a strange nipple damn near poking him in the eye.

Maybe he should take his own advice before he started dishing it out to others.

The bartender came by and Reid ordered a Coke with extra ice.

"Coke?" Anthony looked at him as if he'd lost his mind.

Reid put both hands up. "All that drinking last night got me in enough trouble. I'm not looking for a repeat."

"Trouble, huh? With the way you strolled out of The Hard Court with that honey draped all over you, I would have thought you'd be okay with how last night turned out."

"The problem wasn't with last night. It was this morning when I woke up and had no idea who was in my bed with me." Reid shook his head. "I couldn't even remember her name until after lunch. And I'm still not sure if I'm right."

Anthony belly-laughed. Reid didn't find anything particularly funny about the situation.

"You done?" he deadpanned when his friend finally stopped laughing.

"Wait a minute," Anthony said, and started laughing again. Reid was just about to get up and leave when his friend finally got control of himself. Asshole.

"I'm sorry, man," he said, wiping tears of mirth from his eyes. "I'm just glad I don't have to worry about stuff like that anymore. I may have to pick up some flowers for Ciara on the way home, just to show her how much I appreciate that I no longer have to play those games."

The effort it took not to begrudge his friend's relationship became more arduous with every mention Anthony made of how sweet life was with his long-time girlfriend. At one time, just the thought of settling down with a single woman made Reid break out in hives. He wasn't as allergic to the idea as he once was. Between Myron's recent engagement and constant reminders of Anthony's relationship, the string of random hook-ups Reid had engaged in over the past few months seemed downright pathetic. Maybe it was time he thought about settling down.

Settling down?

What in the hell was he thinking? A relationship of any kind was the last thing he needed right now. Didn't the debacle that took place in his apartment prove that?

Desperate to redirect his thoughts away from their current path, Reid shifted on the stool and asked, "So, what's up? Why'd you want to meet?"

"You know what's up," Anthony said, all traces of

amusement vanishing. "Why haven't you talked to the lawyer guy?"

The group watching the baseball game erupted in cheers. Reid started to speak once the hoopla died down, but Anthony spoke up first.

"It's been nearly two months since you promised to talk to your brother's law partner about this, Reid."

"I know," he said. "And I will."

"When?" Anthony asked, his tone sharp. He shook his head. "Look, man, you're either serious about going into business together or you're not."

"I told you I'm—"

"Because I'm serious as hell about it," Anthony said, cutting him off. "I've already invested more than twenty grand into having this app developed and will have to finance at least another forty. I'm ready to pull the trigger. You need to decide if you're in or not."

"I know," Reid said. "It's just..."

He threw his head back and released a frustrated breath.

How could he explain to his friend what was holding him back when Reid wasn't completely sure how to explain it to himself? He and Anthony had talked on and off over the years about starting their own construction company, but it had always seemed like a pipe dream. How could two knuckleheads who didn't know shit-all about running a business go into business for themselves?

But about six months ago, Anthony came up with an idea that had lit a fire under his ass unlike any Reid had ever seen. With the help of his techie cousin, his friend developed the concept for a phone app that would allow customers to get help for their small home improvement projects through their phones and computers. According to

Anthony, his design went further than similar apps that were currently on the market because it would allow people to video chat directly with a professional. And it was geared toward specific locales, so that if a customer found themselves in over their head, he or she could request emergency, in-person help with the swipe of a finger.

Reid still wasn't one hundred percent clear on how it would all work, but he liked what he'd heard about it so far. What he didn't like was the thought of leaving Holmes Construction.

It's not as if this new venture Anthony was working on would be competition for Alex's company. The app-based business would cater to residential customers. HCC was now strictly commercial construction.

Yet, the thought of leaving Holmes Construction still made Reid nauseous.

He owed his cousin a lot. Growing up in his brainiac-heavy family hadn't always been easy. Reid had known by the tenth grade that he didn't want to step foot on anyone's college campus. At the time he figured he just wasn't cut out for it. It wasn't until years later, when he'd run across an article on learning disorders, that the pieces to the convoluted puzzle that was his brain began to fall into place. By the time he figured out just why he'd always had such a hard time in school, he'd already settled in at Holmes Construction.

At the time, Alex had been the only other member of the Holmes clan who hadn't gone to college—though he did eventually earn his degree through night school. Alex had seen something in him, recognizing that Reid wasn't college material, and had taken him under his wing. It felt like the height of disloyalty to just up and leave his cousin now, especially when Alex was on the brink of expanding HCC into a multi-regional operation.

But it was more than just loyalty to Alex that had him hesitating.

Working at Holmes Construction was akin to working with a built-in safety net. Alex had cut him more slack than he should have, especially during those early years. Any other boss would have fired Reid's ass over a dozen times for some of the stuff he'd pulled.

What if he wasn't ready to make this kind of move? Owning a business was serious shit. He'd grown a lot in the last few years, but was he *this* grown?

Yet, Reid knew he couldn't go on feeling the way he'd been feeling lately. This sense of being in a rut, like a hamster on a wheel, spinning his legs but not going anywhere, had been steadily building over the past six months.

He figured it was his fast-approaching thirtieth birthday. That impending milestone was having a bigger effect on him than he'd ever thought it would.

Reid had just picked up his drink when Anthony said, "Look, I've been talking to a couple of buddies I went to trade school with. They both work in Baton Rouge, but they're willing to move to New Orleans. If you don't want to do this..."

Reid set the glass down without taking a sip. His jaw literally dropped as he stared at his friend. "You trying to shut me out?"

"No!" Anthony was quick with his reply, but then he shrugged, his expression earnest. "It's like I said, I'm serious about this. You're the one I want to go into business with, Reid. We've talked about building something of our own for a long time, but you have to either shit or get off the pot. I can't sit around waiting for you to make up your mind."

A mixture of panic and anxiety twisted within Reid's chest. He'd never thought in a million years that Anthony would seek out others to take his place. But, hell, could he blame the guy? Anthony had emptied his savings in order to invest in this company, and so far the only thing he'd asked of Reid was to solicit some legal advice from his brother's law partner.

He was damn lucky Anthony had put up with his shit for this long. If the shoe were on the other foot, Reid doubted he would have tolerated this waffling back and forth. It was time he stepped up and made a decision.

"I'm in," Reid said. "One hundred percent."

The skepticism he saw lurking in his friend's eyes hit Reid like a gut punch. Anthony didn't believe him.

"I'm serious." He pulled out his phone and logged into his banking app. "What's your email again?"

"Why?"

"Just give me your email," Reid said.

Anthony rattled off his email address. Reid typed it into the app and hit submit on the money transfer.

"There you go," he said. "I just sent you five thousand to put toward development."

Anthony's eyes bucked. "You serious?" He flipped his phone over on the bar and tapped at the screen.

"It's in there," Reid said. "Now, tell me again exactly what I'm supposed to ask Jonathan?"

"I'll pretend I haven't told you this a million times already," Anthony said as he set the phone back on the bar. "We need to know what kind of legal protections we'll need, against lawsuits and things like that. I've done some research online, but I won't feel okay with it until we've gotten some real talk from someone who knows the law. In the meantime, Gabriela and I will continue developing the app. What she's done so far is pretty barebones, but these things take time, and she works a full-time job. She's working on the app in her spare time."

"Is it possible for her to take an extended vacation?" Reid asked. "Maybe, if she can take a solid two weeks off, we can pay her whatever she would be making at her day job and she can just put everything she has into getting it done."

"She runs the IT department for one of the largest employers in the city. We can't afford to pay two weeks of her salary," Anthony said. "But I'll ask her." He held up his phone. "This five grand will help."

"I'll give you more as soon as I can. But I want to hold on to some to help with the startup cost for my mom's foundation."

Anthony waved that off. "This is good for now. It's the knowledge from people like your brother and Jonathan that's worth more than cash. That's what I need you to focus on."

"I'm going to get in touch with Jonathan this week. I'm not bullshitting around this time," Reid said. He slipped off the barstool. "I need to get going. Alex needs me to fill in for him in the morning, and after being late today I damn sure don't want to be late tomorrow."

"I hear you," Anthony said. "I need to get going myself. I promised Ciara I'd bring dinner. I'm thinking burgers."

They exchanged a half-handshake/half-hug before exiting the bar. Anthony clamped a palm on Reid's shoulder as they strolled down the sidewalk toward their vehicles.

"Hey, be careful when you get to your apartment. Last

time I forgot a chick's name after sex, she was waiting for me with a knife." He shook his head. "Forget the burgers, I'm bringing home steaks tonight. My baby deserves it for rescuing me from that lifestyle."

"Whatever," Reid said with a laugh.

As he slid behind the wheel of his pickup, he tried to convince himself that Anthony's warning held no water. Monique—at least he thought her name was Monique—may have been pissed, but she didn't seem like the stalker type. Then again, how the hell would he know? He wasn't sure he even knew her name.

For a second, Reid considered driving over to Ezra's and crashing on his brother's couch, but he quickly tossed that idea aside. He wasn't sleeping on anyone's couch when he had a nice bed in a nice apartment where he paid a nice sum of money for rent each month. Besides, Ezra probably wasn't home anyway. His brother spent more time at his girlfriend, Mackenna's, place these days than at his own house.

Reid pulled into one of the parking spots adjacent to his apartment complex and looked around, cursing himself for not being more familiar with the cars his neighbors drove. He didn't spot anything out of the ordinary as he made his way to his apartment and cautiously opened the door, but he didn't release his first full breath until he'd searched the entire apartment and was sure it was free of knife-wielding stalker chicks.

Walking back toward the kitchen, Reid nearly jumped out of his skin at the loud clang that rang out, before realizing it was the A/C unit kicking on.

"Son of a bitch," he cursed, clamping a hand over his chest and collapsing against the wall.

He pulled in several deep breaths in an effort to calm his erratic heartbeat.

"You brought this on yourself," he said. Pushing away from the wall, he went to the fridge, grabbed a bottle of water and then plopped down on his sofa. He pitched his head back and stared up at the ceiling. Disgust twisted in his gut.

Just like that, he'd reached a breaking point. He would not put himself in this position again, too afraid to walk into his own damn home because he didn't know if the woman he'd brought in here the night before was stable or some crazed stalker waiting to attack him. No sex—no matter how good—was worth this.

Reid released a bitter laugh as he took a pull on his water bottle.

How was it that he'd painted himself to be the victim in all of this? He was the one who couldn't even remember the girl's name, and he had the gall to question if she was unstable? He couldn't imagine what Monica, or Monique, or whatever Vivian's granddaughter was feeling right now. She was probably telling all her girlfriends about the asshole who couldn't be bothered to learn her name.

Yeah, he'd reached a breaking point. He refused to be that guy again. He couldn't.

The next time Reid brought a woman into his bed, he would make sure he knew way more than just her name.

CHAPTER THREE

BROOKLYN REACHED FOR HER CELLPHONE, preparing to open her Pandora app, but then remembered she only had one more skip this hour. It would be just her luck that Nickelback would come up next and she'd have to suffer through Chad Kroeger's straining voice for four minutes. She decided it would be better to endure one of her least favorite Green Day songs.

A minute later, she nearly choked on the water she'd just sipped when Nickelback's "Photograph" came through the phone's speaker. Brooklyn quickly switched to her Stevie Wonder station. She'd listened to enough alternative rock for today anyway.

Using a set of Command Strips from the stash she'd found in what she'd discerned was the supplies drawer—based on the hodgepodge of ink pens, carpenter pencils, tape and other office supplies crowding it—Brooklyn tacked the small cork board she'd brought from home to the wall. Just a few feet from the cork board hung a series of white boards she'd found mounted to the wall when she came in this morning, courtesy of her new boss. She'd mentioned that she preferred white boards to help keep track of timelines, but never imagined that Alex had actually paid attention to such a tiny detail.

When it came to bosses, Brooklyn knew she'd hit another goldmine. She could already tell that Alex would go out of his way to make her work life as easy as possible. The only thing that could make a boss better was if he were her own flesh and blood, and she'd been lucky enough to have that for eleven years.

The trailer's door opened and Alex walked in carrying a flat, rectangular box.

"Good morning," he greeted. He set the box on her desk. "I brought doughnuts. I was supposed to have them for you yesterday, but forgot. A little welcome to the job gift."

Cue heart melting.

"That's so sweet," Brooklyn said as she immediately opened the box. She never said no to a sugar rush. "Wait." She licked glaze from her knuckle and pointed her doughnut at Alex. "What are you doing here? I thought you were going to the site on the Westbank?"

"So did I." His expression was the textbook definition of weariness. "But I have to go to my daughter's school this morning to meet with one of her teachers and the principal."

"Uh-oh. It's never good to be called to the principal's office."

"It's even worse when the principal happens to be your wife." He lifted a jelly doughnut from the box, but then set it back down. "Just my luck, I'd take one bite and get raspberry all over my shirt. It's not worth it."

Brooklyn laughed hard enough to choke on her doughnut. "Here, have a regular glazed. It's safer."

"Thanks." He wrapped the doughnut in a napkin, then lifted a leather-bound planner from his desk. "This is the other reason I'm here. Left this yesterday. I'm trying to transition to an all-electronic system, but can't seem to let this one go."

Brooklyn nudged her head toward her own desk, where her personalized Erin Condren LifePlanner sat. "Right there with you, boss."

She and Alex fist bumped over planner love.

"I'm due at the school in twenty minutes and then I'm going straight to the Westbank site," he said. "If you need anything—"

Brooklyn cut him off with a wave of her hand. "We're good here. I just ran some projections and with the stretch of good weather the meteorologists are predicting for the week, this build should be back on schedule by Friday. Of course, this is New Orleans, so that good weather can turn bad in an instant, but I put on my optimist hat today."

"I hope you have more than one of those hats," Alex said. He looked at his watch. "I gotta get going." He started for the door, but stopped as his eyes arrested on the walls. "Wait a minute," he said. "When did you do all of this?"

"This morning," Brooklyn said. The blank whiteboards he'd attached to the walls were now lined with color-coded timelines.

Brooklyn gave him a quick rundown of her charting system, which she'd implemented years ago, back when LeBlanc & Sons began to expand. Her dad's company wasn't nearly as big as Holmes Construction, but she had no doubt her system would work just fine here.

"It's all computerized as well, of course. But I find having a visual helps everyone stay on track."

"I don't know if we've ever been this organized," Alex said. A smile stretched across his face. "You're going to work out even better than I first thought."

As Alex exited the trailer, Brooklyn felt a familiar warmth course through her at his praise. If she'd managed to impress him already, she couldn't wait to see his face when she *really* settled in and got down to business. She would have this place running with the agile seamlessness of the U.S. Olympic relay track team in the 400-meter dash. Alex Holmes would wonder how he'd ever got along without her.

Brooklyn ignored the sudden pang that shot through her chest. The sensation tended to arise whenever she acknowledged the value she brought to construction sites. She knew she was good at what she did. She'd been at it for eleven years, working part-time throughout high school and college, and full-time since earning her bachelor's degree in construction management. She wasn't just good at it, she was friggin' fantastic at it. And there was no bigger ego stroke than constantly hearing that you're indispensable.

But being indispensable came at a cost.

Being indispensable meant giving everything to a job she had zero passion for.

Her dad always told her that it's better to do one thing really well than to try to do a bunch of other things and just be okay at them. She'd proven time and time again that when it came to this job in particular, she was one of the best out there. But giving 110% to this job meant sacrificing the other thing she held so dear to her heart.

She couldn't ignore the ache this time as she tried to swallow past the lump in her throat.

"Stop your bellyaching and be grateful you have a job," she muttered underneath her breath.

After the way she'd bumbled things with her family's business, she was lucky to find a good paying job doing the one thing that she knew how to do well. It's not as if the construction business was the goldmine it used to be. She'd been given a second chance, one Brooklyn wasn't sure she even deserved. She would not waste it lamenting over something that apparently was never meant to be.

She spent the next hour using colored duct tape to create a checkbox system on one of the white boards, then began the arduous task of hanging up the flowcharts she'd printed this morning on the huge plotter printer. LeBlanc & Sons had never been big enough to justify owning one of the big machines, so whenever she had to print charts or blueprints, she'd have to make a run to the printers. She was going to love having that thing at her disposal.

Brooklyn stood before the wall, the flowcharts in her hands. This would be a lot easier if she possessed another five or so inches. Because she didn't, she climbed up on a chair and, using the fluorescent push pins she'd brought from home, tacked the first of five flowcharts above the row of whiteboards. The up and down on the chair should count as her workout for the day—if she was one to go to a gym, of course.

She'd just finished hanging the last chart when the door to the trailer opened. Brooklyn turned to find Reid striding toward her.

A tiny breath whisked from her lungs.

Great. Just two days in and they were already at the breath-stealing stage. No doubt about it, this crush would be an epic one. Much worse than the one she'd had on Donovan Johnson, the bricklayer who'd worked on and off at LeBlanc & Sons for a couple of years. Donovan was cute and all, but he couldn't hold a candle to Reid.

She couldn't get over the sheer size of him. Brooklyn was used to huge men whose muscles were built buy hard construction labor, but something about Reid Holmes's body took on an almost comic book hero likeness. His biceps were like boulders, yet not so big to look unlifelike. It would be a joy to watch him work. She was already imagining the way those muscles would undulate underneath his sweat-dampened Holmes Construction T-shirt.

"Well, damn," Reid said as he looked around. "You sure made yourself at home." He pointed to the chair she still stood on. "You realize that's a safety violation, right?"

Brooklyn's face heated. Yes, she knew that, but she'd mentally used the excuse that it would only take a minute to tack up the charts to justify not having to look around for a step ladder. It was stupid.

"You're right," Brooklyn said. "I know better. That's the last time you'll see me standing on a chair."

Reid responded with a simple nod. He crossed his arms over his chest and peered at the various charts and white-boards now adorning the once empty walls. He hooked a thumb at the inventory chart.

"What's all this?"

"A site-wide inventory list," she answered. "It's a way for workers to let me know if they need anything. If supplies are running low, I want people to write it down on the chart. I'll check it at the end of the day and make the order."

He nodded and moved to the next chart.

"That one will be used to track the progress of the various jobs," she said.

He looked over at her, one sardonic brow cocked. "The 'Job Progress' written across the top kinda gives it away."

"Oh. Right." Brooklyn glanced down at her feet, wondering if there was anything she could do to magically produce a nice big hole that could swallow her up. When she peered back up at Reid, a slight grin tipped up one corner of his mouth.

Good. Lord.

That little tilt to his lips didn't even amount to a real smile and it was *still* enough to make her heart flutter like a butterfly on crack.

Epic. This crush would be epic!

"Are you ready to make the rounds?" he asked.

She blinked twice and shook her head. She'd been momentarily mesmerized by that hint of a smile. "I'm sorry, what?" she asked.

He released a low chuckle.

Oh, nice. He was laughing at her. Perfect. That's exactly the reaction she was going for.

Of course, if she started laughing then he would be laughing *with* her. But Brooklyn wouldn't categorize this little episode as funny. More like excruciatingly uncomfortable and diving full-speed into mortification territory.

She hated feeling this way. She thought she'd built up enough confidence in herself that she would never feel this way again. Except, apparently, around guys like Reid. Just...ugh.

Enough with the awkward, self-conscious bullshit. He was just a guy. No need to feel weird around him.

"What did you ask?" Brooklyn tried to tamp down the irritation in her voice. It wasn't Reid's fault she had a stupid crush.

Well, actually, it kinda *was* his fault. He could try harder to look like a normal guy and not like some Nubian god in worn jeans and a T-shirt with sweat rings under the arms. Seriously, what normal human being made that look sexy?

"I asked if you were ready to make the rounds," he said. "One of your job responsibilities is to tour the work site twice a day. Alex wants me to join you this first week."

Brooklyn emphatically shook her head. "No. Don't worry about it. I've worked on enough construction sites to be able to find my way around."

"You haven't worked on a Holmes Construction site." He tipped his head toward the door. "And I already told you, what you want doesn't really matter here. Alex left instructions. He's the boss."

He pulled a hardhat off the peg on the wall and handed it to her, but Brooklyn had already grabbed the purple one with the Iron Man stickers that she'd been wearing since Robert Downy Jr. won her heart in the first Avengers movie.

Reid lifted the hardhat from her grasp, an even bigger grin stretching across his lips.

Best to get this out in the open.

"I'm into comics and I like stickers, okay? Sue me." She reached for the hardhat, but he extended it just out of her reach.

"What's with the attitude?" Reid asked. "Did I say anything about your stickers?"

"No, but I can tell you want to."

His grin morphed into a full-on smile and the breath that had managed to accumulate in her lungs rushed out again. Dammit.

Reid set the hardhat on her head and gave the crown a playful thump, as one would do to his kid sister.

Okay, that's definitely not what she was going for.

"I like the purple," he said. "Means you'll be easy to keep track of while out in the field."

Of course. Because that was his ultimate concern, keeping track of her. Because Alex had told him to do so, not because Reid wanted to be in her company. Best to remember that whenever her foolish brain felt tempted to read anything more into the smile on his handsome lips.

Remember your lane, girl.

She followed Reid out of the trailer, determined to find a replacement for the role of her workplace crush. Having him play that part was just plain unhealthy, especially with Alex's insistence that Reid act as her guide while on the jobsite.

Her task would be a lot easier if her tour guide made himself scarce for a few minutes. Brooklyn couldn't help but compare every construction worker they came across to Reid, and, well, there was no comparison.

He pointed out the state of the build as they toured the area. Instead of working from the ground up, they were tackling the build by wing. Some walls were up, but not yet painted. The parking lot had been framed, but the concrete would not be poured for another week. Pipes protruded from the floor, but there was still a lot of plumbing work to be done.

As they moved to the northeastern quadrant of the worksite where back-out framers were building additional interior walls, Reid asked, "So, what have you observed so far?"

"Is this a test?" she asked, peering over at him. He even made those goofy ass safety goggles look good. So not fair.

He hitched a shoulder, but shook his head. "No. I just want to know what you see when you look at all of this."

"It looks as if everything is moving at a steady pace," she offered. "According to the project manager, the job is running just five percent over budget and only a couple of days behind schedule, despite the weather delays, which I find impressive. However," She stopped when she realized that Reid was no longer walking alongside her.

She looked back to find him a couple of feet behind her, the skin between the brim of his hardhat and top of his safety goggles creased with confusion.

"What?" she asked. "You don't think that's impressive?"

"What's impressive is that you know where we stand on both the budget and schedule already. This is only your second day."

She shrugged. "It's my job to know."

"Shit," he cursed after expelling an irritated breath. He rubbed the back of his neck. "I guess you really are good at this."

"You don't sound particularly happy about that."

"I just hate it when I'm wrong and Alex is right."

She frowned. "What?"

"Forget I said that." He gestured at the network of wooden planks they'd been walking on during their site tour. "Come on. Let's take a look at the rest of it."

As they made their way around the site, Brooklyn counted three women working among the men in the field. That was three more than LeBlanc & Sons had ever employed, present company excluded. Her dad's unwillingness to hire women had been a bone of contention between them for years. Even though he'd had no problem dragging Brooklyn onto construction sites all her life—and teaching her everything from floating drywall to running electrical wire—he never thought to hire women to do the actual work.

Yet another notch in the plus column for Holmes Construction. At least they seemed to be progressive and not stuck in a 1950s mindset when it came to gender roles.

She wouldn't hold that catcall from yesterday against Alex or the others on the worksite either. She knew from experience that assholes were everywhere, and some of them happened to be good at installing insulation or roofing. She hadn't encountered anything along those lines today that made her feel uncomfortable. Whether it was due to Alex's warning or the fact that Reid had accompanied her, she couldn't be sure.

Maybe having him as a bodyguard wasn't such a bad thing after all.

———

BY THE TIME they returned to the trailer, Brooklyn had decided to put the bodyguard thing back into the big fat no column. Any positives she could come up with were overshadowed by the single biggest negative: her heart could not take being in such close proximity to Reid Holmes for an extended period of time. Twice while touring the site she'd stumbled on the uneven ground and Reid had caught her by the arm to steady her. Her skin still tingled where he'd touched, and her heart rate had yet to return to a normal pace.

She nearly wilted in relief once she reached her desk, looking forward to an afternoon without her entire body suffering through this heightened state of awareness. Seriously, this could not be good for her heart.

But instead of going back out into the field as she expected him to do, Reid walked over to Alex's desk and plopped down in her boss's rolling chair. He picked up a pen and repeatedly tapped it against the palm of his other hand as he studied her.

Brooklyn attempted to ignore him, turning to her

computer and logging into her email. She could feel his eyes on her the entire time. After a full sixty seconds ticked by without him saying a word, she was the first to cave.

She swirled her chair around to face him. "What?"

He tilted his head to the side, tossed the pen on the desk and asked, "What made you decide to work construction? I took a look at your resume this morning. You have a degree in...what is it in?"

"Construction management."

"Yeah, that." He slowly swiveled the chair from side to side, a faint creak chirping every time he twirled to the right. "To be honest, I didn't know that was even a thing you could study in college. Why did you choose that as your major?"

"I come from a long line of construction workers," Brooklyn answered.

"I know that. Your family has been in the business for years, but it's LeBlanc & Sons, not LeBlanc & Daughter."

She cocked a brow. "Sexist much?"

His wry grin returned. "Sorry. I didn't mean to be. I'm just curious. You don't—" he started, then stopped.

Brooklyn perched her elbow on the desk and rested her chin on her fist. "I don't what?" she queried.

He released a dry chuckle as he ran a hand down his face. "This is going to sound as bad as the LeBlanc & Daughter comment, but you don't really fit in with the whole construction site crowd."

Yeah, like she hadn't heard that before.

"Really? So, what would make me fit in?" she asked, unable to keep the humor from her voice. "Should I go out there and drive a few nails into two-by-fours, because I can do that too. In fact, I can do *your* job if necessary."

Amusement shone in his keen eyes. "Should I be worried?"

She stuck her nose up in the air. "Nah, I don't want your job. You couldn't pay me to work out in that heat."

His sharp laugh echoed off the trailer's faux wooden walls. "Spoiled by the A/C."

"Damn right." She tossed him a cheeky grin, enjoying this back and forth way more than she should. "I'm starting to suspect that you're still in this trailer for the same reason."

"I'm still in here because you still haven't answered my question."

"Which is?"

"What made you decide to work construction?"

She expelled a deep sigh. "Simple. It's all I've ever known. I've been doing this for over ten years."

He sprang forward from his relaxed pose, those whiskey-colored eyes teeming with incredulity. "Ten years? How old are you?"

"And that's your business how?"

"Come on," he said.

"How old are *you*?" Brooklyn countered.

"I'll be thirty in a few weeks," he answered without hesitation.

Interesting. She'd pegged him as a couple of years younger than thirty. How she wished the age difference could make him seem less attractive, but it didn't. Not even a little bit.

"So?" he asked.

"So what?"

"How old are you?"

"You're just full of questions, aren't you?"

"I'm told it's my most annoying and endearing trait," he answered, that grin lifting the corners of his lips again.

Wait. Was this flirting? Was he *flirting* with her?

"Still waiting," Reid said.

Okay, so maybe he really did just want to know her age.

"I'm twenty-six," Brooklyn answered. "I started working for my dad when I was fifteen."

He nodded and leaned back in the chair, resuming the lazy back and forth swirl. A couple of moments ticked by before he abruptly rose and started for the door.

Hold on. Was that it?

"Where are you going?" Brooklyn asked.

"Back to work. Unless you want to trade places for the rest of the day. You can go out there and inspect a couple hundred CPVC fittings and I'll stay here in this nice air-conditioned trailer."

She looked him up and down, deliberate with her side-eye action. Then Brooklyn made a production of turning her chair back to her computer screen. "Have fun inspecting those pipe fittings."

His rich, teasing laugh wove its way through the air, baiting her until she twisted her chair around and stuck her tongue out at him. Was she really engaging in lighthearted, witty conversation with this unbelievably sexy man? Was this her actual life right now?

"Smart *and* funny," Reid said. Then he winked. "There're more sides to you than you first let on."

He walked out of the trailer and Brooklyn's heart skipped a good five beats. She couldn't be sure that's exactly what happened, because, well, her heart had never skipped a beat before, but she was *pretty* sure that's what the skitter and thump within her chest amounted to.

He *had* been flirting with her. That's what that wink and teasing amounted to in her book. Of course, guys like Reid probably engaged in that kind of lighthearted teasing all the time. But, so what? She was the one on the receiving end. Brooklyn was more than happy to have some of it directed her way.

That said, she was also smart enough to not read anything into it. Just because he'd tossed a couple of smiles her way, it didn't mean she had to lose her head. Who knows, maybe they could be friends. It would make dealing with this crush easier, wouldn't it?

Yes. Definitely.

It was settled. She and Reid Holmes would be friendly co-workers. No pressure. No awkwardness. No expectations that were certain to be unmet, thus plunging her into a heaping ball of disappointment.

Whew. Nice to have that all squared away. Maybe now she could get some actual work done around here.

Brooklyn turned her attention to several subcontractor agreements Alex asked her to review. She tried to downplay the anxiety cascading along her nerve endings as she pored over the documents, but couldn't deny that it was there. It would probably always be there when doing this particular task. After all, if she hadn't missed a clause in that last contract she'd reviewed for LeBlanc & Sons, maybe her family would still be in business.

Brooklyn pushed her chair away from the desk and stretched her arms out in front of her, clutching and then releasing her palms in an effort to relieve the tension building within her veins. She could *not* allow those past mistakes to affect her for the rest of her life.

She managed to put that unfortunate episode out of her head and concentrate on the task at hand. She also went the rest of the afternoon without seeing her new friendly co-worker. Until it was time to leave the worksite, that is. Brooklyn was walking to her car when he fell instep beside her.

"You know you can't do this every day, right?" she asked after several moments skated by without him saying a word.

"I'm just going to my truck." He pointed toward the Chevy Silverado parked a couple of spaces ahead of her car. That truck had not been there when she'd parked here this morning. She would have noticed it. Had he moved it during the day?

They arrived at her car and Reid stopped. Brooklyn turned to face him.

"So, if you were just going to your truck, why'd you stop?" she asked.

He pulled his cellphone from his pocket and swiped at the screen. "I don't know what you're talking about. I only stopped walking so I could check Facebook. It has nothing to do with making sure you get to your car safely."

She cocked a hip to the side and folded her arms across her chest. Reid continued to play with his phone.

After a solid minute had passed, Brooklyn threw her hands in the air. "I give up."

"About time," he said. He slipped the phone in his pocket, reached over and opened her car door. "Damn, you're stubborn."

She belted out a laugh. "Don't think for a minute that I didn't know what you were up to. Stick to plumbing, because you suck as an actor," she said, sliding in behind the wheel.

He leaned into the car and, with another of those killer grins, said, "And just when I was preparing to give Idris a run for his money."

He winked at her. *Again.* Then closed the car door and continued up the sidewalk toward his truck.

"Holy shit," Brooklyn whispered as she watched his perfect ass walk away. She was still trying to recover from that second wink as she pulled away from the curb. She couldn't remember the last time her heart had raced as much as it had today. Maybe back when she fancied herself a runner and jogged a half mile on the treadmill?

"Nope. Not even then."

As she waited for the traffic light at Carrolton and Bienville, Brooklyn debated whether to make the right turn or keep straight. Just a few blocks away, in the upstairs room at Tubby & Coo's Mid-City Book Shop, sat a worn leather armchair that cradled her body like a lover's arms. That chair, that room, that space had become a place of respite for the last few years.

It was in that room that Brooklyn had found solace after she'd foolishly engaged in an online war with a stupid dude-bro who made the proclamation that women didn't belong in comics. It was in that room that she'd perfected her newest iteration of Iansan, the mythological African goddess of war and wind, and the inspiration for her latest comic. It was a place she could escape to when the world began to close in on her. She'd needed that escape more in the last four months than a single person should.

But not today.

With all the preparations for her new job taking up her weekend, Brooklyn hadn't visited her parents' since Thursday evening. She rarely went more than two days without seeing her dad.

Decision made, she drove past the blue and white bookstore and made a right at Orleans Avenue, heading for the two-story Italianate she'd grown up in over in the Treme neighborhood. Seeing her mom's minivan in the driveway, Brooklyn parked on the corner and, minutes later, used her key to enter the house.

"Hello?" she called.

"In here," came her dad's husky voice. She walked into the living room to find him in his recliner, a plastic cannula in his nose, an oxygen generator pumping air into his weakened lungs.

"Hey, Daddy." She planted a kiss on his cheek. "Rough breathing day?"

He wasn't on oxygen 24/7, thank goodness, but had been instructed by his pulmonologist to use the machine whenever he started to feel out of breath.

"Just a little," her dad answered.

Brooklyn looked around. "Where's Mama?"

He pointed to the stairs. "On the Facebook with her sister."

She didn't bother to correct him. No matter how many times she told him it was just Facebook, her dad insisted on adding the *the* to the social network's name. She immediately began straightening up the living room, picking up the mail scattered on the coffee table and bringing an empty cup into the kitchen.

"No food?" she called from the kitchen. "I'm not used to seeing a cold stove in this house."

"Felt like Chinese tonight," he said when she returned to the living room. "Should be here...in a few minutes." He patted the arm of his recliner. "Come over here. Want to know how things...are going at the new job."

"Stop trying to talk," Brooklyn said. "Your job is to concentrate on pulling air into those lungs."

She repositioned the plastic tubing behind her dad's ears, making sure the cannula fit correctly. He'd stopped slapping her hands away a long time ago, surrendering to the fact that her fussing over him was now a part of his reality.

She perched on the arm of his chair and gave him a broad rundown of her first couple of days at Holmes Construction, leaving out the catcalling from yesterday and assuring him that her new boss was the stand-up guy her dad remembered him to be back when Alex worked for LeBlanc & Sons.

She knew he worried about her. Brooklyn was convinced that one of the reasons he'd nearly worked himself to death was because he didn't want to put her in the position she now found herself in—having to find a job outside of LeBlanc & Sons. He'd hidden his illness until it could no longer be hidden, camouflaging his cough and blaming construction dust for the COPD that now imprisoned his lungs.

"Do you like the job?" he asked.

"It's only my second day, but so far, yes. Holmes Construction is a lot bigger than what I'm used to, but give me a week. I'll know everything there is to know about how it operates."

"That's because you're the best at the job."

Brooklyn barely managed to hold in her sigh as she thought about that brightly-painted room at Tubby & Coo's.

Yes, she was one of the best construction site coordinators out there today. Lucky her.

———

FRUSTRATION BUILDING with every second that ticked by, Reid thumped his head against the headrest, willing the stationary cars surrounding him to move. Fifteen minutes ago, the flag guy said it would only be another five minutes. If he'd known there was roadwork being done today he would have stuck to the side streets instead of hopping on the freeway.

Another couple of minutes passed without an inch of motion.

"Son of a bitch," Reid released on an irritated breath.

If they remained at a standstill much longer he was going to lose his shit. He needed to get to Harrison's. Now. He didn't want to give Indina any reason to think he'd blown off the meeting and didn't care what happened with their mom's foundation.

Reid snatched up his phone from the passenger seat and fired off a text to his three siblings.

Stuck in traffic. Will be there soon.

A few seconds passed before Harrison replied. ***Still waiting on Indina and Ezra to get here.***

"Thank God," Reid said.

His phone chimed with an incoming text. It was Indina.

I'm here. Walking up the driveway.

"Shit," Reid cursed.

Don't start without me. He texted back.

Yeah, okay. Came Indina's reply.

They were definitely going to start without him.

He tossed the phone on the seat next to him and turned up the radio. The Aria Jordan song that had been playing when Reid first got on the highway was playing yet again.

"Oh, hell no." He quickly switched to another station.

He was a huge Aria fan, and not just because the girl could sing her ass off, but because his record-producer cousin, Toby, had discovered the R&B singer years ago. Reid was all about supporting family, but he would go insane if he had to hear that song one more time.

Unable to find anything interesting on the radio, he picked up his phone again and searched for the podcast app. Until about three hours ago, he'd never listened to a podcast in his life. Hell, he didn't even know they were available on his phone. But earlier today, when he'd helped Brooklyn place an emergency order for more insulation material, she'd been listening to an interview with one of his favorite actors. She explained that it was a popular podcast that apparently everyone in the free world had heard of, except for Reid. Even after they'd completed the order, Reid had hung around the trailer so he could hear the end of the interview.

Yeah, okay, so maybe there was another reason he liked hanging around the trailer these days. He still wasn't sure what to make of that, so he'd rather not think about just why he'd come up with a half dozen bullshit reasons to walk into that trailer over these last couple of days.

He found the podcast app, opened it and stared.

What the hell?

There were *hundreds* of them. How was he supposed to find the one Brooklyn had been listening to?

He scrolled through the list of top podcasts, but nothing stood out to him. Faced with the choice of the radio, a podcast he wasn't sure about, or silence, Reid chose silence. Stealing a bit of time to clear his mind was necessary every now and then. The problem, of course, was that his mind didn't handle silence all that well. His thoughts soon drifted to Holmes Construction's newest hire and Reid caught himself grinning.

He immediately felt like a traitor.

He'd forgotten for a second that he was still bent out of

shape over Brooklyn LeBlanc even being a Holmes Construction employee, something that had slipped his mind several times this week. He'd lost count of the times he'd caught himself teasing her and had to remind himself she'd taken a job that rightfully belonged to Donte—a job Reid had *promised* Donte.

Sure, she was smart and efficient, well-organized and capable of juggling several tasks at one time. She was also funny and got along with just about everyone on the job site.

And cute. She was pretty damn cute.

Not that it mattered. None of that changed the fact that Donte should be the site coordinator. Did he have Brooklyn's experience? No. But, if given the chance, Reid had no doubt Donte would have grasped the information as quickly as Brooklyn had.

"Sure he would have." He snorted.

It was time he stop telling himself that lie. Brooklyn hadn't been there a week yet, and it was clear that she could run circles around Donte.

Reid had been wrong. Alex had been right.

Damn, it sucked to admit that.

How could he trust himself to make sound business decisions when he'd gotten this one so patently wrong?

Thankfully, traffic started to move before Reid could spend any more time questioning his decision-making skills. He'd save that for another day. Less than ten minutes later, he pulled up to his brother's two-story brick home in the Lakeview neighborhood, just outside of New Orleans. He noticed Ezra's car parked alongside Indina's, and cursed.

He was hoping Ezra had gotten caught up in the construction on I-10. But his always prepared, pragmatic brother probably had the foresight to check the traffic before getting on the road.

Reid knocked on the front door and, moments later, was greeted by his sister-in-law, Willow.

"Hey you," she said, a huge smile gracing her lovely face. "I wondered if you'd make it this time. You missed the last few times we've gotten together to discuss the foundation."

He had to crouch in order to kiss her cheek. "That's because I had no idea you all were getting together. No one thought to tell me."

"Are you serious?" Irritation flashed across her face as she glanced back toward the kitchen, where he figured his three older siblings were. "I'll make sure you're in the know from now on."

"That's why I love you," Reid said, giving her another peck on the cheek.

He loved his sister-in-law as if she were flesh and blood —sometimes *more* than he loved his own flesh and blood. His brothers could be pains in his ass. But Willow? Willow was his boo.

He'd had a crush on her since middle school, when she and Harrison first started dating. Reid had experienced true heartbreak when he came to the realization that she wouldn't leave his older brother and wait for him to reach puberty. He'd settled for having her as a sister-in-law. But Willow had always been so much more than just a sister-in-law. She'd been a true friend. Like Alex, Willow recognized that Reid was different from his older siblings. She was an ear when he needed someone to listen without judgment.

A few months ago, Reid learned that she and Harrison had been having problems in their marriage. Genuine fear raced through him at the thought of his brother and sister-in-law's relationship being on shaky ground. He couldn't imagine a life without Willow in it.

They seemed to be getting along better over the past few weeks. Reid had even walked in on them embracing in the kitchen at his dad's house as they cleaned up after Sunday dinner. Whatever Harrison had done—because Reid had no doubt it was his fault—it looked as if his brother had made things right.

He followed Willow into the kitchen where Indina, Harrison and Ezra were all seated at the table in the breakfast area.

"Look who finally showed up," Ezra said.

"I would have thought you'd be surprised to see me here," Reid said. "If Indina hadn't sent me that text by mistake on Monday, I wouldn't have known about this meeting at all. What's up with leaving me out of the plans?"

His sister had the decency to look guilty. His brothers, however, didn't.

"What do you know about planning a gala?" Harrison asked.

"As much as you do," Reid shot back.

"It's not a gala," Willow said. "It's just a kickoff party. And, yes, Reid should have been included. All three of you should feel ashamed for leaving him out."

God, he loved that woman.

"Fine, I'm sorry," Indina said. "You're here now, so take a seat and let's get started."

Reid headed for one of the benches at the breakfast bar, but thought better of it. He wanted a seat at the table. Literally. He refused to be isolated from this process any more than his siblings had already isolated him. Taking the seat next to Ezra's, he accepted the glass of iced tea Willow immediately placed in front of him and smiled when she rounded the table and eased onto Harrison's lap.

Oh, yeah, something had *definitely* changed here. It wasn't that long ago these two were barely speaking to each other. Thank God they'd come to their senses. It would be devastating for the entire family if something were to happen to their marriage, especially for his niece and nephew.

As if his thoughts had conjured them, both Liliana and Athens came strolling into the kitchen.

"Can I take the car to Amina's house?" Lily asked.

"Well, hello to you too," Indina said.

"Sorry. Hey y'all," Lily greeted with an impatient wave. She returned her attention to her parents. "So, can I take the car?"

"Amina lives ten minutes away. You can walk," Harrison said.

Lily rolled her eyes, and Reid suppressed a laugh. He remember what it felt like to have a brand new driver's license burning a hole in his pocket.

"Actually, we can use some milk," Willow said, rising from her perch on Harrison's lap. She pulled her wallet from the purse on the counter and handed Lily some cash. "Why don't you run to the store to get some, then you can go to Amina's."

Harrison wore the expression of the defeated. "Make sure you put the milk in the fridge at Amina's," he said.

"Duh, Daddy," Lily called, already halfway to the door that led to the garage.

Willow turned to Harrison. "I told you that when it comes to that car we have to pick our battles." She went over to the pantry where Athens had been rummaging for the past few minutes. "Now, when she asks to use it tomorrow night to go to the high school football game, we can tell her that she's used up all her driving time for the week."

"Smart woman," Harrison said. He and his wife shared a grin that sent another dose of relief flowing through Reid's veins. Those two were going to be okay.

Her eyes still on her husband, Willow took the Little Debbie's snack cake out of Athens's hand and replaced it with an apple. She gave the ten-year-old a look that dared him to say anything. "I'll be up in a half hour, and that homework had better be done," she said.

Athens frowned, but kept his mouth shut. Once his nephew was out of the kitchen, Willow held the snack cake up. "What's this doing in the house?" she asked Harrison.

"I thought I'd hidden them well enough," his brother said.

"You know what the doctor said."

"*What did the doctor say?*" Reid, Ezra and Indina all screeched at the same time.

"Calm down," Harrison said. "It's nothing serious."

"What did the doctor say?" Indina asked again.

Harrison shrugged. "Just that Athens needs to lose a little weight."

"It's more than just that," Willow said. "Athens is pre-diabetic. We have to monitor his sugar intake. That means no more junk food." She went to toss the snack cake in the trash, but Reid stopped her.

"Throw that over here. I'll get rid of it for you," he said. He caught the chocolate cake his sister-in-law tossed his way. "You can bag up the rest of the junk food. I'll take it with me tonight."

Harrison looked at him and mouthed, *put the chips in my car.*

No, Reid mouthed back before stuffing half the cake in his mouth.

Asshole, his brother returned.

"So, what's the plan for the kickoff celebration?" Willow asked as she returned to her perch on Harrison's thigh.

Indina spread several pictures out across the polished breakfast table.

"These are a few of the ideas I came up with. I was thinking we could rent one of the ballrooms at the Windsor Court to hold the event. I know it's a little ritzy, but we want to make a good impression with the kickoff party." She fished through several of the photographs before finding the one she'd been looking for. "I *love* how elegant this is. Just look at these centerpieces."

"This looks like a wedding," Ezra said.

"Well, I got it from a bridal magazine, but that doesn't mean we can't use it for the kickoff party."

Reid rolled his eyes as he leaned back in his chair and picked at the crumbs littering the snack cake wrapper. His sister had just become engaged last month and now everything was about the wedding. Reid could only take Indina and his future brother-in-law, Griffin, together in small doses. The two of them were so damn sickeningly in love he could barely stomach it.

A frown pulled at the edges of his lips. When had he turned so sour at the thought of people in love? He'd had the same reaction to Myron mooning over getting engaged. He hadn't always had this cynical outlook, had he?

Shit. Maybe he had.

"What about renting out Snug Harbor?" Ezra asked. "Mama used to love going there to listen to jazz."

"That's a good idea," Harrison said.

"No, it isn't," Reid countered, returning his attention to the conversation at hand.

"What's wrong with Snug Harbor?" Ezra asked.

"It's been done before. All of this stuff has been done before. Can't y'all come up with something that hasn't been done a thousand times already?"

"You have a brain, don't you?" Harrison asked. He tapped the table. "Lay *your* plan down."

Reid ignored his brother's challenge as he gathered several of the photographs and thumbed through them.

"I don't know just yet," he finally admitted. "But I know it'll be better than this. We need to come up with something that'll stick out. Something that's going to get people talking. What's so special about people in dressy clothes eating tiny food and drinking champagne in a ballroom at the Windsor Court? The same goes for Snug Harbor. Something like that may stand out in another city, but this is New Orleans. There's nothing special about holding an event at a jazz club. All this stuff has been done to death. Let's be different."

"If you think you can come up with a better idea, have at it," Indina said. She pushed the other photographs toward him and dusted her hands. "You're in charge of coming up with the theme for the kickoff party."

"You can't be serious," Harrison said.

"Why not?" Willow and Reid asked at the same time. Although Reid's voice didn't hold nearly as much conviction as his sister-in-law's.

"What's wrong with Reid being in charge of coming up with the kickoff party's theme?" Willow asked.

"Because he'd have a bunch of strippers jumping out of cakes," Ezra said. "What kind of party has he planned other than a bachelor party?"

"Don't be an asshole," Reid shot at him.

"No, no. This is good," Indina said. "Actually, it's perfect timing. I have a huge project coming up at work so I won't be able to work on this for the next few days. Why don't you take that time to come up with an idea," she said.

Panic instantly rose in Reid's throat, threatening to cut off his air supply. Just a few days ago his sister couldn't be bothered to even tell him they were planning the kickoff party, and now she was leaving him in charge of coming up with the theme? How in the hell had *that* happened?

"Um, are you sure about this?" Reid asked.

"Why not?" Indina asked. "You said you want to be involved."

"I'll help," Willow said, her sweet smile easing some of the anxiety that threatened to overwhelm him.

"Nah," Ezra said. "He says he can do it, let him do it."

Reid caught the sly smiles Indina and Ezra shared and realized they were just placating him. They didn't really trust him with this.

Instead of feeling relief over the fact they really didn't expect him to do this, it pissed him off. What did they think, that he would throw just anything together? Didn't they realize how important it was to him that his mom's foundation got off to a good start?

Reid clapped his hands together and rubbed his palms. "Okay, I'll get started tonight."

"Come on, Reid. We don't have time to joke around anymore," Ezra said.

"No, I'm doing it." He looked at Indina. "How long do I have to come up with a theme? Should we meet the same time next week?"

His sister leveled a look at him that any other time would have had Reid backtracking. Not today.

"Well?" he asked.

She sat back in her seat and folded her arms across her chest. "You really think you can come up with a viable theme in that time?"

"Yep. And it won't be something that's been done a million times already either," he added.

Indina lifted a shoulder in a casual shrug. "Fine with me."

"Deenie," Ezra said.

His sister pointed at Ezra. "I've told you not to call me that. And if Reid wants to take this one, I say we let him."

"Well, I think you'll do a fabulous job," Willow said. She rose. "I need to go check on Athens's homework." She walked over to where Reid sat and put her hands on his shoulders. "I know you can do this" she said. She leaned forward, kissed his cheek and whispered, "You know I'm here if you need me."

He. Loved. This. Woman.

"Thanks," Reid said, blowing her a kiss as she left the kitchen.

"Now that Mr. Party Planner is done flirting with my wife, can we get back to what we're here to do?" Harrison asked. "We still need to work on the criteria for the scholarship."

Ezra blew out a breath and shook his head. "Fine," he said.

As his brothers and sister talked over the qualifications for those vying for the scholarship they'd set up in his mom's name, Reid tried to calm the panic once again building within his chest. What in the hell had he been thinking, offering to come up with the theme for the kickoff party? Ezra was right. What did he know about party planning, other than beer and strippers?

His dad used to tell him all the time not to write a check that his ass couldn't cash. Had he done just that?

They'd all put so much into getting this thing off the ground. The Diane Holmes Foundation would be his mother's legacy. This kickoff party would be its first introduction to the world. It had to be perfect.

And he'd just signed up to come up with the theme?

Shit.

Next time maybe he would just keep his fool mouth shut.

CHAPTER FOUR

BROOKLYN SAVED the changes to the database she'd spent the majority of her afternoon updating, then sat back in her chair and released a satisfied sigh. Today marked the end of her first week at Holmes Construction. To say she felt relief was an understatement. Not just relief; she felt happy, lucky even.

The anxiety she'd harbored at the beginning of the week now seemed foolish. She'd allowed her past mistakes to get into her head, heaping unwarranted pressure on herself without fully knowing what the job would entail.

In fact, she felt even *less* pressure working for Alex than she had working for her dad. Sure, she had a vested interest in making sure every single person on this worksite did a good job, but it didn't have the same gravity as it had when the success of a job meant food on the table for LeBlanc & Sons workers. Holmes Construction was big enough to handle minor setbacks. Everyone would eat tonight, no matter what happened out there in the field.

Brooklyn logged off her computer, grabbed her hardhat from the peg next to the door and exited the trailer. She'd already fallen into a comfortable routine, ending her day with a cursory walk around the site to make sure everything was running smoothly and that all needs were being met. She'd learned pretty quickly that she would have to be more hands-on with this crew. Despite her pleas that needed supplies be notated on the convenient white boards she'd so graciously provided, she'd twice had to make emergency orders this week from panicked construction workers afraid of falling behind schedule because they were running low on materials.

As she made her way through the job site, the familiar sights and sounds of construction work covered Brooklyn like a warm blanket. It felt like home. The smell of fresh cut lumber was as comforting as the aroma of an apple pie baking in the oven on a crisp autumn day. The whirl of the buzz saw, the methodical puff of the nail guns, the grinding of the gears on the backhoe; it was the soundtrack of her life, going back to those early years when her dad would bring her on renovation jobs. She'd sit there with her coloring book as her dad and her grandpa worked.

Brooklyn stopped for a moment and wrapped her arms around her body, the heat of the day no match for the chill that raced through her at the knowledge that she would never experience the magic of watching her dad work again. She inhaled a deep breath and made a concerted effort to push those sullen thoughts away. She had no problem indulging in them, but this was neither the place nor the time.

She made it to the framed-out rear of the urgent care center, where wheelbarrows of sand were being hauled to elevate the ground. A potential sinkhole had been detected yesterday, so all work in this area had been halted while an outside civil engineering company came in to inspect the zone. It was one of those unforeseen headaches that tended to pop up on construction sites. It would put them behind, but it was better to uncover something like this now than to have it happen later, once the building was done.

She came upon several of the workers from the general labor crew who stood to the side, shovels in hand, waiting for their cue to start packing in the sand.

"Look who's here! What's up, Wonder Woman!"

It was the infant with the earring. Jarvis? Jared? She couldn't remember his name, but she had no problem remembering his cheesy pickup line from the other day.

Are you Netflix? Because I could watch you all day.

Lord, save her. The boy was barely out of his teens.

"Hey, Brooklyn," Anthony Hernandez called, resting his chin on his shovel's handle. "I'm surprised you didn't get this sinkhole fixed overnight. We all know you've got magical powers."

"Ha ha," she deadpanned. She'd inoculated herself against becoming agitated over good-natured ribbing a long time ago. They joked, but she knew they were all damn grateful for those "magical powers" they liked to tease her about. She'd saved Anthony's hide just yesterday, driving out to a local home improvement store to buy replacement safety goggles after one of the guys on his crew accidentally crushed a box of them with a steamroller. She'd earned their respect by going above and beyond the call of duty.

Brooklyn caught Reid looking at her and inwardly sighed.

She'd earned the respect of *some* of them.

When it came to reading this one, she was clueless. Brooklyn doubted he was into cosplay, but if he was she had the perfect costume for him: Jekyll and Hyde. Because the man was like night and day, depending on their surroundings. The Reid who joked around with her in the trailer seemed completely different from the Reid staring her down out here in the field right now. Gone was the light-hearted teasing. He turned into this non-smiling, no-nonsense hard ass whenever they were around the other workers, as if it was a crime to get caught being a pleasant, decent human being in her presence.

Why couldn't she have a crush on that damn infant with the tired pickup lines? At least she could read that one like Japanese manga.

"Hey, we're still meeting at Pal's tonight, right?" one of the other guys asked.

"It's Friday, ain't it?" Anthony replied. He playfully nudged Brooklyn with his elbow. "Why don't you join us?"

"Join you where?"

"Pal's Lounge. The guys—and some of the girls—hang out there on Fridays. It's our way of unwinding at the end of the work week."

Reid, who hadn't said anything up until this point, chose now to step forward. "I don't think that's a good idea," he said. "It's for the people who work in the field."

Anthony's mouth twisted downward with an incredulous frown. "No, it isn't. Claude used to join us all the time."

The look Reid shot Anthony's way was lethal enough to kill, but Brooklyn was too pissed at his deliberate attempt to cut her out of their Friday night ritual to care. She looked directly at Reid as she spoke to Anthony.

"Count me in," she said.

Reid ran his hand over his face and heaved out a sigh.

"What?" Brooklyn asked. "I am over twenty-one, you know. I'm allowed in bars."

He remained silent, but she could sense the frustration radiating from him.

What in the hell is his problem?

Where was the guy who'd walked her to her car these past four evenings? The guy who'd hung out in the trailer and listened to the *Another Round* podcast with her yesterday, then provided his own comical commentary? Why couldn't he be *that* guy all the time?

He didn't know it, but he was *sooooo* close to being written off as her workplace crush. She didn't care how nice his ass looked in a pair of worn jeans. This hot and cold attitude he had toward her overshadowed any warm feelings she'd started to developed.

And it sucked. Because over these past few days, Brooklyn had discovered that she and Reid got along surprisingly well when he wasn't being such a hard ass.

Maybe she could direct her crush toward Anthony. He was sorta cute, kinda funny *and* a Black Panther fan. Definitely crush material.

As she continued her survey of the worksite, Brooklyn tried to put the notion of workplace crushes out of her mind, but she couldn't deny the steady hurt that remained, pinching her chest and turning her usually bright mood dark. Why wouldn't she be hurt, knowing a fellow co-worker had something against her for no apparent reason? She just did not get it. Not at all.

There was nothing she could do about Reid's unwarranted attitude against her, but there *was* something she could do about her attitude toward *him*. Just because they were co-workers, that didn't mean they had to be friends. They didn't even have to be acquaintances. If Reid Holmes could not bear to be her friend when they weren't alone, he couldn't be her friend at all.

Brooklyn returned to the trailer and locked it up for the weekend. There would be a skeleton crew here tomorrow, but only because they offered to work on Saturday to make up for the time lost to the sinkhole. Alex had objected to it—not because he didn't want to pay overtime, but because he thought the guys should spend the weekend with their families. She'd worked in construction for more than a decade, and had never seen a boss so committed to his workers having a life outside of the job.

She exited the gate and, within seconds, Reid appeared alongside her, as he had every day this week.

Brooklyn rolled her eyes. "Are we still doing this?"

He gave his usual answer. "Just walking to my truck."

"Yeah, okay," she deadpanned. "Do me a favor. Stop parking near my car."

"Hey, what's with the attitude? It's been a week. You should be used to me by now."

He had the nerve to ask her about *her* attitude? Seriously?

"If you really want me to stop, I'll tell Alex that I don't think escorting you to your car is necessary," he added.

Brooklyn refused to acknowledge the twinge of sadness she felt at the thought of their little end of the day strolls coming to an end. Instead, she said, "Yes, please tell Alex that this is unnecessary."

He was quiet for a moment before he said, "Hey, are you serious about going to Pal's?"

"Why wouldn't I be?" she asked. "I was invited."

"That doesn't mean you have to go."

Brooklyn stopped walking and turned to him. She'd been mentally practicing the excuse she would give Anthony on Monday about why she chose to skip their little Friday get-together because, in all honesty, she was beat after this long first week on the job. But the look she saw in Reid's eyes, as if he was hoping she wouldn't join them, was enough to make Brooklyn change her mind.

"I'm going," she said. "Sorry if my being there makes you uncomfortable."

"Hey, I didn't say all that. I'm just looking out for you, okay?"

"So, you not wanting me to hang out with the rest of the crew tonight is for my benefit? That's the story you're going with?"

His head flinched slightly. "It's not a story. It's the truth. The crowd at Pal's can get a bit rowdy. Same goes for some of the guys from the crew once they've gotten a few beers in them. Once we're off these grounds, I can't tell them what to do."

Ignoring the sincerity in his voice would be the smart thing to do. She'd seen the look on his face when Anthony invited her to join them tonight. She would be a fool to believe that his not wanting her at the bar had anything to do with him looking out for her. Yeah, right.

"You know how we just established that I don't need you walking me to my car?" Brooklyn asked. "Well, the same goes for Pal's or anywhere else. I don't need you looking out for me, Reid."

He crossed his arms over his chest. "Really? So, if Jarvis gets drunk and tries to grab your ass tonight, how would you handle that?"

Brooklyn mimicked his pose. "I would knee him in the junk and tell him to fuck off."

His lips twitched with amusement and she could tell she'd shocked him. In a good way. Brooklyn cursed the flutter that skated through her belly. She'd made him laugh. So what.

He held up both hands again in a gesture of surrender. "Okay, fine," Reid said. "I'll lay off."

"Thank you," she answered with a firm nod.

When she resumed walking, Reid stopped her, catching her by the shoulder and urging her to turn around and face him. The sincerity had returned to his expression.

"But if you find yourself in a situation that makes you uncomfortable tonight, just signal and I'm there, okay?"

The concern in his voice nearly did her in. Where was *this* guy earlier today?

Brooklyn swallowed and nodded. "I will. Thank you," she said again.

Neither spoke as they continued along the sidewalk. An inkling of fall teased the air, the humidity of the summer barely noticeable in the crisp evening breeze. Leaves littered the ground, short piles collecting against the curb. The urge to make excuses for tonight remained, but she would see it through, if only to prove to Reid that she really would be okay without his playing bodyguard.

They were still several yards from her car when she unlocked her door with her key fob. As usual, Reid walked ahead of her, opened her car door and waited for her to get in.

"Thank you," Brooklyn muttered. It was the phrase of the hour.

Instead of closing the door, he draped his arm over the rim and dipped his head. "Do you know how to get to the bar?"

Brooklyn held up her phone. "I looked it up before I left the trailer."

He nodded. "See you there."

With that, he closed the door and crossed the street to where he'd parked his truck. There'd been a service of some kind at the church in the next block, so most of the parking spots along the street had been occupied this morning.

Brooklyn clutched her steering wheel and lowered her head against it. She was so friggin' confused when it came to that man. One minute it seemed as if he would give up both thumbs to have anyone but her as Holmes Construction's new site coordinator, and in the next he's offering to play her knight in shining armor against drunken, ass-grabbing construction workers. He needed to pick a damn role. Either he was her enemy or he was her friend.

By the time she arrived at Pal's Lounge there were at least a dozen of Holmes Construction's crew taking up several of the small, round tables.

"Hey, Brooklyn. Over here!" She looked left and found Anthony straddling a chair at a table occupied by three others who worked in General Labor.

"It's Wonder Woman." This from one of the guys whose name Brooklyn had yet to learn.

She rolled her eyes at the nickname they'd started to call her. She'd worn T-shirts featuring five different comic book heroes this week: Green Lantern, Iron Man, Captain America, Wonder Woman and The Flash. Of course, it was Wonder Woman that stuck out to them. Gender stereotyping was a son of a bitch.

"Let me be the first to buy you a beer," Anthony said, motioning for her to take the chair he'd just vacated as he dragged another from a nearby table. "It's the least I can do after you saved my ass this week."

"And how exactly did I save your ass?" Brooklyn asked, helping herself to a French fry from the basket in the middle of the table. "Wait, don't tell me. The safety goggles," she said.

He nodded. "And the tax forms."

"That's right! I forgot about that."

While familiarizing herself with the personnel system, she'd noticed several important tax documents missing from Anthony's file. He would have paid a ton in penalties and interest if Brooklyn hadn't caught it. "I think you owe me *two* beers," she told him.

Anthony threw his head back and laughed. He clearly didn't realize she was serious.

Someone at the table brought up the big rivalry game between the Saints and Falcons in the Superdome this weekend, and Brooklyn was quickly reminded of why she usually had no interest in hanging out with construction workers outside of work. She couldn't give a flying hockey puck about sports of any kind.

While the guys went on about quarterback passer ratings, Brooklyn scanned the room, mulling over just how long she would put herself through this before she feigned fatigue and went home. There was a brand new set of Copic watercolors with her name on it—literally, she'd had them personalized—and she was eager to break them in. She continued her perusal of the bar until her gaze connected with a set of intense brown eyes.

Reid sat two tables away, one arm draped over the back of his chair, the other resting on the scarred table. His palm wrapped around a bottle of beer. His expression unreadable. Brooklyn did her best to ignore the heady sense of awareness coasting across her skin with each second his intense gaze remained on her.

Reading people had never ranked high on her list of skills, but when it came to *this* particular person, she royally sucked at it.

Which Reid had walked into Pal's Lounge tonight? Was it the one who'd listened with rapt attention the other day as she shared the procedures she'd implemented over the years in her dad's business to help increase productivity? Was it the one who'd just walked her to her car less than a half hour ago, who claimed that looking out for her was actually a bullet point on his priority list? Or was it the guy who basically ignored her existence once they stepped foot outside that trailer?

And if he *was* the guy who ignored her whenever they were around their coworkers, why wasn't he doing so now? Why were those deep brown eyes locked on her?

As if he'd heard the words echoing through her mind, his eyes widened, as if shocked to find himself staring, and he quickly brought his attention back to the guy next to him —Donte, she thought his name was—and assumed the role of the Reid who ignored her.

Well, at least she had her answer.

She could deal with the Reid who ignored her. In fact, she preferred the Reid who ignored her. At least with *that* Reid she knew what to expect.

Nothing at all.

————

REID TIGHTENED his grip on the condensation-slicked longneck he'd been nursing for the past half hour—the only alcohol he planned to partake of tonight. He vowed to never put himself in the position he'd found himself in last weekend, being so inebriated he wasn't even sure who he'd taken into his bed. The fact that a chill ran down his spine every time the door to Pal's opened revealed just how much that episode with Vivian's granddaughter had shaken him. He kept expecting her to walk through the door with her friends and start whaling on him.

A potential run-in with a past one-night stand wasn't the only thing causing this weird, edgy feeling to claw at his skin tonight. Every time he heard that melodious laugh coming from the other table, an unnerving sensation that felt too much like jealousy washed over him.

Jealous? Me?

It had been so long since he'd even come close to being jealous over a woman that it had taken Reid a while to recognize the emotion for what it was. But damn if that wasn't jealousy causing his palm to tighten on the beer bottle every time one of the other guys from the crew made Brooklyn laugh. He'd worked with these guys for years. Their jokes weren't even that funny.

At the moment Brooklyn was the one causing the raucous laughs to erupt at the table as she told a story about a mishap she'd caused while trying to carry on her grandmother's tradition of holding a fish fry for the work crew at LeBlanc & Sons during the Lenten season.

"You have to keep in mind that I was only sixteen," she said. "And my cooking skills at the time consisted of heating up frozen chicken nuggets in the microwave. I dumped about four pounds of catfish in the fryer and half the cooking oil spilled over the sides and onto the propane burner." She shook her head, her self-deprecating humor charming the pants off just about everyone in the bar. "I nearly burned poor Smitty's eyelashes off."

The guys damn near fell off their chairs with their laughs. Reid couldn't help the grin that edged up the corners of his own lips. Having spent several hours with her in that trailer over the course of her first week on the job, he'd had ample opportunities to witness her sense of humor. The fact that it bothered him so much that others were now experiencing it would bug him for the rest of the night.

As he nursed his beer, Reid settled back in his chair and studied her. Brooklyn LeBlanc did not fit in with this group. She just didn't. If he were basing it on looks alone, he'd have pegged her as a quirky preschool teacher, the kind all the kids talked about incessantly because she always came up with fun games and didn't pressure them to take naps. If he had encountered her on the street, never in a million years would Reid have once thought she'd spent over a decade working for a construction company.

Yet, to say she kicked ass at her job was the biggest understatement of the millennium. The improvements she'd made after just a week on the job were mind-boggling. Reid had made fun of all her charts when he first saw them on Tuesday. By this morning he found himself using her timeline to figure out how best to adjust his plumbers' work schedules to fit around the work being done with the sinkhole.

And he wasn't the only one. The head of each unit had praised the new charting system instituted at HCC. What would have taken hours of going around in circles to figure out who should go first, and which crew would need the most time to complete their work, had been done in about twenty minutes. Having everything laid out and color coordinated had made all the difference.

So, yeah, not only was she funny, easy to get along with, and the owner of an apparently endless supply of super hero T-shirts that pulled perfectly across her dream-worthy breasts, she was also on track to being the best site coordinator to ever work at Holmes Construction. It shouldn't come as a surprise that the resentment he'd felt over her taking Donte's job had been superseded by an attraction Reid was still trying to come to grips with, and one he knew damn well he couldn't act upon.

His fist tightened so hard around the bottle Reid was surprised it didn't shatter in his hand.

His reluctance to even consider examining the magnetic pull he'd felt with each encounter he'd had with Brooklyn this week had nothing to do with loyalty to his friend. Once he'd acknowledged she was the better person for the job, Reid hadn't given Donte a second thought. It was the promise he'd made to Alex that had him so damn conflicted. He'd promised to watch over her. Reid doubted the watching he'd found himself doing this week was what his cousin had in mind.

His directive from Alex also played into this unnerving, unfamiliar urge to pummel so many of the men he usually called his friends. For the better part of an hour, every time one of them even *hinted* at something that even *seemed* like flirting, his blood started to boil. An old D'Angelo song from the late '90s came on and Jarvis Collins tried to coax Brooklyn into dancing. It took every ounce of restraint Reid possessed not to launch himself across the table and choke the living daylights out of the little shit.

And that's when he realized he had a problem.

His orders from Alex did not extend beyond the work-site. He had no say in who Brooklyn danced or flirted with on her own time. The rational part of his brain knew this. It was this other part—the part that selfishly believed Brooklyn's teasing smile and dry sense of humor was reserved for those times when they found themselves in the trailer back at the job site—that had Reid ready to climb the walls.

He had to get a handle on this, which would require ignoring the irrational part of his brain. It was the only way he would make it through the next hour.

Another five minutes passed with Jarvis making yet another corny ass attempt at flirting, and Reid decided removing himself from the situation was the best game plan. He didn't want to have to explain to Alex that he was down one laborer because Reid couldn't stop himself from knocking the guy's teeth down his throat.

He pushed away from the table and walked past the occupied high-backed barstools on his way to the bathroom. Notorious for the vintage photos from *Playboy* Magazines from the '60s and '70s that plastered the walls, the men's room at Pal's could usually take his mind off just about anything. Not tonight. Reid's brain hardly registered the naked starlets on the walls.

He braced his palms against the porcelain sink and stared at the face reflecting back at him in the mirror. It was the same face he'd been staring at for years, so why did he all of a sudden feel like a stranger residing in his own skin? Why in the hell was he so conflicted about every damn thing these days?

"Shit," Reid released on a frustrated breath.

Between leaving Holmes Construction to join Anthony with this new business, questioning whether he was capable of coming up with a theme for the kickoff party for his mom's foundation, and navigating these feelings for a woman who, just a week ago, he wouldn't have even considered his type, Reid couldn't decide which had him more discombobulated. What happened to those days when his most pressing worry was whether or not to have Chinese food or pizza delivered for dinner? Why couldn't he go back to *that* lifestyle?

"Because you can't," Reid said to his reflection.

He'd made a promise to Anthony a long time ago that they would eventually go into business together. He'd made a promise to his siblings that he would take this business with his mom's foundation seriously. And he'd made a promise to himself that he was done being the guy who woke up to strange women in his bed.

Did that mean he should be making room in his bed for Brooklyn? Hell no. Never mind the fact Alex would probably kick his ass if he tried to start up anything with her, but who's to say she *wanted* to be in his bed? She didn't even want him walking her to her car in the evenings.

But Reid could no longer ignore the obvious. If the enigmatic pull he felt whenever he was around her wasn't enough of a clue that he was venturing into new territory when it came to Brooklyn LeBlanc, his reaction to seeing her chumming it up with the other guys from the crew sure as hell was. She had awakened something within him that left him both confounded and intrigued. Which begged the question...

"What are you gonna do about it?"

Releasing a heavy breath, Reid took another minute to collect himself and readjust his mood before joining the crew again. He had to remind himself that connecting his fist with Jarvis's stomach was not the way he wanted to end his night.

When he exited the restroom a solid thump to his chest met him at the door.

"What the—"

"Just what in the hell is your problem?" Brooklyn asked.

He took a step back, his eyes widening at the vehemence in her voice. How long had she been out here waiting for him?

"What's my problem with what?" Reid asked.

"With *me*," she said. "What is your problem with me, Reid? Everyone else on the crew freaking loves me. They think I'm the best thing since wireless headphones. Except for you."

Was she serious right now? He liked her too damn much. *That* was the problem.

"Brooklyn, I don't know—"

She pointed toward the tables where the rest of the HCC crew sat. "We've been having a blast over there, sharing stories and stupid jokes, while you've spent the entire night glowering at me. Are you really that pissed that I tagged along for your little Friday night get-together? Is it really *that* bad having me around outside of work?"

"That's not why—"

She thumped his chest again. "You treat me like dog shit stuck to the bottom of your shoe, and I want to know why."

What the hell?

"I do not treat you like dog shit!" Reid said.

"Yes, you do. Actually, dog shit gets treated better. At least dog shit gets acknowledged. You don't even acknowledge me when there are other people around." Her voice hiccupped on the last word and Reid's chest nearly caved in on itself.

She backed away and lifted her chin in the air, fearless and breathtaking and phenomenal in her refusal to show weakness. She might be small in stature, but she was big in attitude. Yet another thing for him to admire.

"Look, Reid, I don't know what your problem is, and to be honest I no longer care. You don't have to like me. But if you don't like me in public, that means you don't like me in private either. Don't come in the trailer pretending to be interested in the podcast I listen to or my T-shirt collection or anything else that doesn't relate to work. We're co-workers. There's nothing that says we have to be friends."

But he wanted to be her friend. He wanted to be *more* than just her friend. For the first time in longer than he could remember, he'd found a woman who actually sparked his curiosity. He was aching to get to know her better. And she thought he didn't *like* her? Damn. Could he have possibly fucked this up any more than he already had?

Yes. He was pretty good at fucking things up.

But unlike his previous mess ups, he was not about to let this one stand. He had to make this right, because the thought of the light banter they shared when he stepped in that trailer at work coming to an end was enough to make Reid's stomach turn. She'd only been around for a week, yet she'd become one of the brightest spots in his day.

But if he told her that right now she'd probably call bullshit.

Because she was right, he had been treating her differently in public than he did in private. It started out as loyalty to Donte. He hadn't wanted to be seen as a traitor. But that excuse sounded weak even to his own ears.

He had to make this right.

"I'm sorry," he started. "I don't dislike you." Reid huffed out a laugh. "God, if you only knew how far off base you are."

She folded her arms across her chest and hit him with that look Indina used when she thought he was lying.

Reid pitched his head back and rubbed the spot between his eyes. This would not be easy. Not that he deserved easy.

She, however, deserved the truth.

"I wanted your job to go to someone else," he finally admitted. Her head jerked back and Reid could tell that wasn't the explanation she'd been expecting to hear.

"I'd recommended Donte for your job. I'd practically guaranteed it to him. And when Alex up and hired you without even telling me that he was passing on Donte, it... well...it kinda pissed me off." He shrugged. "I was determined not to like you from the minute you started working for Holmes Construction. Not because there was anything wrong with you, but out of loyalty to Donte. I didn't want it to seem like I was cozying up to the person Alex had hired for the job I'd promised to him."

She nodded slowly. "I get it. Because of something I had absolutely no control over, you decided to treat me like shit."

"No! Well...shit, I guess," Reid admitted. "But once I saw how good you were at the job, I knew that Alex had made the right decision. I finally came to terms with that after I left the job site yesterday. You're the better person for the job."

"So if you decided yesterday to stop blaming me for something Alex did—because I'll remind you that I am completely innocent in all of this—why the shitty attitude tonight?"

Because I'm not used to seeing you joking around with the other guys on the crew.

Great, now he was both jealous *and* possessive. What in the hell was happening to him?

No way would he tell her that he'd been seething with jealousy over how well she was getting along with the other guys. If there was one thing he could say that would make him look like an even bigger asshole, that was it.

"I have no excuse," he said. Reid held his hands out in a plea. "Can we just start over?"

She looked him over, skepticism teeming in her brown eyes. "What exactly does starting over mean? Does it mean you finally start treating me like just one of the guys?"

He definitely didn't see her as just one of the guys, but Reid figured it was a safe place to start. There was still Alex to contend with. His cousin had ordered Reid to look out for her. Maybe it actually *was* best to think about her as just one of the guys. No matter how hard that would be for him.

"Yeah," Reid answered. "With Alex dividing his time between the two worksites, we may find ourselves working together more often than we did already this week."

She stuck her hand out. "To being friendly co-workers."

He grasped her hand. "Friendly co-workers."

CHAPTER FIVE

"I'M SO good I scare my damn self," Brooklyn murmured as she keyed in the last bit of data on the pivot table she'd just created to keep track of sick time. Not that there was anything wrong with the spreadsheet Holmes Construction had been using to monitor sick leave, but this would make the task much more efficient. She saved the file to the local server, then opened up her cloud drive to save it there as well.

Her heart gave an emphatic thump when her eyes landed on the file she'd named FELLOWSHIPS in her cloud drive. It just sat there, taunting her to open it. But opening it was unnecessary. She knew exactly what she would find if she clicked onto the little file folder icon.

Brooklyn had spent the summer researching various grants, scholarships, and fellowships throughout the country, and even a few in Canada and the U.K., searching for a way to kick up her comics game. There were new opportunities for writers and illustrators sprouting up every day. After talking herself out of applying for them for the last two years, she'd finally summoned the nerve to seek out a few programs that seemed the most open to welcoming women into their fold.

But then Dad got sick.

Whenever she even contemplated filling out one of these applications, the guilt nearly suffocated her. How could she be so selfish? How could she even *consider* leaving her mother to take care of her dad on her own? Just so she could work on this pipe dream of writing comics?

She should just delete this folder from her drive. Even if Dad were to get better—and, God, how she prayed his condition eventually improved—Brooklyn knew there was no way she could apply for one of the fellowships. She'd just started a new job. She couldn't go to Alex and tell him she needed three weeks off to fly up to Chicago and attend one of the premier comic book consortiums in the country, could she?

"Of course not," Brooklyn said with a sigh.

Yet, as the pointer hovered over the folder on the screen, something inside her would not allow her to click the computer mouse. Maybe it was just a foolish pipe dream, but it was *her* foolish pipe dream. She couldn't give up on it just yet.

The trailer door opened and Reid walked in.

His eyes immediately sought her out, a tentative, slightly tense smile lifting one corner of his mouth as he greeted her with a soft, "Hey."

"Hey," Brooklyn returned, hearing the caution in her own voice, despite her attempt to sound normal.

She wasn't really sure what normal looked like when it came to this new, fresh start she and Reid embarked upon following their run-in at Pal's Friday night. It was as if they were still feeling each other out, trying to decide what it meant to be friends-slash-co-workers-slash-something Brooklyn wasn't sure how to define just yet.

She studied him as he turned to hang up his hardhat and remove the neon-yellow, mesh safety vest all the guys were required to wear while out in the field.

She'd anticipated the awkwardness. It wasn't as if it could be avoided after the way she'd whaled on him outside the restroom at the bar. It was not knowing the scale and scope of the awkwardness that had gnawed at her all weekend long. Would he go back to being the guy he was her first day on the job, the one who didn't want her there? Would he be the Reid who leaned back in Alex's chair and lobbed silly, nosy questions at her? The one who'd walked her to her car her first week on the job? Would he acknowledge her at all?

Worry about how this would all play out when they saw each other Monday morning had hounded her the entire weekend. To both her surprise and relief, things had been okay.

Of course, Reid had been in the field most of this week, so the opportunity for awkwardness to rear its head between them had been scarce. Even so, the few times she had run into him during her daily morning and afternoon tours of the site, he hadn't been distant or cold. He'd been...normal.

As each day drifted by, Brooklyn did her best to convince herself she was just fine with the two of them coexisting in this ordinary, run-of-the-mill way. This was how things usually worked with her workplace crushes, wasn't it?

She felt the floor vibrate as he made his way to her desk. Brooklyn twisted her chair around before he arrived, pasting a smile on her face.

"Been a busy start, huh? How are things going out there?"

"The dump truck just arrived with the fill soil," he answered. "They're going to start filling the hole in another ten minutes."

The situation with the sinkhole had gotten worse over the weekend, requiring all hands on deck in order to get things under control. Work had been halted on the left wing of the urgent care center while the engineering firm Holmes Construction had contracted scrambled to redesign the drainage system with one that would alleviate the water pressure if something like this were to happen again.

"Are they certain they've found the culprit?" she asked.

He nodded. "They're pretty sure it's a natural underground flow. I don't have to tell you that New Orleans is basically a bowl, and Mid-City is at the bottom of it, so there's runoff coming in from all the surrounding areas that are at a higher elevation. Alex had a soil study done well before we started this build, but according to the engineer, these pockets can develop at any time. I don't think this was avoidable."

"It sucks," Brooklyn said. "It's going to put this project behind, something I know Alex has been trying to avoid." She pointed to her progress chart. "I've been staring at this thing all day, but can't figure out how to shift the work to make up for the time lost."

Reid came around her desk and perched on the edge, stretching his legs out and crossing his ankles. Brooklyn swore she could feel the heat radiating from his firm thigh. It sat just inches from her arm; the way his worn jeans stretched over the solid muscle taunted her to touch it. He crossed his arms over his chest and looked up at the white boards, undoubtedly clueless to the way his nearness caused her heart to race.

Relief swept through her as she reveled in the familiarity of it all. *This* is how a workplace crush worked. She would sit here and pine over Reid's hotness while he had no clue that he was being mentally undressed by her overactive imagination. At the end of the day, they would bid each other good night and go their separate ways until he arrived in the morning for a cup of the coffee with chicory that Alex kept here in the trailer.

This is what she wanted. The lighthearted teasing as he walked her to her car, the playful banter that tipped-toed too closely to the edge of flirting; it had muddled her thinking and thrown her expectations out of whack. Juxtapose that with the distance he'd kept once they were outside of this trailer, and it was no wonder she was so confused when it came to reading him.

She would not put herself in that position again. She was prepared to mentally fistfight any foolish thoughts about Reid Holmes being anything more than a friendly coworker on whom she had a normal, safe, and *totally innocent* crush.

Damn, girl! Way to get back on track! As soon as he left this trailer she would give herself a high-five.

Reid continued to peer up at her progression chart. After another minute or so of studying it, he released an exhaustive sigh and shook his head.

"I'm not sure there *is* a way to make up for the lost time. The framers have already built as much of the walls off-site as they can. They'll just have to wait until the new cement is poured before they can begin erecting them." He shrugged. "It's just the way these things work out sometimes." He quickly stood and slipped his hand into his pocket. "I almost forgot why I came in here. The lead civil engineer suggested we install something to capture the runoff water and reroute it so that it can be used to irrigate the landscaping." He nodded at her computer and handed her a sheet of paper. "You mind?"

Brooklyn snatched the paper from his fingers. "Only because I'm getting paid to do it."

She should have known her quip would lead to a grin from him, and that his grin would lead to her heart doing that pitter patter thing again.

Nothing wrong with a pitter pattering heart when it came to a workplace crush, she reminded herself.

"Ah, there's the smart-aleck," Reid said with a laugh as he reclaimed his perch on her desk. "I haven't been in here much this week. I'd forgotten about that attitude."

If her cheeks even so much as *tried* to blush...

Shit. She was totally blushing.

Brooklyn stuck her nose up in the air. "Don't expect some things to change just because we decided to start over."

His expression shifted from amused to thoughtful. "I wouldn't want you to change a thing," he said, the wistful tinge to his voice knocking her off-balance.

A ripple of awareness quaked through her belly at his softly spoken words.

She caught the moment Reid recognized that he'd caused the conversation to veer off the innocuous, easygoing course it had been on. He straightened and said, "Besides, I'm the one who needed to change his attitude, remember?"

"And have you?" she asked. "You're no longer holding the fact that I took Donte's job against me?"

"No." He shook his head. "Even Donte doesn't hold it against you, not after the way you saved his ass by shifting his schedule so that he can attend his sister's homecoming ceremony this coming Friday. He's been the father figure in her life since their dad died. Thanks for finding someone to cover his shift so he could be there."

Being a daddy's girl, Brooklyn's heart broke for Donte's sister. She'd played Tetris with the work schedules until she found one that worked, simply because she knew how important it meant for a girl to be crowned homecoming queen and didn't want Donte to miss it. She'd had no idea just how important it was to their family.

Brooklyn shrugged as she swallowed past the lump in her throat. "Like I said, it's my job."

"No, that's going above and beyond your job." His eyes locked with hers and the sincerity she witnessed staring back at her arrested the air in her lungs. "Holmes Construction is lucky to have you."

It would suck if she died from lack of oxygen right now, so despite every instinct that urged her to continue holding her breath, Brooklyn willed herself to exhale.

"Thank you," she said. "It means a lot to hear you say that." Why did her voice sound so husky? Oh, yeah, lack of oxygen. "So," Brooklyn said, turning back to her computer and hopefully out of the dangerous territory she suddenly found herself wading through. "What size catch basin am I ordering?"

"Right," Reid said after a moment's pause. He leaned closer to her computer and she instantly realized the mistake in summoning his help. He smelled like a sweaty construction worker. As far as she was concerned, if someone slapped Sweaty Construction Worker on a candle she would buy up the entire stock.

"The forty-eight by thirty-six inch should work, but make sure the inlet and outlet match the piping we already have. It would put us over budget if we had to buy all new pipes just to fit this basin."

His phone dinged and he took a step back. *Thank God.*

He pulled it from his pocket, glanced at the screen, and cursed.

"Shit." He wiped a hand over his face. "As if I don't have enough crap on my plate today."

Not your business, Brooklyn reminded herself. So why did the words, "Something wrong?" come out of her mouth?

Reid tapped his thumbs against the phone, then stuck it back into his pocket. "It's taken nearly thirty years, but I've finally learned the meaning of the phrase biting off more than you can chew," he answered.

Brooklyn's mouth twisted in confusion. "You're going to have to give me more to go on."

He reclaimed his earlier pose, leaning against the edge of her desk and folding his arms across his broad chest.

Ignore the biceps. Ignore *the biceps.*

"It's a family thing," he started. "I volunteered to come up with the theme for this thing...this kickoff party. And I have no idea what the hell I'm doing."

"Okay." Brooklyn nodded. "Umm...actually, not okay. I still need more. What exactly are you kicking off?"

He looked as if he was about to indulge more, but then shook his head. "Don't worry about it. I'll figure something out by tonight."

"Reid, come on. I've thrown a party or two in my day." Exactly two, but he didn't need to know that. "Maybe I can help."

He released another of those deep sighs and readjusted his perch on the desk. "My family is starting a foundation in honor of my mom. She died earlier this year. In March."

"I'm sorry," Brooklyn said.

"Thanks." His lips tilted in a sad smile. "Anyway, the goal of the foundation will be to educate women, specifically those in the black community, about the dangers of heart disease, which is what took my mom from us. And we want to provide scholarships to young black women who want to major in medicine. That's the focus for now. We'll eventually branch out as it grows, but we're starting small."

"Small? That's huge, Reid. What an amazing tribute to your mother's memory."

"That's the thing, it needs to be amazing. This kickoff party is the official launch of the foundation, and my brothers and sister put me in charge of coming up with the theme." He put his hands up. "Okay, I volunteered to do it. But I didn't think they would take me seriously. They *never* take me seriously."

He pushed up from the desk and started pacing. Brooklyn tracked his steps as he marched back and forth between her desk and Alex's. He stopped, looked up at her, and said, "I don't know what I'm doing. What the hell do I know about coming up with party themes? The last three parties I went to were bachelor parties."

"I doubt that's the vibe your siblings are going for."

"No shit," he said with a desperate laugh. He pitched his head back and ran both hands down his face. "I don't know what I was thinking. I should have just let Indina roll with her bougie gala idea. But that's so damn tired." He looked at her again. "I want something different. Something that's going to stand out. Something that—"

He stopped. His forehead furrowed and his eyes narrowed as his gaze focused on her breasts.

"Hey." Brooklyn crossed her arms over her chest. "Stop that."

"Wait. No." He shook his head. "No, I wasn't staring at

your chest. Okay, I was, but not for the reason you think." He pointed at her. "Your shirt."

She uncrossed her arms and looked down at her well-worn Wonder Woman T-shirt. She had at least a half-dozen she wore to profess her love for her favorite Amazonian princess, but this one was, hands down, her favorite.

"What about my shirt?"

"My mom's foundation is all about creating a space where girls can grow into strong, capable women. Who's stronger than Wonder Woman?"

"Well, if we're talking pure physical strength, The Hulk or Thor would win out."

"I mean women."

"In that case." Brooklyn pointed to the emblem on her chest. "This is your girl."

And, great. She just directed his attention back to her breasts. And, oh shit, her nipples were now responding to the fact that he was once again staring at her breasts.

She quickly put her elbows on her desk and folded her hands, surreptitiously blocking his view.

"Are you sure it would work as a theme for that kind of party?" Brooklyn asked. "I had a Wonder Woman birthday party when I was six years old."

And ten. And twelve. And twenty-two.

"I'm not saying we blow up a ton of balloons and hand out those little paper whistles. I was thinking something a bit classier than that, but still fun. People can even dress up if they want."

"Are you talking full costumes, or just a She-Ra crown?"

He hunched his shoulders. "Not sure yet. I just came up with the idea. My brain doesn't work that fast," he answered with a grin.

She *reeeeally* needed him to put the brakes on the sexy

grins. They were coming too fast and too furiously for her heart to maintain a healthy rhythm.

Brooklyn cleared her throat. "So, sophisticated super heroes."

"Yeah." He nodded as he returned to her desk, his relaxed gait a stark contrast to his frantic pacing from moments ago. "I'm picturing something fun and not boring, but that people who've paid five hundred dollars just to walk through the door will still feel comfortable attending."

"Five hundred a head? Are you sure you don't want to go the ball gown and tuxedo route?"

He shook his head. "No. Superheroes. Because that's exactly what my mom was to countless people." He braced his palms on her desk and leaned forward. "It's perfect. Thank you."

His proximity made speaking damn near impossible, but Brooklyn still managed to say, "All I did was wear a shirt."

"You wore the *perfect* shirt." His eyes crinkled at the corners and his smile had a devastating effect on her ability to form a coherent thought.

Recognizing that her already tentative grip on her promise to not move past the harmless infatuation stage was beginning to slip, Brooklyn pointed to the short hallway that led to the bathroom and said, "I'll...uh...I'll be right back."

She raced to the trailer's tiny restroom and closed the door behind her. Resting her head against it, she let her eyes slide shut and counted to ten, imploring her heartbeat to return to normal.

Maybe it was time she redefine exactly how her workplace crush operated. Because *this* feeling was unlike any she'd ever experienced before.

REID SAT on the edge of Alex's desk, his palms gripping the lip, his nails meeting resistance as his fingers tightened against the cold metal. He pulled in a deep breath and slowly released it in the hope of finding some control before Brooklyn made it back.

As far as his plan went, he'd failed.

The plan had been set into motion the moment Brooklyn extended her hand Friday night in a show of agreement that they start over. Prior to that moment, Reid's intention had been to move in the opposite direction of where he found himself this morning, pretending that he was okay with being just her co-worker and nothing more. He was the one who'd erected these mental barriers, using the fact that she took Donte's job, and because Alex would be upset, to justify his staying away. But as he'd watched her enjoying herself with the guys from the crew Friday night, he'd decided to stop fighting the obvious attraction he felt toward her.

Until he witnessed just what those mixed signals he'd been sending had done to her.

Because of his selfish desire to keep the budding camaraderie they'd started developing last week between just the two of them—because he didn't want to share her infectious laugh and enchanting smile with anyone else— he'd caused her to think that he saw something wrong with *her*. When, in reality, nothing could be farther from the truth.

The hurt he heard in her voice during her tirade Friday night would haunt him for ages. He didn't deserve her laugh and her smile. He didn't deserve anything more than whatever she was willing to give him. Which is why Reid's new plan had been to allow their fresh start to be exactly what she'd asked of him, friendly co-workers.

But, damn, it was hard.

He liked her. He wanted to get to know her better. He wanted to learn where this love of super heroes had come from, and how she decided which wild, bright color to streak through her hair, and how she could possibly be as sweet as she appeared to be. He wanted to know what it had been like to work, as a fifteen-year-old girl, on a construction site, instead of doing the normal things fifteen-year-old girls did. There was so much he wanted to know about her. He'd never been the least bit interested in learning anything past the name of women he'd been with before—and sometimes not even that.

But this woman? God, he wanted to know it all.

He would have to *earn* the right to know those things. He would have to earn the right to be seen as anything more than just another plumber on the payroll at Holmes Construction. If she saw fit to open her world up to him a bit more, that's when he would move in. It was her call.

Being out in the field this week had been a blessing he hadn't deserved, but one Reid appreciated all the same. It made it easier to respect her boundaries and gradually test what this new, fresh start they'd agreed upon would entail. The past twenty minutes had demonstrated the ease with which they slipped into that playful pattern of flirting. It seemed to happen whenever they were in this trailer together.

He'd fought the impulse to escalate the easy, light-hearted teasing into something more, something that would make the color on her smooth cheeks deepen into an even more beautiful dark brown. But he could not be the one to push them in that direction. It had to be Brooklyn's choice.

Thank God he was needed in the field. The effort it took to go against his natural inclination to flirt was unsustainable. He would have to limit his time in the trailer to allow whatever might develop between them—if anything actually *did* develop—to happen organically.

Reid stood at the sound of the bathroom door opening. She came around the corner, her steps faltering at the sight of him.

"You're still here," she said.

"Yes," he answered. "But I'm about to go back out into the field, so—"

Just then, the trailer door burst opened and Alex walked in. "Good. You're both here."

He hung up his hardhat and made a beeline for the coffee pot.

"Hey," Brooklyn greeted him, her forehead creasing with the same confusion Reid felt. She pointed to the old-school wall calendar behind Alex's desk. "I thought you had an AGC meeting in Baton Rouge this morning?"

"I couldn't make it," his cousin answered. "In fact, I'll have to step down from my position on the safety committee. I won't have the time to commit to the Association of General Contractors with the amount of work HCC is about to take on." Alex look over at Reid. "I've been down at City Hall. We won the bid."

Reid's heart started to pound within his chest. "For the new annex?"

Alex nodded.

It had been two years since voters approved an annex building for one of the city's courthouses. Holmes Construction had been involved in the bidding war, but quickly lost out to a larger company that came in nearly twenty thousand dollars cheaper.

Less than a month ago, in a scandal that rocked the local political scene, two members of the city council—Cecil Washington and Russell Babin—were arrested for accepting bribes from the company. According to his soon-to-be sister-in-law, Mackenna Arnold, who sat on the council and who'd just thrown her hat into the mayor's race, this was just the tip of the iceberg when it came to the council's two disgraced members.

Instead of going through the bidding process again, the city decided they would choose from the previously submitted bids.

"Why didn't you remind me that this was all going down today?" Reid asked.

"Because I needed you here supervising the work on the sinkhole. I've been back there checking it out. It looks like everything is under control."

Reid nodded. "Brooklyn just ordered a catch basin. Everything's handled."

"That's good because things are about to get even hairier than they have been around here. Everybody will need to step up."

Alex rounded his desk and sat in front of his computer.

Reid stood there, waiting for him to elaborate. When it was clear he wasn't planning to, Reid asked, "You want to explain what you mean by that?"

Alex held up a finger. "One minute." He pecked at the keyboard with his two-finger typing method, clicked the mouse, and swung the chair to face both Reid and Brooklyn. "There's been a change of plans with the library on the Westbank. The grand opening date has been moved up by two months to coincide with the birthday of Alice Dunbar Nelson, who it's being named after."

"Whoa, Alex, you think we can make that deadline?"

Reid asked.

"It doesn't matter what I think. Only thing that matters is that we have to make it. Full stop. If we pull a few guys from this job and if there aren't any more mishaps on the French Quarter job, we can make it work."

"What about hiring more subcontractors?" Brooklyn asked.

Alex and Reid both shook their heads. Reid turned to her. "HCC only uses subcontractors that have been completely vetted. The ones we use are all booked."

"Are there people who can pull double duty?" she asked. "Like framers who are also dry-wallers?"

Alex snapped his fingers and pointed at her. "Yes." He turned to Reid. "You'll need to check with the guys on the crew. See who has double licenses."

"I can tell you that in a couple of minutes," Brooklyn said. She raced over to her computer. A minute later, she grabbed several papers from the printer bed and handed a set to Alex and another to Reid. "I'm not completely comfortable with the personnel management software, so I built a temporary database like the one I used back at LeBlanc & Sons. I also added a couple of fields that aren't covered in your software, including licenses. Here's a list of everyone who holds more than one license, both alphabetically and by trade."

Reid flipped through the printout, his mind sufficiently blown. If someone had told him he'd have to talk his dick out of getting hard over a database, he would have called bullshit. The joke was on him.

"Damn, I may have to give you a raise your second week on the job," Alex said.

"When did you even find time to do this?" Reid asked.

She shrugged. "It didn't take long." She turned to Alex.

"So, do you want to go through the list and figure out who you want to pull from this job to bring over to the Westbank site?"

"Jason and I will go over it once I get over there," Alex said. "Right now, I want to make sure everything here is in order before I leave." He pointed at Reid. "Who can take over your duties out in the field?"

Trepidation skittered along Reid's spine. "Why?" he asked.

"Because I'm going to need you in here," Alex said, confirming what Reid had suspected—and feared—would be his cousin's answer.

"You also need me out in the field," Reid said.

"Mainly in a supervisory role. Next to you, Craig and Rolando are the best two plumbers on this job, right?" Alex asked. Reid nodded. "Get those two to pick up the slack. I need you in the trailer, even if it's just in the afternoon."

The finality he heard in his cousin's voice told him that Alex had already made up his mind.

Was this payback for past misdeeds? What other explanation could there be for the field day karma seemed to be having with his life right now? He'd spent all these years going from one random woman to the next, only to now be forced to sit in this trailer with the one woman he actually *wanted* to get to know better, but whom he'd just vowed to lay off until she was ready?

Yeah, karma was definitely paying him back.

Alex gathered a stack of papers and manila folders, then grabbed his coffee cup and stood. "I need to get going. Now that we're GC on the annex project, I need to meet with the three biggest subcontractors. Jennie is going to set something up in that back room at Superior Grill," he said, speaking of his longtime assistant, Jennie Marconi. Alex snapped his fingers. "That reminds me. I may have found a place for Holmes Construction's new headquarters. I'm meeting with the real estate agent tomorrow." A smile drew across his cousin's face. "Ten years ago, when I was still running this business from my kitchen table, who would have thought we'd be here, huh?"

It had been so long since Reid had seen the normally stoic Alex like this; he thought his cousin had forgotten just what it felt like to be excited about his business. But there was definitely excitement dancing in Alex's eyes right now.

He stuffed the papers under his other arm and clamped a hand on Reid's shoulder, giving him a thoughtful squeeze. "Thanks for sticking with me all these years. I don't tell you enough, but I appreciate it. And I need you now more than ever."

Aaannnd cue the biggest fucking guilt trip in all the guilt trips that had ever been taken. Just when Alex needed him the most, he was preparing to leave and start up this business with Anthony.

Reid watched as Alex left the trailer. The man damn near had pep in his step.

"So," Brooklyn said, jerking him out of his thoughts on one problem and reminding him about another. "It looks as if we'll be working together a lot more."

Reid nodded. "Yeah, looks that way." *Lord, help me.* He hitched his head toward the door. "I should get back out there. I need to explain what's about to go down to the various crew supervisors so they can share it with the guys on their crew."

He hightailed it out of the trailer. He would have more time in here with her than he'd ever bargained for. He needed some time away so he could get his mind and body ready for it.

When he pulled up to Harrison's house later that evening, Reid's stomach performed an uncomfortable flip flop at the sight of a black Tesla Roadster in the driveway.

This laid all doubt to rest: the universe had decided to drop-kick his ass.

What other explanation was there to account for his running into the one person he'd been trying to avoid for weeks? He'd promised Anthony he would talk to his brother's law partner months ago. It was the only thing Anthony had tasked him to do. But Reid had made a sport out of thinking up excuses to evade Jonathan.

With a sigh, he climbed out of his truck. It was time he stopped playing this avoidance game and handle his business.

He started up the driveway and spotted Harrison and Jonathan standing next to the fountain that had just been installed in the landscaping in the front of the house. His brother had joined Jonathan's small law firm years ago. Just last year, they'd officially become partners, renaming the firm Campbell & Holmes, and hiring their first associate. Reid figured it was only a matter of time before they hired Holmes Construction to build a fancy new building for their growing law practice.

Which is why Reid needed to get this free legal advice now, before their law firm became even more in demand.

"Hey," Reid said as he came upon them.

"Hey man! It's been a minute since I've seen you," Jonathan greeted, pulling Reid in for a half hug and thumping him on the back.

"Yeah, I've been meaning to come by," Reid said. "I... uh...been needing to run some stuff by you." He glanced over at his brother, who—*shit*—was definitely paying attention.

Jonathan glanced over at Harrison as well. Reid could tell by the slant to Jonathan's brow that he understood that whatever Reid had to talk to him about, it was something he didn't want Harrison to know about.

"Yeah, sure," Jonathan said. "Hit me up when you have a minute. You know I always make time for family."

Although he wasn't technically family, no one would refute that statement. Jonathan had been family from the time he'd accompanied their cousin Toby down for Christmas break back when the two were in college together.

Jonathan turned to Harrison. He held up an expandable file folder. "I cancelled a date in order to go over these tonight. You owe me."

"Yeah, I owe you," Harrison said. "Lunch is on me for the rest of the week."

"She's a former Ms. Louisiana. Lunch is on you for the rest of the *month*." He tapped Reid on the shoulder. "I'll catch up with you later. Good luck with the party planning. Oh, I almost forgot." Jonathan stuck his hand in his pocket and retrieved a piece of paper, which he handed to Reid. "This is for the kickoff party."

Reid unfolded the paper. It was a check for a thousand dollars.

"Whoa. Thanks, man. This will help out a lot."

"The firm will make a formal donation to the foundation at the kickoff party—something nice and big to get the ball rolling. This is just a personal donation from me to help with the party expenses." He held up the foil-covered paper plate he'd been holding. "Tell Willow thanks for the brownies," he said to Harrison before heading to his ridiculously badass car.

Reid turned to his brother. "Wills made brownies?" he

asked before taking off for the front door.

"Don't get too excited," Harrison called. "They're made using black beans instead of flour. She's trying a bunch of diabetic-friendly recipes."

Reid stopped and waited for Harrison to catch up with him. "How serious is this pre-diabetes thing with Athens? Will he have to start taking insulin shots or something?"

"Not if we get a handle on it. He has a doctor's appointment at the end of the week. Hopefully they can tell us if the changes to his diet are having an effect."

Harrison ran a hand down his face, and for the first time in a long time, Reid noticed how exhausted his brother looked. Exhausted and stressed.

"Hey, man," Reid said, putting his arm around Harrison's shoulder. "You okay? Is there something I can do?"

"You can tell me about whatever cloak and dagger shit you and Jonathan have going on."

He dropped his arm and took a step back. "You've got more important things to worry about."

"I can worry about more than one thing at a time. Are you in some kind of trouble?"

"No."

"Reid."

God, he *hated* that tone. It was one usually reserved for parents, but being the eldest of the four and the only one with kids of his own, Harrison had perfected it.

Reid blew out an irritated breath and folded his arms over his chest. "A friend from work is trying to start a business. He had some legal questions and I told him I'd ask Jonathan."

"When your own brother is a lawyer?" Harrison asked.

"You've got enough on your plate," he answered.

Even before he'd learned about his nephew's medical

issues, whatever was going on between Harrison and Willow had been enough for Reid to avoid bringing his brother into this. But Harrison's family troubles was just one of the reasons Reid hadn't wanted his brother to get involved. He knew what Harrison would think if he learned that Reid was considering leaving Holmes Construction. He would think Reid was abandoning his family.

Well, that *is* what he would be doing.

No, it wasn't. He wasn't abandoning Alex; he was making something happen for himself. This was his first step on the road to building his own legacy.

Swallowing past the guilt that continued to build whenever he even thought about leaving HCC, Reid followed Harrison into the living room where Indina and Willow were already seated on the sofa, each with a glass of white wine in hand. A moment later, Ezra and Griffin came through the French doors that led out onto the patio.

"How's it been going?" Griffin asked, greeting Reid with the same half-arm hug he'd just shared with Jonathan. His future brother-in-law pointed to the patio. "Have you seen the new grill that one just bought? Next party will have to be here. I want to see what that thing can do."

"I'm grilling burgers for the Saints game on Sunday," Harrison said. "I will be giving demonstrations."

"*He's* giving the demonstrations. I'll bet that's because *he's* the only one allowed to touch the grill," Ezra chimed in.

"You damn right. Don't even think about laying a hand on it."

Indina snorted. "I swear I will never understand men and their toys." She held up a hand when Harrison started to speak. "I don't want to understand. I want to get started with this meeting. Griffin and I are trying to catch an eight o'clock movie."

"On a Thursday?"

"We've been working late every single night this week," she said. "With the way things are at the office these days, I wouldn't be surprised if we're stuck there tomorrow night too. I don't want to chance it." She pointed her wineglass at Reid. "You ready to wow us with your ideas?"

Sweat instantly broke out in the middle of his back.

How in the hell had he landed himself in this position? Oh, right. He'd opened his big mouth. Maybe next time he'd keep it shut. It wasn't so bad being the charming slacker who no one ever took seriously. That was his role, and he played it to perfection.

Stop it, dammit!

You can do this.

With Brooklyn's help he'd come up with a damn good idea. He was fully prepared for his siblings to hate it, but Reid wasn't going down without a fight. He would *make* them love it.

His gut clinched as he began.

"When you think about foundations like the one we've set up for Mama, what usually comes to mind? Stuffy. Serious. Boring. But Mama wasn't any of those things. She was the cool mom on the block. Instead of making us come inside after the streetlights came on, she'd come outside and shoot lay-ups."

"And make more shots than all of us combined," Ezra said.

"Because she was..." Harrison started.

"...the best point guard in the land," they all finished, quoting one of their mom's favorite lines.

"And she never let us forget it," Indina chimed in.

"But it was all in good fun," Willow said. "Your mother was never one to brag."

"Exactly." Reid jumped on his sister-in-law's perfect segue. "If there's one thing Mama believed in, it was having fun. That's why I think the traditional, stuffy gala is the wrong way to go."

No pitchforks had emerged yet. That meant he was doing something right.

"In my mind, and in the minds of many people around here, Mama was a real life superhero," Reid continued. "I think the kickoff party should reflect that."

"I'm not following," Griffin said. "Are you saying we should have a superhero theme for the kickoff party?"

Reid nodded. "That's exactly what I'm thinking. Something fun and bold, but still upscale and classy."

He held his breath.

No one spoke. There was an awkward strain in the air. Reid's discomfort grew with every second that passed as five sets of eyes stared at him.

He held his hands out. "Okay, somebody say *some*thing."

"I love it." Reid's head jerked around at the sound of his sister's soft, awe-filled voice. "I absolutely love it."

"Damn, so do I," Harrison said. He turned to Willow. "Remember when my old firm held that Halloween ball a few years ago? It was fun, but still sophisticated."

"Sophisticated superheroes," Ezra mused. A slow smile drew across his face as he stared at Reid. "Damn, dawg. I didn't think you had it in you, but you came through on this one."

The wave of relief that crashed through Reid's veins was strong enough to bring him to his knees.

"It's brilliant," Willow said. She rose from her seat and walked over to him. Still holding onto her wineglass, she reached up and wrapped her arms around Reid's neck. "I knew you'd come up with a killer idea, honey."

He *loved* this woman.

"Thank you," Reid said, planting a kiss on the top of her head.

"We could still rent out one of the ballrooms at the Windsor Court, or even the Hilton Riverside," Indina said. "We could get one of those big spotlights to shoot the bat signal over the Mississippi River!"

She hopped up from the sofa and clapped her hands together in that no-nonsense way of hers.

"Okay, we're *definitely* going with this. It's unique and no one will be expecting it." She turned to Reid and hooked a thumb toward where Harrison and Ezra sat. "Those two had me scared you'd have a stripper jumping out of a cake, but this is fantastic. Remind me not to listen to them." She turned to Griffin. "Sorry, baby, but we're not seeing a movie tonight. I wouldn't be able to pay attention to it anyway. I have too many ideas popping up in my head. We need to get this ball rolling."

And, just like that, Indina was off to the races.

Reid took a seat on the raised ledge of the stone fireplace and silently observed as his sister posed questions and threw out suggestions about how to incorporate the kickoff party's new theme. He'd been so certain they would all hate the idea that he hadn't prepared himself for what would happen if they actually liked it. Reid should have known Indina would take over, as usual.

A part of him resented the way they'd so easily shut him out yet again, but he'd done his part. He'd delivered a killer theme for the foundation's introduction to the world. No doubt his Mama was smiling down on the job her baby boy had done.

CHAPTER SIX

BROOKLYN SIFTED through the collection of sticky notes, old envelopes and tattered napkins she'd accumulated during her walk-through this morning. She'd given up on convincing the workers to use the white boards she'd hung up around the worksite to keep a running tab on needed supplies. The guys back at LeBlanc & Sons had never caught on to her brilliant idea either.

As she filled out the inventory list, she did her best to put the reminder that had popped up on her Outlook calendar out of her head. She would have better luck getting each of those workers out there to turn their timesheets in on time and without a single error. Basically, zero chance.

The deadline for the Vulcan Comics Grant ended tonight, at midnight. She'd filled out her application weeks ago. It sat in her cloud drive, waiting to be uploaded. All that was left for her to do was pull the trigger.

Yet, she hadn't.

Why was she having such a hard time making up her damn mind? Chances were she wouldn't get in anyway. What was the harm in applying?

But Brooklyn knew exactly why she got the shakes whenever her computer mouse hovered over the file folder. It wasn't the thought of *not* getting the grant that would hurt, it's the pain she would feel if she did. Because if she was lucky enough to win that $5,000 grant and a spot in their three-week long comics writing intensive, there was no way she would be able to attend. Not with the mountain of responsibilities weighing her down—responsibilities she'd added to her own plate because of her bad judgment and mistakes.

Maybe if you'd been doing your job instead of playing around with your comics, LeBlanc & Sons would still be operating and your Dad wouldn't be tied to that oxygen tank.

Brooklyn closed her eyes and swallowed past the lump of guilt and disgust lodged in her throat.

She knew she wasn't the cause of her dad getting sick. That was from years of his working construction and putting everyone else's well-being ahead of his own. But it was due to her ineptitude that her family was in the financial bind they now found themselves in. The medical bills were piling up, and the blame for that rested squarely on Brooklyn's shoulders.

Thank God she'd landed this job.

Thank God. Thank God. Thank *God.*

This job had been a godsend in more ways than one, but one of the biggest bonuses to her new position at Holmes Construction was that it had come with a twenty-percent salary increase over what she'd been making at LeBlanc & Sons. Last week, Brooklyn opened a separate savings account to stash away the extra cash she would be taking in. The money would be there to help every three months when her dad's prescriptions needed to be refilled. She'd already talked it over with her mom. Her dad would throw a fit if he knew, which is why Brooklyn would make sure he never found out.

The alarm she'd set went off, causing her to jump so high she hit her knee against the underside of the desk.

"Elegant as always," Brooklyn said with a snort.

She lifted her purse from the drawer, grabbed her hardhat from the hook next to the door and headed outside. She'd made it only a few yards past the row of wooden pallets stacked with cinderblocks before she spotted Reid walking toward her.

She would never understand how this man made a simple T-shirt with sweat rings underneath his arms look so damn enticing.

"I'm on my way," he called. "Just let me wash up." He pointed to the non-potable water bin installed for quick clean ups out in the field. He splashed water over his face, then reached behind his head, caught his shirt by the neck hole, and pulled it over his head.

Sweet. Baby. Jesus.

She would have appreciated the chance to prepare herself for the onslaught of lust that crashed over her. Instead, Brooklyn was left with having to hide her erect nipples, which instantly hardened at the sight of all that ridiculously gorgeous chocolate skin.

Reid soaked the shirt with water and used it to wipe down his chest and torso, and for the first time in her life Brooklyn knew what it felt like to be jealous of an inanimate object. She would give anything to trade places with that T-shirt.

Reid unzipped the backpack he carried with him and pulled out a clean shirt, quickly donning it. Thank God he was able to tuck the shirt in his jeans without undoing them, because she had no doubt she would have fainted at the first sound of that snap coming undone.

"What time did Alex say the real estate woman would be there?" he asked as he came upon her.

Brooklyn was still trying to roll her tongue back in her mouth.

She cleared her throat before she spoke. "We're...uh...supposed to meet her there at three p.m.," she finally said. "We have to pass through two school zones to get there, which will tack on another ten minutes to the drive, so I figured we need to head out earlier."

"There's construction on the St. Charles Streetcar line, too. I say we try to avoid that area altogether," Reid said as they started for the gate.

"Do you mind if we take your truck?" Brooklyn asked. "My car started doing this jerking thing this morning. I don't want to drive it too much."

"Transmission?"

She hunched her shoulders. "When it comes to cars, my knowledge bank is pretty much empty."

"They're not my strong suit either, but I know enough to check the level of the transmission fluid. I can take a look at it once we get back if you want me to," he offered.

A delicate tremor fluttered in her belly. There was something altogether too domestic about the thought of him playing underneath the hood of her car.

"Uh, thank you," Brooklyn said. "I'd appreciate that."

"It's not a problem," he replied. They quietly traversed over several yards of uneven sidewalk before he spoke again. "I'm surprised you don't have someone to do that for you," he said, a curious lilt to his voice.

"My dad used to, but—"

"I'm not talking about your dad," Reid interrupted. "I'm talking about a boyfriend."

Her heart skipped a beat and she nearly tripped over her own two feet. Thankfully, there was a jagged piece of sidewalk that she could blame her clumsiness on.

"I..." she started, but couldn't think of anything to say. Her skin flushed with heat.

"Well?" he pressed. "Why don't you?"

"Why don't I have a boyfriend?" she asked.

"That is what we were talking about, isn't it?"

"That's what *you* were talking about," Brooklyn answered as they came upon his Chevy. He opened the passenger door for her and she had to grab onto the door frame in order to lift herself into the behemoth of a truck. Reid rounded the front and climbed in on the driver's side.

He buckled his seatbelt, then draped one wrist over the steering wheel and turned to her.

"So are you going to answer my question?" he asked.

"Which question?"

His brow arched in indulgent exasperation.

Brooklyn threw her hands up. "How am I supposed to answer that question? I don't know why I don't have a boyfriend. Maybe my *OkCupid* and *Black People Meet* profiles aren't interesting enough."

The grin that tilted up the corners of his mouth would have been cute if the smile wasn't at her expense.

"Don't you dare laugh at me," she warned. "There is absolutely nothing wrong with online dating."

"I didn't say there was anything wrong with it, did I?" he asked as he revved the engine and pulled away from the curb.

"You've done online dating?"

"I didn't say that either." They turned onto Carrolton,

heading uptown. "I can help you with your profile," he said. "I'll bet you're too honest to lie on it."

"What's the point in lying? If I lie on my profile, that means I'll have to lie in the relationship."

"Wait a minute. You're looking for an actual relationship online? I thought people just used those things to hook up."

"That's *Tinder*."

"You're on *Tinder* too?"

"No!" Brooklyn said. Why were they even having this conversation? "Can we please stop talking about my online dating habits?"

"Hey, I'm just trying to be a friendly co-worker," he said, a tinge of amusement coloring his voice.

This was a game to him. Her heart broke a little.

"Co-workers don't talk about their dating lives," Brooklyn murmured.

"Says who? You need to spend more time in the field. I know more about girlfriends and fiancés than I ever wanted to know."

"Well, as far as *I'm* concerned, co-workers don't share that kind of information." She then turned her head, putting an end to the conversation. She had to put an end to it, because Brooklyn doubted she would be able to speak past the disappointment clogging her throat. She stared out the passenger side window, and tried her hardest to ignore the hurt resonating within her chest.

If his reaction to discovering that she was on online dating sites was to help with her profile so she could find dates with *other* men, it revealed a lot about how he felt. Clearly, he didn't see them moving past the friendly co-worker stage.

That's what you wanted, right? A typical workplace crush. Nothing more.

Brooklyn mentally pointed her middle finger at the annoying voice in her head.

Okay, fine. So maybe she had insisted that she would be satisfied with Reid being nothing more than the object of her little workplace fantasy, but come on. Seriously. *Come. On.* Would it be too much to ask that he at least *try* to see her as desirable? Could he not pretend for a minute that there was something a bit more amorous behind his teasing smile?

Apparently not. Because if last week's flirting really meant anything to him, he wouldn't be offering to help her find a date.

Brooklyn barely contained her growl.

Her neighbor's six-year-old daughter was right. Boys were stupid.

As they pulled up to a two-story building on Magazine Street, Brooklyn decided that Reid's obliviousness to her feelings for him would not take up any more space in her head. She was on the clock. Alex wasn't paying her to obsess over his clueless cousin.

She opened the door before he could make his way to her side of the truck and climbed down onto the sidewalk.

"This is it, right?" Reid ask as he came around the truck.

She glanced at the address she'd saved into her phone. "Looks like it."

The front of the building was done in sage green stucco. Black ironwork ran along the upper balcony, resembling the townhouses found in the French Quarter. There was a logo for an accounting firm on one door, and a For Lease sign in the window of the other half of the building.

"This is pretty nice," Reid said. "I already know one reason Alex likes this place. It isn't too far from his house."

The door to the unleased side opened and a blonde dressed in a sensible pants suit and ballerina flats walked out.

"Hi there! Alexander?" she asked, extending a hand to Reid.

"No, I'm the Deputy Project Manager at Holmes Construction, Reid Holmes. This is Brooklyn LeBlanc, the Site Coordinator. Alex is tied up at one of our worksites and asked the two of us to take a look at the office space."

"Well, welcome," she said. "My name is Shania, like the country singer."

Brooklyn looked at Reid, who looked back at her. They both turned to the real estate agent.

She waved her hand. "Never mind about that. Why don't I show you around?"

As they followed her into the building, Brooklyn leaned over and whispered, "Deputy Project Manager?"

"Sounds better than head plumber," he murmured.

"Mr. Holmes was very specific in his requirements," the Realtor called over her shoulder. "He requested a space that could house a staff of ten, along with two conference rooms. I think he will be very happy with this particular office space. There are twelve offices, two conference rooms and a decent size kitchen-slash-break area. And this stretch of Magazine Street has seen major development in the last few years, so there's a number of restaurants within walking distance."

She brought them upstairs first, where eight of the twelve offices were located. Brooklyn was disappointed to discover the French doors leading to the balcony were faux. Why have a balcony if you couldn't use it?

The Realtor then led them back downstairs, giving them a quick tour of the kitchen space, the smaller of the two conference rooms, and what would likely be Alex's spacious corner office. They ended the tour in the second conference room.

"So, what do you think?" Shania asked.

"It fits Alex's criteria. What about parking?"

Based on the grimace that flashed across her face, it was obvious Brooklyn had asked the one question Shania-Like-the-Country-Singer had hoped to avoid answering.

"I'll be honest, parking may be a bit tricky," the woman answered. "There's a small lot behind the building with four designated spots for this suite, but there's ample street parking in the residential neighborhood behind us. I frequent this area and have never had a problem finding parking, even during the lunch hour."

Brooklyn nodded. "I like it, but I'm not the one who will be making the decision." She looked over her shoulder to find Reid perusing the space, a thoughtful expression illuminating his face.

"Reid?" she called.

"What?" he asked, startled, as if he hadn't heard a word they'd said. "Sorry, I wasn't paying attention."

Well, guess that answered that.

He walked over to them and, shoving his hands in his pockets and looking around the conference room, said, "Knowing Alex's style, I'm pretty sure he'll like this one." His lips tilted up in a smile. "It's amazing to think that the little construction company he ran out of his kitchen for so long has grown to the point where he needs something like this to house it."

Brooklyn's heart swelled at the admiration she heard in

his voice. She naturally had a soft spot for family run businesses. Witnessing Reid's pride over his cousin's success tugged at the part of her soul that would celebrate every small achievement her dad was able to accomplish with LeBlanc & Sons.

Some of that animosity she felt over the online dating thing started to subside. It was foolish to hold it against him just because he didn't have the reaction to her that she wanted him to have. In the end, if all she could have is Reid's friendship, she would take it.

"I'm going to take some pictures and video to bring back to Alex," Reid said.

"Absolutely," the Realtor replied. "There's also a 360-video online for this listing, which I emailed to Mr. Holmes. But you two understandably have a better idea of what he would like to see." She turned to Brooklyn. "You should also take pictures so we'll have all our bases covered."

As Reid used his phone to record virtually every square foot of the building, Brooklyn went around snapping pictures and trying to get a feel for how the office would be set up. Given the nature of her job, she would be stuck in a trailer most of the time, but Alex informed her yesterday that her home base would be in the new office space.

She'd visited the place that served as Holmes Construction's headquarters when she interviewed for the job. At the time she'd thought the two-hundred square foot room attached to Alex's house—about ten minutes from where they were right now—was nice, but it wasn't sufficient for a company that was growing at the rate in which Holmes Construction was growing. His assistant, Jennie, and HCC's official project manager, Derrick Lawson, were the only people who worked there, but according to Alex, he was planning to hire two additional project managers and an in-house quality control expert. He also hoped to add a small engineering department so that he no longer had to rely on contractors.

It was exciting to come into this company just as it stood on the precipice of this massive growth spurt. Yet another reason why she could forget about taking time off to attend a several-weeks-long comics writing program. She couldn't leave now, not with everything happening at Holmes Construction.

Shania thanked them both for coming to view the rental space and promised to be in touch with Alex later in the day. They followed her out of the building and Reid started for his truck, but Brooklyn stopped him.

"Hey," she called, still standing on the sidewalk in front of the building. He looked back over his shoulder, one brow spiked in inquiry. "You up for some ice cream?" she asked.

He turned around fully, and by the serious look on his face, Brooklyn was certain she was about to get a lecture about them being on company time. But then he said, "What kind of question is that? Of course I'm up for ice cream."

She burst out laughing. "Good, because I rarely get over to this part of the city, and one of my favorite ice cream parlors is just a few blocks away. Alex wouldn't mind if we take a few minutes to grab a couple of cones, would he?"

Reid closed the distance between them, and with the most delectable twinkle gleaming in his brown eyes, said, "Who says Alex has to know?"

———

AS THEY STOOD WAITING for a utility truck to pass at the corner of Chestnut and Upperline Streets, Reid strove to temper the thrilling charge that raced along his skin. A damn near impossible feat. He'd spent the better part of the last hour pushing back against the urge to touch her every time she came near him.

Apparently, Brooklyn's confirmation that she wasn't seeing anyone was the green light his brain had been waiting for. All those excuses he'd drummed up over the past two weeks had crumbled away like the corroded thread on a rusted-out pipe. He was through pretending he was okay with this "let's just be friendly co-workers" bullshit. He wanted more.

His new goal: convince Brooklyn that he *deserved* more.

He couldn't rush this. And he couldn't be stupid about it either. He would have to rethink his usual method of pursuing a woman. If he went with his normal approach—a smile, a wink, and a quick invitation to his bed—he would either get a) a slap, b) a knee to the nuts, or c) both.

But he'd already acknowledged that his normal approach wouldn't work this time, because there was nothing normal about the way any of this felt.

He didn't *do* relationships. He'd never wanted to. Not until the woman who'd just invited him to join her for ice cream had crashed into his world and tempted him with her beguiling smile and array of superhero T-shirts. As he glanced over at her and took in the mass of thick, crinkly curls he'd been dying to shove his fingers into as he held her head steady against him, Reid realized what he had to do.

He would court her.

He'd never made much of an effort to win a woman over, but when he thought about the look that would come over his mom's face when she talked about how his dad courted her back in the day, Reid knew he had to at least try. Brooklyn was worth it. He would take the time to get to know her, to learn her likes and dislikes, and actually listen when she talked. But he would take it slow and give Brooklyn the chance to determine if her feelings mirrored his own.

God, please don't let me mess this up.

They turned onto Prytania Street and, moments later, came upon a green building that looked like a throwback to the 1960s.

"Wait, this is the old McKenzie's Bakery, isn't it? When did it become an ice cream parlor?" Reid asked.

"Years ago," Brooklyn said. She huffed. "And you call yourself a real ice cream lover. You can't really love ice cream and not know about The Creole Creamery."

He reached over and held the glass door opened, motioning for her to go ahead of him. He leaned in close as she walked by him and said, "I guess you *really* love ice cream."

She looked at him over her shoulder. "Like most parents love their children. Probably more. Kids can be little shits sometimes, but ice cream? Ice cream never, ever disappoints."

He couldn't control the laugh that shot from his mouth.

"I've never met someone who takes their ice cream this seriously. I'm fascinated." He slid onto the seat next to her, perching on one of the vinyl barstools that lined the old-school counter. "How does this obsession compare to the superhero T-shirts and stickers? Does it come close?"

"No," she said, her dark brown cheeks darkening even more as an adorably abashed grin stole across her lips. "The

T-shirt obsession is worse, but only because too much ice cream would pack on the pounds."

Reid let his eyes drift over her curves. "I don't think you have anything to worry about."

She pulled her bottom lip between her teeth and turned toward the ice cream display, but not before Reid glimpsed the heat that flared in her eyes.

The air arrested in his lungs as a wave of cautious hope rippled through him. That touch of awareness he'd caught in her gaze had to mean something, right? Like maybe she wasn't all that interested in keeping up this friendly co-workers charade either.

Reid sucked in a swift breath.

It would be hard enough sticking to his vow to take this slow. If Brooklyn showed him even the barest hint that she was interested in moving quicker, there was little hope he'd be able to resist the temptation to make a full-court press.

Slow down, Reid reminded himself. He would not rush this.

"So," Brooklyn started after clearing her throat. "Since you haven't been here before why don't you let me order for you?"

He nodded, his gaze falling to her mouth. "I think you'd know what I like," he answered, his tone dipping to a low, sensual timbre.

What. The. Fuck?

Didn't he *just* vow to scale back the aggressive come-ons?

But how could he when that alluring blush flared yet again on her cheeks? Reid knew damn well he was coming on too strong, too fast. He would have to go against every single one of his instincts if he didn't want to mess this up?

He stood. "It's a nice day out. How about I go outside and grab the bench."

He pulled his wallet from his back pocket, but Brooklyn shook her head.

"No, the ice cream is my treat. Consider it payment for the offer to look at my transmission."

"Do I actually have to explain that the car stuff is free of charge?" Reid asked.

She rolled her eyes. "Just go outside."

He did as he was told, leaving her to buy the ice cream while he snagged the bench that sat in front of the green and white storefront. Even though it was nearly October, the last of the summer's heat lingered in the air. It made the forthcoming ice cream a welcome treat on this sultry afternoon.

As he parked himself on the bench, a number of things clawed at his attention. Two birds squabbling over a piece of bread someone had dropped on the sidewalk outside of the restaurant next door. A mother singing nursery rhymes to the baby she pushed in a stroller. But eventually Reid's eyes moved to the ice cream parlor's huge window, and the woman standing in line at the counter.

He studied Brooklyn as she pointed at the curved glass display case.

A month ago, he would have said that she wasn't his type. He would have said it two weeks ago. But Reid now realized he didn't *have* a type, at least not one that was based on anything other than the most superficial qualities. He'd never had a serious girlfriend. Not one.

Oh, he'd had his share of women. His share, his friends' share, enough to share with an entire football team. But when it came to getting to know a woman, the most thought he'd ever put into it was deciding whether or not he trusted her enough to share his real name. Who in the hell lived that way?

Apparently, he did. But he didn't want to live that life anymore.

If he bought into any of that weird woo woo shit, Reid could almost believe the universe had placed Brooklyn in his world at this precise moment as a remedy to the sense of restlessness that had been building inside him for months now. She was the breath of fresh air he'd been seeking, a welcomed contradiction to the kind of women he'd grown so weary of. Given his indefensible track record with members of the opposite sex, Reid wasn't sure he even deserved her, but he wasn't about to look a gift horse in the mouth. He would just be grateful that she hadn't yet figured out she was too good for him.

She came outside carrying an ice cream cone in one hand and a long dish piled with six scoops of ice cream in the other.

He laughed as she handed him the dish. "Did you buy every flavor?"

"You've never been here before, so I wanted you to get a good sampling of what the Creole Creamery has to offer." She grinned. "Don't worry, whatever you don't finish I'll be more than happy to help put away."

He ate a spoonful of his treat, then stopped.

Reid had no doubt he would spend the rest of his life wondering why he hadn't prepared himself for the sight of her licking ice cream. The moment her tongue connected with the creamy concoction, his mind damn near imploded with enough filthy thoughts to make a sailor blush. He sat there, mesmerized. And it wasn't as if she was doing anything overly sexy. She was just eating freaking ice cream. But as far as his mind was concerned, she was eating ice cream while sliding down a stripper pole and losing her G-string on the way down. That's just how turned on he was.

"So, do you think Alex will like the office space?" she asked.

He heard the question, but his mind was still too focused on her mouth to completely register it. Somehow he managed to tear his eyes away from the most innocent porn flick he'd ever seen in his life and he asked, "Sorry, what was that?"

"The offices we just toured," she said. "Do you think Alex will go for it?"

Reid nodded. "Probably." He concentrated on his own ice cream so he wouldn't get distracted, scooping up a spoonful of what he thought was vanilla, but he swore he tasted a bit of rum in there.

"For one thing, the place on Magazine Street is a steal compared to how much the same amount of space is leasing for downtown. It's also closer to his house and to the school where his wife, Renee, is principal." Reid shook his head. "I still can't believe he's at the point where he needs to move into a place like that."

"You sound like my dad," Brooklyn said. "He's so proud of him, you would think Alex was his son instead of someone who worked for him well over a decade ago."

"The respect is mutual," Reid said. "I've lost count of the number of times Alex has reminded me that Holmes Construction wouldn't exist if not for everything Warren LeBlanc taught him back in the day."

The smile that appeared on Brooklyn's face brighten every corner of his day.

"It would make my dad so happy to hear that. He truly

does think of Alex like a son. He thinks of many of his old employees that way."

"Do you have brothers?" Reid asked.

She shook her head. "Only child."

He tilted his head in question. "So where did the 'sons' in LeBlanc and Sons come from?"

"Ah, the burning question that's always on everyone's mind," she said, her musical laugh flowing over him like a warm breeze. "My dad is actually the son in LeBlanc & Sons. Well, he and my Uncle Roland. My grandfather started the business when my dad and his younger brother were still in high school. It was always his intention that Dad and Uncle Roland would take over, but my uncle joined the Navy instead. He lives in Maryland. And, like dad, he only has daughters." She looked down at her ice cream cone. When she looked back up, her smile had dimmed. "I guess this was destined to be the end of the road for LeBlanc & Sons no matter what."

There was a mournfulness to her voice that immediately stirred up his protective instinct. He felt the need to reassure her that all would be okay. He hadn't thought of how the closure of her family's business had affected her.

Reid started to ask her why her father decided to close the business instead of just scaling back his personal workload, but before he could, she gestured to his bowl and said in an overly sunshiny voice, "Try the purple one."

He decided to let it go for now. Maybe one day she would be open to sharing a little bit more about what had to have been a difficult reality to accept.

Reid stuck a spoonful of the purple ice cream in his mouth and tried his best to keep his expression as neutral as possible.

She looked expectantly at him, then grimaced. "You don't like it."

He made himself swallow it down as he shook his head. "No. Sorry."

"Your tastebuds are messed up," she said. "The honey lavender is one of my favorites."

Reid held the dish out to her and tried to hand her his spoon.

"As if." Brooklyn regarded the spoon with repugnance. "I don't even want to imagine where your mouth has been."

"Hey," he balked. "What's that supposed to mean?"

She leveled him with a look that told Reid exactly what she meant by that.

He listed toward her, and despite the voice in his head reminding him of his vow to ease off the heavy flirting, whispered, "Just what do you think I do with my mouth?"

She pulled her bottom lip between her teeth again. God, she couldn't possibly know what that did to him.

"I don't even want to speculate," Brooklyn answered.

Reid's brow tilted up. "You sure about that? You trying to figure out all the different things I can do with my mouth sounds like a fun time to me." Reid looked at his phone. "By the way, we're no longer on the clock, so you can't sue me for sexual harassment."

She grinned. "I think I can still make a case."

"I'm sorry," he said, shoving a bit of false contriteness into his voice. "I'll try to behave."

Her eyes dropped to his lips. "Want to hear something really crazy? I'm not sure I want you to behave." She looked up at him. "What's going on here, Reid?"

He eyed her with skepticism. "Was that question rhetorical, or do I really have to spell it out for you?"

"I think you have to spell it out. Is this just typical

flirting for you, or is it..." She released a bewildered laugh. "It's too ridiculous to even finish the sentence."

He took her ice cream and dumped it on top of his, then he set his dish on the bench next to him.

"What about this is ridiculous to you?"

She shook her head. "Never mind."

"No, tell me. Because I'm trying really hard not to mess this up, and I need to know if I'm doing a good job."

"What is *this*?" Brooklyn asked. "What is it you're trying not to mess up?"

Rubbing the back of his neck, Reid released an uncomfortable laugh. When was the last time he'd felt this self-conscious around a woman?

"This is me trying to court you," he finally admitted.

Her eyes widened. "Court me?"

"Yeah, you know. It means—"

Brooklyn cut him off. "I know what it means." The sweetest smile traveled across her lips. "I'm just...surprised that you would go to the trouble."

"I didn't realize I would be so bad at it," he said. "I know it's old-fashioned, but my mom loved to talk about how my dad used to court her. I figure if smooth-as-barbwire Clark Holmes could pull it off, I at least have a shot." He looked over at her. "Please don't tell me my dad is smoother than I am."

"You're pretty good at it," she said.

He blew out a relieved breath. "Thank God."

She folded her hands together and stretched them out in front of her. Lifting her shoulders in a casual shrug, she asked, "So, what exactly are you hoping to accomplish with your smooth courting moves?"

"You're making fun of me," Reid said at the amusement coloring her voice. He wasn't totally upset about that. He liked the thought of making her laugh, even at his own expense.

"I'm not," she said, though the grin still creasing her face suggested otherwise. "I'm just...flattered. It will take me a while to wrap my head around the thought of a guy like you...you know."

Reid frowned. "A guy like me...what?"

She shook her head. "Nothing. But I do want to know what the end game is here."

"There is no end game," Reid said. "When I asked you if we could start over, you said you wanted to be friendly co-workers. I'm still onboard with that. We can be friendly co-workers...at work. But I don't want our time together to be limited to just work."

There was a long pause before she said, "You're asking me out." It was a statement, not a question.

"To be fair, you asked me out first. You bought me ice cream. If my mom was still here, she'd say we were going steady." He joined her in her laugh, but then added a dose of seriousness to his voice when he continued. "I'm not pushing, Brooklyn. I'm not used to going slow, but I can. In fact, I want to. This is...nice. It's different. Just sitting here talking to you—getting to know you. I like it."

That deep blush stained her cheeks again. "Me too," she said. She reached across him and picked up the dish of melting ice cream. "But I'm not letting this go to waste."

Reid held his hands up and chuckled. "Sorry. Now, if my mom was here she'd chew me out for wasting food. That was an outright violation in her book. I became a pro at hiding peas." He pulled the neck of his T-shirt out and peered inside. "I may still have some hidden down here."

His silliness garnered the reaction he'd hoped for, earning him another dose of her musical laugh.

"That sounds familiar," Brooklyn said. "Mine was cabbage. Not as easy to hide, so I just stubbornly refused to eat it." She bumped him with her elbow. "Speaking of your mom, you never told me what your sister and brothers thought about the idea."

Reid was still getting over the shock of how seamlessly they'd moved from the seriousness of him revealing his intentions to court her, to talking about mundane stuff again. Is this how relationships worked? Why hadn't he tried this before?

Maybe because you never found a woman you wanted *to be in a relationship with before Brooklyn.*

"I'm sorry I forgot to mention it," he said. "They love it."

Her eyebrows spiked. "Really?"

"Yeah." He nodded. "I went in there just knowing they would laugh me out of the house, but they honest-to-God love it. My sister, Indina, is already moving full steam ahead with the idea. It'll be interesting to see what she comes up with."

Brooklyn's brows went from arched to slanted. "Wait, so you're not going to be involved in the actual planning?"

He shrugged. He would never admit to the disappointment he felt, but after coming up with the concept for the super hero party, it sucked that he wouldn't have any input in how to pull it off.

"You'd have to know my family to understand," Reid said. "The fact that they even listened to me in the first place surprised the hell out of me."

"But you're an equal part of the family," she argued. "You should be able to have your ideas heard and taken as seriously as any of the others."

Her reaction validated the disgruntlement he'd been

experiencing lately. He was tired of Indina, Harrison, and Ezra treating him as if he didn't have anything to offer.

"She was your mother too, Reid. What would she say if she knew you were being cut out of the decision-making?"

"She would be pissed. When I was younger, she used to make Ezra bring me along when he would go out with his friends. He hated that," Reid said with a laugh. "She really was a super hero, at least to me." He tipped his head to the side. "Not just to me. Long after we'd all grown up, she was still running the children's bible study at the church, and volunteering to mentor young girls at the high school we all attended. She didn't know the meaning of the word selfish."

"She sounds amazing," Brooklyn said.

"She was." Reid swallowed past the lump that had formed in his throat. "I miss her so damn much. I knew life would be hard without her, but I never thought it would be *this* hard. I was never aware how often I picked up the phone and called, just to talk to her, until I couldn't do it anymore."

Brooklyn reached over and placed her hand over his. And in that moment, Reid realized this was the most he'd ever shared with anyone when it came to his feelings about losing his mother. He hadn't even hesitated; that's just how comfortable Brooklyn made him feel about opening up to her. It made him want to share more.

Reid slipped his hand in his pocket and pulled out his phone. He flipped through his photos until he found the picture he was looking for. He smiled at the image, then held the phone out to Brooklyn.

"This is the last picture I took with her," he said.

His mother sat up in the hospital bed, her shoulders covered in a pink, white and green shawl Willow had knitted for her. Reid stood just to the side of her, his arms wrapped around her as they stared at Liliana, who'd taken the picture.

"She was beautiful," Brooklyn said.

He couldn't speak, so he nodded in answer.

She looked up at him as she handed him the phone. "I think your mom would be so proud of you for wanting to continue her legacy of doing for others." She gestured to his phone. "She would want you to be a part of this. Don't let them cut you out of it, Reid."

He slipped his phone back into his pocket.

"You're right," he said. "And I won't."

CHAPTER SEVEN

NESTLED in her favorite comfy chair in the upstairs room at Tubby & Coo's, Brooklyn tapped the marker against her temple as she contemplated the length of the cape on her newest superhero. For some reason, cape length had become her newest thing to obsess over. Too long seemed to buy into the over-feminization of women superheroes, while a short cape didn't seem superhero-y enough.

"Ugh. Just draw one already!"

Deciding on mid-back for the length, Brooklyn quickly added the flowing cape, shading it in with a midnight blue to match the logo on the heroine's chest. The time it took to decide on the length for the cape was nothing compared to the hours she'd spent hemming and hawing over the inter-locking Ds design for the logo. When it came to this super-hero in particular, she'd debated every single detail. And for good reason. For the first time in three years, Brooklyn was preparing to share her drawings with another human being.

The immediate tightness that pulled at her chest gave the tiniest indication of just how monumental even the *thought* of sharing her work truly was for her. Candice, the owner of the bookstore, was the only person who even knew Brooklyn came up here to draw. But, showing the utmost respect for her customers' privacy, Candice had never once pressured her into sharing her work. Other than in the solitude of her own apartment or under her favorite secluded tree in City Park, this was the only other place where she felt comfortable drawing.

Brooklyn knew she couldn't keep her secret passion hidden forever. She would have to share her work if she ever summoned the nerve to apply for one of those fellowships. Of course, now that yet another had slipped past the deadline, the likelihood of doing so grew slimmer by the hour.

But the illustration she'd spent the past week working on wouldn't be shared with a grant or fellowship committee. It would be shared with a man she worked with every day. A man who'd swiftly turned into more than just an innocent workplace crush.

Brooklyn set the sketchpad in her lap and covered her face with her hands.

It felt as if she was living in an alternative universe. For years she'd maintained that like people went for like people, and super sexy, fine-ass men like Reid Holmes didn't go for cute, but average women like her. She accepted that. She *counted* on that. Acknowledging those facts as her reality made it easy to crush on guys like Reid without setting herself up for a huge letdown when her feelings weren't reciprocated. But this thing with Reid was not following the normal course.

What had once been casual flirting had turned into something much more meaningful since their afternoon at the ice cream parlor. He called himself *courting* her for God's sake!

They'd established a pattern since that day. He worked

out in the field in the morning, then moved into the trailer in the afternoon to manage the work piling up on Alex's desk. They'd attempted to keep the talk in the trailer strictly work-related, but there was only so much either could say about the activity going on around the worksite. Their conversations eventually meandered onto more personal avenues.

Yesterday, Reid had shared more about his mother. He talked about how hard it had been on his family to see their once vibrant matriarch deteriorate due to heart disease, and how proud he'd been of his dad for remaining strong throughout all of it. But then he broke Brooklyn's heart when he spoke about the day he'd walked into his parents' home about two months after their mother's passing, and discovered his dad bent over their wedding photo, sobbing.

Reid's heartache had been palpable as he talked about his uncertainty in trying to decide if he should comfort his dad or allow him to mourn in peace. He'd chosen the latter and had never mentioned to anyone—neither his dad nor his siblings—what he'd witnessed that afternoon.

His pain was still raw. It was undeniable. She ached for the self-professed Mama's Boy who was trying to figure out how to navigate a world his beloved mother was no longer a part of.

It touched Brooklyn on a personal level. Being a Daddy's Girl, it was apparent with every day that passed that she was moving closer and closer to that same fate. One day, sooner than what was fair, her mother would become the widow who clutched memories of her beloved in her hands and wept over what had been lost. Brooklyn prayed that the multitude of medications currently keeping her dad from getting sicker would continue to do their job, but there was only so much his body could take, and his COPD would only continue to worsen.

She rubbed her chest in an attempt to wipe away the ache brought on by thoughts of what she would one day have to endure. But at least she still had her Dad with her, unlike Reid, who bore the pain of losing his mother already. That was just one of the reasons Brooklyn was willing to do the one thing she had not had the courage to do in years.

Her chest did that tightening thing again as the memory of what happened the last time she'd shared her drawings with other people flooded her senses. She would *not* let the trauma inflicted on her by that horrible bastard from that stupid online chat room get the best of her again. She'd allowed that faceless asshole to bully her into hiding for years; allowed his harsh critique of her illustrations to strip away her confidence.

Not this time.

She had not spent the entire week working on these drawings, taking time away from her own comics, just to let it go to waste. If there was a reason to finally share her talent with the world again, this was it.

"You can do this," Brooklyn reminded herself.

Candice poked her head into the room and knocked twice on the wall. "Sorry to do this, but I have to close a little early today."

"Oh, no problem," Brooklyn said. She closed her sketchpad and pushed herself up from the comfortable chair. "You mentioned you were closing early when I first came in."

"If you're not done, I recommend finishing up at the coffee shop next door. They're brewing their special fall blend and it is amazing. I plan to have it as many times as I can before the season is over."

"A nice cup of coffee sounds fabulous."

Brooklyn stuffed her sketchpad and markers into her beat up messenger bag, then made her way down the curving staircase. Its walls were peppered with floating bookshelves that made it seem as if the stacks of Young Adult novels were floating on air. She navigated around the pillars of bookcases that commanded the bottom floor of the tiny bookstore, waving to Candice on her way out.

"See you next weekend," Brooklyn said as she pulled on her sweater. She exited the store and turned left, heading toward the Bean Gallery Coffeehouse and Cafe.

"I wondered how long you would be up there."

Brooklyn yelped and turned, finding Reid perched against the hood of her car, which she'd parked at the curb in front of the bookstore. He wore his signature worn jeans paired with a long-sleeve black T-shirt that molded to the arms crossed over his chest.

"What are you doing here?" She clamped a hand over her erratically beating heart. "Are you stalking me?"

He lifted a shoulder. "Maybe. You're pretty stalkable."

"Is stalkable even a word?"

A grin stretched across his face. "I don't know. I'm just a lowly plumber, remember? I leave all wordy things to smarty-pants like you."

With anyone else, Brooklyn would have taken those words as a dig, but the smile on his face told her that his joke had not an ounce of maliciousness behind it.

"Whether or not stalkable is an actual word, I'm going to take a guess that stalking me was not your original intent," she said.

"No, it wasn't." He pushed away from her car and covered the two yards that separated them. He stuck his hands in his pockets and tipped his head toward

The Bean Gallery. "I happened to be on my way to the coffee shop when I noticed your car parked on the curb. When I didn't see you in there, I figured the bookstore was the most logical place. I've never been to it, but I know Anthony has. They sell lots of Sci-fi stuff, right?"

She nodded. "It's funny that I've never seen him there before. Of course, I'm usually in the upstairs room, and all the adult books are downstairs."

"What's upstairs?"

She hesitated for a moment, the sketchpad in her messenger bag suddenly feeling as if it weighed three tons. "Kids' books and a game room. It's a cool place to hang out and read comics," she answered. *Coward.* "I was actually on my way to get some coffee."

"You mind if I join you?"

As if she would ever in a million years deny herself the opportunity to be in the same space with him. She was so fully immersed in this fantasy, Brooklyn doubted she would ever recover.

They climbed the stairs to the huge porch at the entrance of the coffee shop, but before Brooklyn could reach for the door handle, Reid stepped in front of her and pointed to one of the outside tables.

"Coffee's on me. I still owe you from our ice cream. What are you having?"

"Well, I was going to have just a cup of brewed coffee, but now that you're paying I want something fancy and expensive."

His rich laughed filled the air around them, and her body warmed from the inside out.

"So, I'm ordering the most expensive drink on the menu?"

"I'll go easy on you this time. Get me just a regular latte."

She sat at a table, and minutes later, Reid returned with her drink and a muffin wrapped in plastic wrap.

"Thank you," she said as she accepted the cup and took a sip. She sat up straight. "Did you sweeten this?"

He nodded. "I've noticed you put two packets of sugar in your afternoon coffee."

The significance of his admission sent all kinds of feelings traipsing throughout Brooklyn's bloodstream.

"How is it?" Reid asked.

She took another sip and looked up at him. "Perfect."

His eyes dropped to her mouth and her heart began to pound like a base drum against the walls of her chest. She was walking the edges of very dangerous territory here. Ever since Reid made his intentions known, she'd made an effort to temper her propensity to fall headfirst. It wasn't the easiest thing she'd ever done. Reid Holmes made it extremely difficult not to fall headfirst in ridiculously sappy, infatuated love with him.

Brooklyn quickly tore her eyes away from his kissable lips and looked out at the sun gently setting over the trees of Mid-City.

"So, what brings you to this neighborhood on a Saturday evening?" she asked. "It isn't a typical party place."

"I'll be thirty next week. I'm getting too old to party," he said. She rolled her eyes. "I was down at Delgado," he finished.

Her eyes widened. "Are you going to school?"

"Hell no." He laughed. "The only time you'll catch me on a college campus is for the occasional LSU football game or if I'm visiting my brother, Ezra. He teaches journalism at the community college. We were supposed to meet up at his place today, but he has a class on Saturday afternoons and decided to stay a bit later to grade some papers."

"That's dedication."

"Yeah. He's trying to get as much off his plate as possible before his life gets crazy. His fiancé is Councilmember Mackenna Arnold. She's running for mayor."

"Wow! I know who Councilmember Arnold is. She sponsors a toy drive for her district at Christmas. LeBlanc & Sons has been a donor for years. She's going to be an amazing mayor."

"She has to win first, but I agree," Reid said. "Anyway, I like the coffee here, so since I happened to be so close, I decided to stop in. Noticing your car parked at the curb was a sweet bonus." He gestured his head back toward the bookstore. "You may think I'm a crazy stalker once I admit this, but I sat out there for an hour waiting for you. How long does it take you to buy books?"

Brooklyn nearly choked on her coffee. "You've been here for an hour? Why didn't you just come inside the bookstore?"

"I wanted to surprise you," he said. "I'm not sorry. You jumped a foot in the air when I called your name. That reaction was worth the wait."

Brooklyn burst out laughing. "And I thought I was twisted."

"You want to hear something *really* twisted?" He waited for the bright red streetcar that rolled along Carrolton Avenue to pass before continuing. "I've never done anything like this before." Resting his forearms on the table, Reid clamped his hands together and looked at her with a curious expression. "I looked at my watch at least a dozen times while I waited for you to come out. Every time I did, I told myself this was crazy." He slowly shook his head. "But I couldn't leave. I wanted to see you."

Brooklyn's chest felt as if it would burst. "Okay, so that may be the sweetest thing anyone has ever said to me."

"That's pretty sad, because it wasn't even that sweet. I can be a lot sweeter." He winked. "Just give me time."

Goodness, he was such a flirt. She just so happened to love his flirting.

"So, do you just hang out at the bookstore?" Reid asked as he unwrapped the muffin he'd bought. He produced a plastic knife and cut the muffin in half. Then he put half of one half in his mouth and pushed the half that was still on the plastic wrap in front of her.

"Thank you," Brooklyn said. She quickly took a much smaller bite of the muffin, buying herself some time to decide how to answer his question. He'd unknowingly given her the opportunity to do what she'd been building up the courage to do. Before she could talk herself out of it, she said, "Actually, I go there to work."

He frowned. "You know how Alex is about the whole work/life balance thing. You shouldn't be bringing work home with you."

"Not that work," she said.

She sucked in a deep breath and slowly released it. She knew this would be difficult, but it wasn't until this very moment, when she had to mentally talk herself out of having a full blown panic attack, that she realized just how much that online incident had impacted her.

It pissed her off.

She worked hard at her comics. She'd put more time and energy into this than anything else in her life. The fact that she'd allowed a random stranger on the internet to have such power over her sickened her. She was done hiding her light under a bushel.

Still, as she unbuckled the latch on her messenger bag, she could hardly hear past her heart's loud thumping. She set the closed sketchpad on the table, and kept her eyes on its plain gray cover.

"I draw comics," she finally said. She opened the sketchpad to the drawing she'd been working on all week. "This is my newest. I call her Dynamo Diane." She looked up at him. "It's your mom."

Reid just sat there, staring at the illustration, not saying anything. Brooklyn's anxiety escalated as she silently contemplated grabbing her stuff and running away, clear to Mississippi if she could manage it.

After several long, silent moments passed, he reached for the sketchpad, but then jerked his hand back.

"Can I?" he asked.

Brooklyn nudged the drawing toward him. "Of course."

He lifted it from the table and held it out, examining the picture with the attention one would a masterpiece hanging in a museum.

"You drew this?" He looked over at her. "You *drew* this? You didn't trace it from somewhere else?"

She shook her head.

"This is fucking amazing!"

He stood and, before she knew what he was doing, came over and lifted her from her chair. He swirled her around, her foot kicking the back of an empty chair at a neighboring table.

Brooklyn released a breathless laugh. She closed her eyes for a moment and relished in the heady sensation of her breasts being pressed up against his chest.

"I'm guessing you like it?" she asked when she was finally able to find her voice.

"Did you think I wouldn't?" he asked as he set her back down. She kinda wished he hadn't. She could stand to spend another hour or two in his arms.

She reclaimed her seat, picked up her drink and took another sip before answering.

"I wasn't sure if you would think it was crossing a line or something. It's not as if I asked permission." Brooklyn looked over at him and lifted her shoulders in a shrug. "But, I thought since you're doing a superhero theme for your mom's foundation's kickoff party, your mom should be the star of it."

He sat down, moving his chair a bit closer to hers. He picked the sketchpad up again and held it out. "I don't even know what to say. *You* drew this."

"Yes, *I* drew that." She didn't even try to keep the pride out of her voice. She *should* be proud of herself. It was a damn good illustration.

His eyes still on the drawing, he asked, "What in the hell are you doing working on a construction site with this kind of talent? Why aren't you working for Disney or somebody like that?"

Brooklyn laughed. "I have a loooong way before I'm ready for Disney."

"Bullshit. This picture is incredible." His head popped up and a puzzled expression flashed across his face. "You didn't know my mom. How did you get this to look so much like her?"

Busted.

She could tell him that she remembered the picture he showed her outside the ice cream parlor, but that lie was too farfetched for her to try to sell it. Brooklyn decided to come clean.

"I'm not sure if you know this, but both your Facebook and Instagram accounts are public."

His brows shot up. "Well, well, well. Who's the stalker now?"

Despite the crispness in the fall air, Brooklyn's cheeks felt as if they were on fire.

He leaned over, and with the most adorable shit-eating grin, said, "You know, you could have just sent me a friend request."

"You're horrible," Brooklyn said, unable to hold in her laugh. She fiddled with some of the muffin crumbs before pushing it toward him so he could finish it off. "So, it's not a problem that I stalked your IG account for a picture of your mom?"

"Not at all. If I send you a friend request on Facebook, will you accept it?"

"I'm not on Facebook. That's for old people."

Laughing, he balled up the plastic wrap and lobbed it at her. "Didn't you hear me say I'm turning thirty? I'm sensitive about that shit."

Brooklyn laughed so hard her side hurt. "You don't look a day over twenty-nine and a half," she said once she was finally able to catch her breath.

He picked up the drawing again. It was as if he couldn't stop looking at it.

"So, what do we do with Dynamo Diane? Put her on T-shirts and buttons and stuff?"

"I was thinking that if you all plan to do a program for the event—you know, something that highlights the goals of the foundation—it could be in comic book form. Dynamo

Diane on her quest to save women from heart disease. It would be a great keepsake."

Excitement shone in his eyes. "You could do that? I mean, would you have time? The kickoff party is only a few months away. Can you draw an entire comic by then?"

Brooklyn did some mental calculations in her head. She still had several panels to complete on her Iansan illustrations, which would have to be done within the next few weeks if she was going to bring it with her to the Comic Con in Biloxi where Kurt Bollinger, one of her idols, would be in attendance. There was a ninety-nine percent chance she would chicken out when it came to sharing her drawing with him, but she wanted to have it done on the off-chance she found her backbone and gave in to that one percent.

Of course, if she needed a good excuse to push Iansan aside in order to work on something more important—like a foundation that would help hundreds of people—Reid had just handed it to her. She didn't have to feel bad about chickening out for such a good cause. Right?

"I can do it," Brooklyn said. "Now that I've gotten Dynamo Diane just how I want her, the rest won't be as hard."

Reid's expression was filled with appreciation and awe. His voice, when he spoke, heavy with gratitude. "I can't believe you did this," he said. "It's the most amazing, unselfish thing anyone has ever done for me."

He turned in his chair until he faced her. Then he leaned forward and Brooklyn's heart began to dance a quadrille within her chest. She waited until his mouth was mere centimeters from hers before she pulled her head back and said, "Before we do this, I just need to ask if this is going to be a real kiss, or a 'thanks for making my mom a superhero' kiss?"

"Would you stop thinking so hard and let me kiss you?"

Brooklyn pulled her bottom lip between her teeth. "Answer my question first."

She was an idiot. No doubt about it. The man she'd been fantasizing about for a month was seconds away from putting his lips on hers and here she was playing Twenty Questions. But she had to know that the seductive look clouding his face was there because of attraction and not gratitude. It made a difference, at least to her.

Reid captured her chin with his fingers and lifted her face up to his. "What I'm about to lay on you is one hundred percent real. You got any other questions, or can I kiss you now?"

She swallowed. "You can kiss me now."

He was still grinning when his lips finally met hers, but that grin soon faded as his mouth began a tender, effortless exploration. He was both sweet and seductive, teasing her with his soft touch, setting her body ablaze with his sensual skill. A moan escaped Brooklyn's lips as she melted, her insides turning to liquid as Reid's surprisingly soft lips coaxed her mouth open.

It felt as if she'd been transported to another realm, her mind so caught up in the enchantment of his coffee-flavored kiss that she could think of nothing else. It was better than anything she had dreamed up in her daydreams. Reid's gentle, yet hungry mouth imprisoned her, capturing her with every hypnotic thrust of his tongue.

He moved deliberately, as if he were mapping the inside of her mouth. The blood in her veins pumped faster with every slow and steady glide, her nipples growing so tight they ached.

A faint voice roaming somewhere in the back of her mind tried to warn her they were in public, but Brooklyn mentally swatted it away. She refused to allow reality to step in. She wanted to exist in this fantasy for as long as possible.

But when his hand moved from her side to her breast, Brooklyn froze. That reality she'd been fighting off came roaring to the forefront. She wrapped her hand around Reid's wrist and pulled it away, releasing a shaky breath as she willed her chaotically beating heart to calm down.

"I...uh...I'm sorry," she said. "This is going a little too fast."

"Okay," Reid said with a nod. His chest expanded with his swift intake of breath. The stunned look in his wide eyes mimicked what Brooklyn was experiencing at the moment. It was apparent that neither of them had been ready for the aftereffects of that kiss.

"If this is going to happen—oh, God, this is happening, isn't it?" Brooklyn exclaimed.

"If by 'this' you mean me getting to kiss you at least a hundred times by the end of the week, then I sure as hell hope it's happening."

An insane amount of joy and disbelief bubbled up inside her.

"Can we make that a dozen?" Brooklyn asked. "A hundred seems a bit excessive."

A smile drew across his lips as he wrapped his hand around the back of her neck and lightly caressed the spot behind her ear with his thumb. "We can take it one kiss at a time. And if I'm moving too fast, it only takes one word: stop."

Brooklyn leaned into his touch, her eyes falling closed. It was almost too much to grasp, but with every gentle brush of his finger against her skin, the picture became clearer.

Her fantasy had become her reality.

REID LEANED BACK against the thick, centuries-old tree trunk, one leg drawn up, the other thigh serving as a table for the comic he'd been reading since they arrived at what Brooklyn proclaimed was the most perfect spot in all of City Park. As far as Reid was concerned, it was just one shady tree among dozens of other shady trees. She was the one who made it perfect.

He stared at her from underneath hooded eyes, not wanting to break her concentration. She lay on her stomach, her legs bent at the knees, her ankles crossed as her feet bounced to whatever music was coming through her earbuds. Her Thor T-shirt rode up slightly at her waist, revealing a sliver of skin. Reid had lost count of the number of times he'd fantasized about crawling over to her and burying his face against her stomach. He wanted to sink his teeth into that sexy little roll of flesh that folded over her jeans.

He fucking loved her curves. His hands ached with the need to grab hold of that healthy ass and those luscious thighs and, God, those breasts that tested the limits of the T-shirts she loved to wear. He wanted to touch every inch of her.

He leaned his head back against the tree trunk and shut his eyes tight, barely able to contain the frustration of sitting here and not touching her. But he wouldn't make that mistake again. He'd done so last night and it had spooked her. He had to remind himself that when it came to Brooklyn he had to move slow.

If only he knew *how* to move slow. He didn't know how to do any of this. He now recognized that he was in the midst of a life lesson, learning the difference between being in a relationship and just hooking up. But he was willing to learn, because the more he got to know her, the more he wanted this thing with Brooklyn to grow into something more.

He studied her face, how her forehead creased with concentration. She'd been at it for a half hour, all her focus on the sketchpad as she worked on the program booklet for the foundation's kickoff party. She'd first suggested she draw a few sample panels, as she called them, to share with Indina and his brothers. She wanted to make sure his siblings liked the idea before she started working on the actual comic. Reid assured her they would like it. If they didn't he would raise all levels of hell, but he knew his sister and brothers would be as blown away as he'd been at the sight of their mother immortalized as the superhero they all knew her to be.

He still couldn't believe Brooklyn had kept such talent to herself. As he glanced down at the comics encased in sheet protectors that he'd been reading, he acknowledged her talent went far beyond what he'd first suspected.

Reid still didn't know what to make of her reaction earlier today. He'd caught site of this second set of illustrations when she'd opened up the black zippered portfolio where she kept her Dynamo Diane drawings. When he'd asked if he could see them, she'd recoiled. She'd tried to play it off with a nonchalant wave, telling him that the drawings were just something she was messing around with.

Reid wasn't fooled. Her discomfort had been palpable. It was the only reason he hadn't pushed. But then, after a few moments passed, she relented, handing him the drawings. She explained that she'd been working on the comic for months, but as with all of her illustrations, hadn't shared them with anyone yet.

It was a straight up crime that she'd kept this hidden from the world. As he'd pored over the pages, Reid had been pulled so deeply into the story that, for a time, he'd forgotten everything around him. Not only could she draw, she could tell a story in a way that made you feel as if you were immersed in the character's world.

She may not think she was good enough to work for a major company, but she was wrong. She was phenomenal.

"You're staring," Brooklyn said, her eyes still on her sketchpad.

"You're easy to stare at," Reid returned, not the least bit repentant at getting caught.

She glanced over at him, an impish grin tilting up the corner of that gorgeous mouth. She was *so* damn cute. She wore no colorful streaks in her hair today, but the wild, twisty curls still spoke to her personality in a way that made him smile.

Reid jutted his chin toward her. "How are things going over there? Has Dynamo Diane saved the world yet?"

"That usually doesn't happen until the very end," she said. "However, in this story, the world isn't what's in need of saving. A group of young girls who have been told they shouldn't study STEM needs Dynamo Diane to rescue them from this patriarchal society."

"You lost me at STEM."

She laughed. "STEM stands for Science, Technology, Engineering, and Math—all fields that young girls have traditionally been told are much too taxing for their delicate brains." She twisted around on the blanket and her T-shirt rode up just a bit more. Reid shifted his leg to hide the bulge slowly building behind his zipper.

"From everything you've told me about your mom and the objectives of the foundation, encouraging girls to pursue the sciences is exactly the kind of thing the Diane Holmes Foundation will do."

"It is," Reid agreed. "One of our first goals is to provide scholarships for young African American women who plan to study medicine. Can you imagine how amazing it would be if a recipient of the foundation's scholarship one day went on to cure heart disease?"

"You know, your face lights up when you talk about this," she said.

Reid dipped his head, although why he suddenly felt embarrassed, he didn't know. He was proud of what he and his siblings had set out to do.

He shrugged. "I kinda like the thought of being a part of something that can have a real impact."

"You should. This is going to touch a number of lives. And you're playing a big part in it."

If she continued with the compliments his cheeks would soon have singe marks from all this damn blushing.

"Enough about me," Reid said, eager to get the spotlight off himself. "Let's talk about this." He held up the illustration. "This should be in a bookstore, or on an iPad, or wherever people read comics these days."

Now *she* was the one blushing. Good. They were back in familiar territory. He made women blush, not the other way around.

Brooklyn got up and sat cross-leg on the blanket, grabbing onto both knees. "You're just saying that because you want to get to second base again," she said in answer to his compliment.

"I never quite caught on to that baseball/sex analogy thing. Is second base what happened last night?"

She nodded.

He grinned. "What's third?"

"Something you can't do in public."

"You sure about that?"

She burst out laughing. "You're not getting to third base today."

"Not today, huh? So you're saying we can revisit this conversation tomorrow?"

"You, Reid Holmes, are incorrigible."

"Stop it with the big words," he said, moving away from the tree trunk and settling down next to her on the blanket. He propped his elbow on the ground and rested his head against his fist. "And while there is nothing I want to do more than get to third base with you, that's not why I said your work needs to be in a bookstore. I said it because it's the truth. Iansan is badass. How do you even come up with this stuff?"

"I can't take the credit for Iansan. She's based on African mythology."

"Yet another thing you're into?"

She lifted her shoulders in a matter-of-fact shrug. "You can say that. Back when I was in junior high, my mom would bring me to the library used book sales. She used to joke that my reading habit was going to send us to the poor house." She laughed. "Anyway, I picked up a book on African Mythology and became obsessed. You always hear about the popular gods like Horus and Osiris, but there are so many deities—literally hundreds of them. Each area of the continent has its own distinct mythology."

She shook her head. "I'm sorry. I'm probably boring the crap out of you."

"No," Reid quickly reassured her. "Not at all.

He loved to hear her talk about the things she was passionate about. And she was passionate about *so* many different things. He was the one who felt boring compared to her. He didn't have any cool hobbies or hidden talents or any of the things that made her the interesting, remarkable person he was discovering her to be.

"I've never been one for comic books, or well, any kind of books to be honest," Reid admitted. "But this story pulled me in." He dropped his eyes to the drawing, then looked back up at her. "Maybe if I'd been more into comics as a kid, I would have read more. I've always liked pictures more than I like words."

He started to say more, but then stopped. Was he really willing to share this? But then Reid realized if there was anyone he *would* share it with, it was the woman sitting next to him.

"Reading has never been my strong suit," he continued. He tried to play it off with a casual lift of his shoulder. "I haven't been officially diagnosed by a doctor or anything, but it's likely I suffer from something called surface dyslexia."

Brooklyn's eyes widened in surprise, but then her forehead creased with a frown. "If you haven't been given a diagnosis, how can you be sure?"

"Because I know how my brain works. And based on what I've found online, people with surface dyslexia tend to think and learn the way I do."

She rolled her eyes. "Please don't tell me you're one of those self-diagnosing internet people. I'm surprised you didn't discover it was cancer. Every symptom leads to cancer on the internet."

"It's not as if I did one Google search and decided I'm dyslexic," Reid said with a laugh. "I've researched it a lot over the years. It makes sense. I had meningitis as a baby—it wasn't a severe case, but I had it. A lot of the studies say that this type of dyslexia is sometimes caused by infections in the brain."

"Have you thought about seeking help?"

Reid shook his head. "Maybe if I'd said something sooner, my parents could have taken me to whatever kind of therapy handles this kind of thing, but I hid it for a long time. And at this point, I've gotten so used to compensating, I doubt any legitimate treatment techniques would work for me." He shrugged. "I've managed to do okay. Even in a family like mine."

She frowned. "A family like yours?"

He huffed out a humorless laugh. "You'd have to understand my family to know what I mean by that," he said. "My oldest brother, Harrison, is an attorney. My other brother, Ezra, is an award-winning journalist, and Indina is an interior designer. Not the kind that picks out drapes for your living room; the kind that comes up with the designs for entire government buildings, and three-story libraries, and shit like that."

"They intimidate you," Brooklyn correctly assessed.

"Hell yes," Reid said. "It's easy to feel inferior when you're in a family of brainiacs, while you have a hard time making sentences make sense."

She scooted over to him, sitting so close her thigh meshed up against his.

"The fact that you've been able to accomplish all you have is enough proof that you aren't inferior to anyone."

She picked up a blade of grass and traced it along his hand, then dropped it and replaced the grass with her fingertip. Reid's skin burned where she touched it. He relished the innocent, yet intimate contact.

"You're the only other person alive who knows about my dyslexia," he said. She looked up at him, her eyes rounding in dubious disbelief. "You are," Reid confirmed. "My mom was the only other person who knew." He released a gruff laugh. "I tried to keep it hidden from her, but you can't hide shit from your mom."

"I'm touched that you would share it with me," she said, her voice whisper soft.

Reid ran his palm along the supple jean material covering her thigh. "Enough to let me get to third base?"

She slapped his hand away. "You just cannot be serious, can you?"

"I've learned over the years that being serious isn't fun." He shifted onto his back and folded his hands behind his head. "I shouldn't have to tell you that. You write comic books. Having fun should be in your DNA."

"It is fun," she said. "Most of the time."

Reid looked over at her. "Most of the time?"

She stretched out onto her stomach next to him, shoring herself up on her elbows. She reached over the edge of the blanket, plucked another blade of grass, and twirled it between her fingers.

"The drawing is the fun part, but there are other aspects of the comics world that aren't as fun."

Several beats passed before Reid finally asked, "You plan on elaborating here?"

"When did this turn into share our secrets hour?" she asked.

"I'd say the moment you let me read Iansan. You let that secret out of the bag, you might as well spill it all."

She released another of those annoyed breaths. "It's not even a big secret," she said. "It's just that I don't really talk about my comics. Like ever."

"But why?"

She hunched her shoulders. "I'm just not comfortable

putting my work out there. I've seen what happens when people put their work online. The comics community can be brutal."

Reid chuckled. "You're saying there's a bunch of bullies on the internet talking smack about comics?"

"That's exactly what I'm saying." The gravity in her tone caught him off-guard. Before he could question her further, she shrugged and said, "I don't really get involved in the writing and illustrating side. When it comes to the online community, I'd much rather follow the reader forums. I'm an out and proud Blerd."

"Blerd?"

"Black Nerd," she clarified, and Reid burst out laughing. He couldn't help it. "Hey," Brooklyn said, knocking his arm with her elbow. "Nerds are cool. And Blerds are ten times cooler. Despite all the ugly shit that goes on online, for the most part, the Internet has been great for people like me. "

"People like you? You're not some alien life form."

"I've felt that way at times. It's not always easy to find people around here—especially black people—who will admit to liking comics and cosplay."

"Wait." He sat up. "You're not one of those people who's into dressing up as comic book heroes, are you?" She remained silent, but that blush he was starting to find addicting blossomed on her cheeks. "You are," Reid said. He fell onto his back again and groaned. "What I wouldn't do to see you in a sexy ass Wonder Woman costume." He turned to her and pleaded. "Please wear one for Halloween, I'm begging you."

She elbowed him again. "I am not dressing up as Wonder Woman for Halloween," she said, breaking his heart. "However," she continued. "I will be debuting another costume I've been excited to wear at a Comic Con in Biloxi in a few weeks." She tilted her head to the side. "You should come with me."

"To a comics convention?"

"It would be a good place to research ideas for the kickoff party."

Reid reached over and trailed a faint caress along her arm. In a teasing voice, he asked, "Is that the only reason you want me to come with you?"

"That's the only reason I'll own up to." She laughed. "I'm afraid of how big your ego will get if I admit to anything more."

"I can show you how big my ego can get," he said, catching her by the wrist and pulling her on top of him. He quickly rolled them over so that he was on top and, looking upon her gorgeous face, said, "I really, really want to kiss you right now."

"I'm really, really sure that's not a good idea," Brooklyn said.

"I really, *really* think you're wrong. In fact," he whispered. "If you give me a chance, I can prove just how wrong you are."

He felt her chest moving up and down with her quick, shallow breaths. With a warning look in her eyes, she said, "Just remember, no third base."

Grinning, Reid leaned forward and fused his lips with hers.

"No," he said when she closed her eyes. "Open them. I don't want you pretending I'm someone else when I kiss you."

She choked out a laugh. "Yeah, because that's something I would do."

"Maybe not, but I need to be sure."

She slipped her hand around the back of his head and tugged. "I can promise there's no pretending going on here." Then she lifted her head and took his mouth in an achingly slow, decadently erotic kiss, mapping the seam of his lips with her tongue before thrusting it inside his mouth.

Just as he had last night, Reid recognized something was different. He'd kissed more than his share of women, but there was something deeper, something more meaningful with what was happening right now. This wasn't about him at all. Everything he felt, everything he wanted to do, centered around Brooklyn and the pleasure he wanted her to derive from his kiss.

He angled his head so he could thrust deeper, advancing his tongue with determination, applying gentle but steady pressure. He lost himself in her kiss, assailing her mouth with insistent strokes, loving every soft moan that escaped her lips. She tasted like the cherry Now and Later candies she'd been eating earlier, bringing back sweet memories of his childhood. He swept his tongue back and forth, aching to sample more of her flavor, craving the softness and warmth he discovered with every plunge.

God, she was sweet. And sexy. And amazing.

Controlling his body's natural response to the feel of her pliant form stretched out beneath his own was beyond his capabilities. If she was paying any attention at all to the lower half of her body, she would become aware of the erection rapidly gaining strength against her thigh.

He felt her stiffen and knew they were about to have a repeat of last night. But instead of putting a stop to their very public display of affection, she tugged more firmly on his neck and deepened their kiss.

Reid groaned into her mouth. He flattened his chest against her breasts, covering all of her body with his own.

Moving his lips to the slope of her neck, he concentrated on the silkiness of her skin instead of the overwhelming urge to grind his dick into her soft stomach.

Got*damn* he wanted her.

He was so hard his body ached, but it was the ache to get closer to her—not just physically, but mentally—that Reid felt even more. This obsession over her had hit him with a swiftness that left him breathless, but there was no denying it. He was ready to bury those days of meaningless hook-ups and empty flings. That was his past. He wanted the woman in his arms to be his future.

Now, all he had to do was convince her to want the same.

———

"IS this why you asked me to meet you here?" Brooklyn asked, even as she tilted her head to the side to give Reid better access to her neck.

He'd texted her only minutes after they'd both left the job site. It had been her first time hearing from him since he stopped in the trailer for his coffee this morning.

Today had been one of those days, for both of them. Every time Brooklyn thought she'd have a minute to breathe, something else would pop up, demanding her attention. She'd been anticipating seeing Reid for lunch, when he usually switched from his plumbing duties to his role as Alex's second-in-command. Instead, she'd been called down to City Hall to correct a mistake the site foreman had made on the permits that had been filed to cover the new work that would be done to repair the sinkhole.

She'd been looking forward to a long bath and binge-watching old episodes of *A Different World*, but then she'd received Reid's text, asking if she was free this evening. She should be ashamed at the embarrassing rush of giddy excitement that traveled through her, but she refused to feel one ounce of shame. How could she not be excited in the face of her one-time fantasy becoming reality before her very eyes?

Reid had included the address to his apartment in his text, claiming he wanted to look up ideas for the foundation's kickoff party. He assured her he had no ulterior motives, but after this weekend, Brooklyn knew neither of them could be trusted to be alone in his apartment.

Of course, being out in public didn't seem to be much of a deterrent to their inappropriate behavior either. Both times they'd kissed, they had been out for all the world to see. Such was the case right now as they sat in one of the comfortable chairs at another of her favorite coffee shops. Brooklyn nestled in Reid's lap, working on her computer. He'd spent the past hour stroking her arm and placing the sweetest little kisses along her neck, and behind her ear, and on her shoulder.

How was this real life?

She still could not fully fathom the fact that this was really happening. How was it that the man she'd pegged as her harmless workplace crush, the man she'd designated as being out of her league, was currently nibbling on her skin as if it tasted like cotton candy? This didn't happen to her. It just didn't. She'd never bought into the opposites attract theory. She rolled her eyes at those silly romance stories where the hot, popular guy fell for the shy, geeky girl. She'd convinced herself that men like Reid just didn't go for women like her, and she'd been just fine with that.

Yet, here she was, playing the role of his favorite end of the day snack.

"What about a costume contest?" Reid asked.

She looked over her shoulder. "You think the crowd you're hoping to attract for the kickoff party would go for that?"

"I think the crowd we're hoping to attract is so tired of stuffy, tuxedo and ball gown parties that they'll jump at the chance to have some fun. Don't you think so?"

"Sure, but I'm biased. I think it's perfectly fine to wear a costume to go to the grocery store," Brooklyn said.

His shoulders shook with amusement.

"In all seriousness, I think a costume contest is a great idea. It would encourage people to really get into the whole spirit of the event." She grinned. "Have you decided what costume you're going to wear?"

He hunched his shoulders before burrowing his nose against her neck. "I'm counting on this sexy ass comics-loving girl I know to help me come up with something that's going to blow every other costume out the water."

"Oh, who's that girl? I'd love to meet her," Brooklyn said. She yelped when he pinched her thigh.

"Remember, we're no longer on the clock. No turning me into HR," Reid said.

"How long do you plan to use that excuse?"

"For as long as you'll let me," he said, planting a kiss on the tip of her nose.

The innocent gesture affected Brooklyn in ways his deep kisses had not. There was something pure and guileless about it. It reminded her of those couples who unconsciously reached for each other's hand while walking down the street. She'd always been jealous of those people; now she was one of them.

"Maybe I can be a black superman," Reid said.

Brooklyn shook her head. "Nah. That's played out."

"You mean somebody's already thought of Black Superman? Damn, I thought I was onto something."

She laugh so loud at the dejection in his voice, she drew stares from several of the patrons hunched over their laptops. Brooklyn set her computer on the table and twisted around so she could look at him.

"Don't worry," she said. "We'll come up with an idea for you that's going to have everybody talking the night of the kickoff party."

"Okay, then. I'm placing myself in your hands."

The naughty thoughts his innocent statement conjured made her face heat up. Goodness, when had she become this person who read sexual innuendo into every little thing? Maybe ever since one of the sexiest men she'd ever met started treating her as if she was one of the sexiest women he'd ever met?

Brooklyn still couldn't fully grasp that this was her freaking life right now.

"I've been trying to figure out how we can make the theme work for us in ways we hadn't considered," Reid said, jerking her out of her inappropriate musings. "You know, attract people who possibly wouldn't have attended if we were having just a regular ball."

She had yet to mention it to him, but Brooklyn had been mulling over something for the past couple of days that she was convinced would be a game changer.

Or, it could be a flop.

She had no idea. But she'd have never thought Reid or his family members would choose to have a cosplay gala either, so what could it hurt to share?

"I do have one idea," she said. "I'm not sure how it would play out with the crowd you all are anticipating, but..." She shrugged.

"What is it?"

"You can have an auction. If you can convince a few people to donate some memorabilia or rare comics, and advertise that they will be auctioned off at the kickoff party, you'd pull in some serious collectors. Of course, convincing people to part with their valuable memorabilia would be a feat in and of itself.

"Wait." Brooklyn sat up as a thought occurred to her. "They don't have to part with their items at all. You can just have them on display, like a museum that has rare collections on loan from private collectors."

"You think people will pay five hundred dollars just to look at rare comic books?"

"Some will," she said without hesitation. "However, if you want to make it more accessible, you can hold it apart from the actual gala. How didn't I think of this before? It's perfect." She reached over and grabbed her laptop, then pulled up her note-taking app to capture the ideas that were coming to her at lightning speed. "This is what you all should do. A few hours before the gala starts, hold a pre-gala event and charge maybe fifty dollars to attend. If you can get just a few collectors to agree to the display, you'll pull in dozens—maybe well over a hundred—people."

She laughed at the doubt clouding his expression. "Just wait until we get to Biloxi in a couple of weeks. You'll see how serious real fans take this. It isn't just a weekend hobby for some people, it's a lifestyle. Opening your doors to those who embrace the comics and cosplay world is going to introduce the foundation to an audience you never knew existed. I promise you."

"I forget that I have an actual reason for going to Biloxi." He nuzzled the spot behind her ear again and whispered,

"I've been telling myself that you invited me for the sole purpose of having your wicked way with me."

Despite the teasing in his voice, Brooklyn's stomach pulled tight with desire. She wasn't one to jump into bed with a guy. She'd only been intimate with three in her twenty-six years, and, to be honest, Mikal Johnson's five-minute fumbling act in high school shouldn't really count.

When she asked Reid about joining her at the Comic Con in Mississippi, she hadn't completely thought out exactly how he would view the invitation. *Of course*, a guy like him would think it was more than just joining her and a bunch of other comic book fanatics. *Of course*, he would assume an invitation to spend the night at a hotel meant that they would be there together. As in *together* together. Even though, up to this point, the only thing they'd shared were some pretty spectacular kisses.

Most surprising? Brooklyn was inclined to go along with his interpretation. She didn't want to take things slow this time. She'd never been more tempted to jump into bed with someone as she was right at this moment.

The annoying voice that had been hovering on the periphery of her psyche for the past few weeks began to nag at her again, but Brooklyn silenced it.

For once she'd landed the cute, hot guy. And she wanted to enjoy every minute of it.

CHAPTER EIGHT

―――――――――――

"SINCE WHEN DO you not want to hang out?" Anthony asked as he turned onto Esplanade Avenue. "And especially on your birthday. Come on, man. Today is the day you join the Grown and Sexy Club."

"If I ever hear you refer to me as sexy again I'm punching you in the throat," Reid said.

Anthony laughed so hard he swerved into the next lane. Probably because he was flipping Reid off at the same time.

"Pull that sour stick out your ass, man! It's your 30th birthday," his friend unnecessarily pointed out. "We'll grab some beers and wings at The Hard Court and watch a game. It's better than sitting around your apartment."

Reid nodded and shrugged. At this point, he was just grateful Anthony hadn't brought up his meeting with Jonathan, which still hadn't taken place.

"You're right," he answered. "This'll be cool."

Of course, it wasn't cool. Not really. Cool would have been sitting at his apartment with Brooklyn sitting right next to him, or better yet, *on* him. His lap had become accustomed to bearing her weight. Spending his birthday with her would have been preferable to anything else Reid could think up.

And they didn't have to spend it in his apartment either. They could be at a coffee shop, or a movie, or a funeral home for all he cared. As long as he was with her, that's all that mattered. She made everything better, brighter. He could use that ray of sunshine she brought to his life, especially on a day like today.

Reaching this milestone should have filled him with excitement, but for Reid it had been the exact opposite. For months, his thirtieth birthday had been looming over him like a dark, menacing cloud, saturated with questions about what he'd done with his thirty years on this planet, and what lay ahead for the next thirty. He'd tried like hell to push those questions aside and just enjoy his birthday, but it hadn't been easy.

As usual, his family helped. He'd gotten calls from all his siblings and cousins today. Athens had FaceTimed him, and Lily had sent a silly picture of herself with a cartoon dog tongue on Snapchat. Willow arrived around noon with a homemade birthday cake and his Aunt Margo sent a cast iron pot filled with her spicy jambalaya, Reid's favorite dish. He could always count on his family to be there for him.

But when he thought about the person he most wanted here, one image filled his mind. Actually, it was a cascade of images, because he could never decide which color he liked in her hair the best.

"Purple."

"What?" Anthony asked.

"Huh? Nothing," Reid said. *Shit*.

More irritated at being pulled out of his daydream than of being caught fantasizing, he turned and stared out at the homes lining Esplanade. His mind eventually returned to the only place it seemed to want to dwell lately. With Brooklyn.

The past week had been unlike any Reid had ever experienced while with another woman who wasn't a relative. If someone had told him just a month ago that he would look forward to sitting in the colorful upper room at a local bookstore, reading comics while the woman he dreamed about on a nightly basis drew a cartoon version of his mother, he would have offered to find them help for their drinking problem. Instead, he was the one who found himself intoxicated.

He was drunk on Brooklyn LeBlanc and this potent attraction that grew with every waking hour. It didn't even bother him that sex didn't seem to be anywhere on the horizon.

Okay, that wasn't entirely true. He thought about sex with her no less than eight hundred times a day. But, unlike with women in his past, he had no desire to rush it. Something about this slow burn between them felt right. Natural. Rushing her into his bed would change the dynamic between them, and for now, Reid was just fine with how things were going.

He'd wanted her here with him right now. When she'd told him she had a prior commitment—some family thing— it had made the thought of facing his thirtieth birthday even more depressing. He hadn't been looking forward to today, but if he'd had Brooklyn by his side at least it would have been easier to bear. Instead of heading to the Hard Court for wings and a game he wasn't interested in watching, he wanted to be under his and Brooklyn's tree in City Park, trying to sneak kisses from her, or huddled in the nice, comfortable chair at Tubby and Coo's, still trying to sneak kisses from her. More than anything, Reid wanted to sneak a kiss from her.

Well, maybe not more than anything.

All in due time.

The wait might kill him, but it would be worth it.

Anthony drove around to the parking lot behind The Hard Court, but it was so packed he had to drive back out and search for parking on the street.

"Damn, is LSU playing Alabama this weekend?" Reid asked as they finally pulled into a spot two blocks down from the club.

The high-end sports bar tended to draw a crowd no matter what, simply by virtue of it being one of the city's hottest night spots. But this was overkill even for a Saturday night.

"It's a good thing you have access to that VIP area upstairs," Anthony said as he opened his door. He looked back over his shoulder. "You know that's the only reason I brought you here, right? I didn't want to fight over a table."

Laughing, Reid flipped him off as he got out of the car, then he joined up with Anthony on the sidewalk. He cursed himself for not insisting on taking his own car tonight so he could leave early. If he couldn't hang out with Brooklyn, he'd rather sit at home and sulk instead of dealing with people.

"Hey, you don't plan on staying out here all night, do you?" Reid asked.

"Would you stop acting like you're sixty years old? What in the hell has gotten into you? I'm the one who's usually trying to cut out early so that I can head home to Ciara." Anthony stopped walking. "Wait a minute. Do you have somebody waiting for you at home?"

"Not your business," Reid said.

"Oh, no. No, no, no. You gotta tell me what's up."

Reid ignored him as he continued along the sidewalk. But then he, too, stopped short when he came upon a black luxury sedan.

"Is this...?" he started, but then he shook his head. It couldn't be Harrison's car. Even though he and Jonathan were law partners, his brother had never been one for hanging out at bars, even sophisticated sports bars like the one Jonathan owned.

When they arrived at the entrance, Reid reached for the handle to the smoke-gray glass door, but Anthony knocked his hand out of the way and stepped in front of him.

"You think they're gonna run out of hot wings?" Reid drawled.

"Just shut up and come on," Anthony said. Reid followed him into the sports bar and nearly had a heart attack.

"Surprise!"

"What the f—" He slapped a hand to his chest and reminded himself that thirty was too young to have a heart attack. He hoped. "What's going on here?" Reid asked.

His entire family stood before him, including his dad, his three cousins and their wives, and his siblings with their significant others. Even his aunt Margot and her husband, Gerald, had made it out here. The familiar faces of many of his co-workers from Holmes Construction dotted the crowd, as well as some high school friends he hadn't seen in ages.

"Happy birthday," Indina said, enveloping him in a hug. Then she poked him in the chest. "Now your nosy ass knows the original reason for the meeting we were having weeks ago."

Reid frowned, then remembered the text Indina had mistakenly sent to him.

"*This* was the party you were talking about? It wasn't about Mom's foundation?"

His sister shook her head.

"So why didn't you say anything?"

She rolled her eyes before slapping his shoulder and returning to Griffin, who cradled his arms around her middle and nestled his chin against her shoulder.

"Happy birthday," Ezra said, catching Reid by the neck and bringing him in for a one armed hug. "Hope you don't mind the surprise. I needed to make up for the time I had to get my appendix removed and messed up your eighth birthday," he said. "Maybe now you can finally stop it with the guilt trip."

He punched Ezra on the shoulder. "You're full of shit. You know I'd forgotten all about that." Reid turned to Harrison. "I can't believe they got you out of the house and into a club?"

His eldest brother shrugged. "This place ain't half bad. I may have to come here more often."

"Yeah, right." Willow snorted. She bumped Harrison out of the way and wrapped her arms around Reid's waist. "Happy birthday again, baby. You enjoyed the cake?"

"You know I did," Reid said. He patted his stomach. "Probably too much."

Reid hugged his dad, and the rest of his family members, before being dragged to a table that had been set up at the far free-throw line on The Hard Court's dance floor, which was made to resemble a basketball court. The club's basketball motif was a nod to Jonathan's short career in the NBA. He'd hired Indina to bring his vision to life, and she'd done so in the most magnificent way possible.

Reid couldn't deny his sister's imagination and skill was

off the charts. He couldn't wait to see what she did with Dynamo Diane.

That is, if he could ever convince Brooklyn to allow him to share the drawing. Whenever he brought it up, she replied with some excuse about it not being ready. He didn't understand her hesitancy. If he had her kind of talent, he would spend most of his day tossing copies of his drawings from rooftops.

Reid was seated at the table of honor and treated like a king. Forever taking care of him, Willow directed him to stay seated while she fixed him something to eat from the huge buffet that had been set up along the back wall. She returned with a plate crowded with all his favorite foods, including more of his aunt Margo's jambalaya and his cousin Eli's sweet and spicy party meatballs.

As he looked around, Reid slowly came to realize that everyone here was in some way connected to him. Jonathan had closed the entire club down. On a Saturday night. In the middle of college football season and the MLB postseason. All for *his* birthday.

Unbelievable.

How many people had family and friends who would go to this kind of trouble to celebrate their birthday? Could there be a luckier son of a bitch on the face of the earth?

As if in answer to his question, Reid looked up and spotted Brooklyn walking toward him. It was in that moment that he felt his luckiest. She'd been the only thing missing, and here she was, like a dream he'd conjured.

But before she reached his table, Reid heard a sultry voice to the left of him say, "Well, happy birthday. It's been a long time."

He turned to find a woman in a dress so tight it looked

seconds away from busting at the seams. He remembered her face, but the name escaped him.

"Uh, hey," Reid said. "Thanks."

She rolled her eyes. "It's Khyra," she said. "Don't act as if you don't know me."

Except he *didn't* know her. The things he remembered about her could fit in a shot glass.

Just then, Donte came in from the opposite side, hooking his arm around Reid's neck and whispering near his ear, "Your brother asked some of us guys to invite friends we thought you'd want here to help you celebrate. You can thank me later."

Great.

Khyra, who Reid now remembered meeting at last year's Essence Festival, leaned over and hugged him, her breasts nearly spilling out of the neckline of her low-cut dress. In the past, Reid would have relished the feel of those cushiony pillows pushing up against him. But right now all he could think of was creating some distance.

He looked over toward where he'd spotted Brooklyn. She'd halted her steps. She just stood there staring at him, her expression unreadable.

A noxious ball of unease formed in the pit of Reid's stomach.

He couldn't just push this Khyra person away. He'd been on the receiving end of enthusiastic hugs for a solid twenty minutes. To suddenly rebuff her birthday wishes wouldn't just be rude, it would raise eyebrows from everyone around him.

Yet, the absolute last thing Reid wanted right now was to be reminded of the person he'd been just a few weeks ago. And that's exactly what Khyra represented.

Before Brooklyn, he would have grabbed a night like

tonight by the balls and lived it up, going from the arms of one woman to another. At the end of the night, he would no doubt go home with at least one of them. Because it was his birthday, he would possibly go home with two.

Instead, all he wanted to do was count down the hours until he could leave. It was an indication of how far removed he'd become from that guy he used to be. And he didn't miss his old lifestyle at all.

He had Brooklyn to thank for that. She made all the difference.

He wanted to go to her, but every time he so much as tried to leave his place of honor, another person came to the table to wish him happy birthday.

Over the course of the next half hour, two more women he'd gotten to know in the biblical sense emerged from the ever-growing crowd. Reid fought the urge to throttle Donte. It was unfair. He knew his buddy was just trying to be a good friend, and it's not as if any of the guys at Holmes Construction knew how close he and Brooklyn had grown over these past few weeks. She'd insisted they remain professional while at work—a notion Reid supported, seeing as Alex was likely to kick his ass once he learned that Reid had been feeling up the woman Alex had told him to think about as a kid sister.

So, instead of pummeling Donte for putting him in this awkward position, Reid continued to accept the well-meaning birthday greetings. There was at least one bright spot: Vivian's granddaughter hadn't been invited.

Reid must have glanced over at the booth on the far left side of the club where Brooklyn sat with a couple of guys from work at least twenty times before he was finally able to get away, nearly an hour after he'd first spotted her. When he finally made it over there, she was gone.

"Shit," Reid cursed underneath his breath.

Jarvis slid from the booth and clamped an arm around Reid's shoulder. "Man, this party is fiyah. Can't believe you rented out The Hard Court. Maybe I need to get my plumbing license."

"It was a surprise party, fool. He didn't rent the place out," Donte said.

Reid ignored them both. He turned around in a circle, searching for Brooklyn. A relieved breath whooshed out of his lungs when he caught sight of her, off to the right, where the downstairs bathrooms were located. Reid quickly made his way over to her. Taking her by the hand, he brought her to a more secluded area of the club, away from the crowds and music.

"Hey," he said. Fuck, he could hear the guilt in his voice. Why was he feeling guilty? It's not as if he'd done anything he should feel guilty about.

"I haven't had a chance to talk to you all night," Reid said.

She motioned to the dance floor. "Well, you've been pretty busy. It's quite the crowd out there."

He shrugged. "Yeah. To be honest, I can't remember the names of half of these people. Some of them I haven't seen since high school."

"But they turned out for your birthday. I don't think I've ever known this many people in my entire life," she said. "Must feel good to know that so many care about you."

If he shrugged again she may think he had a tick of some kind. Instead, Reid stuffed his hands in his pockets.

"So, when you said you had something planned with your family... That was a lie?"

She held her thumb and forefinger a millimeter apart.

"Just a tiny one. I did have breakfast with my parents this morning, so technically, I did a family thing."

Earlier this morning. Which meant they'd spent the entire day apart for nothing.

Reid shifted from one foot to the other as he tried to think of something else to say. Alarm gripped his chest with each awkward moment that ticked by. He could sense them moving into a territory they'd left behind the day she asked him to join her for ice cream. He had no desire to return there.

Reid forced a smile. "Nice job keeping this a secret from me," he said.

"Uh, actually, I only learned about the party yesterday," she said. "Anthony told me about it when he came in to check on his vacation time."

She didn't know until yesterday?

"Shit, Brooklyn, I'm sorry."

She held up her hand. "It's no big deal. It's not as if your siblings even know who I am."

No, they didn't. That would change right now.

"Come on," Reid said, grabbing her by the hand. "Let me introduce you to everyone."

"No." She shook her head and tugged her hand from his hold. "No, Reid. That's okay. I can meet them later." She jutted her chin toward the club's main floor. "Your family didn't go through all this trouble just for you to spend your time back here talking to me. Go out there and enjoy your birthday."

But here talking to her is where he wanted to be. This was *his* birthday party. And the woman he wanted to spend it with had been relegated to sitting in a back booth. He couldn't allow that to stand.

"If it were up to me, I wouldn't be here at all," Reid said.

"I'd rather be in our chair at the bookstore, reading comics while you worked on Dynamo Diane."

"I can think of a few people who wouldn't agree with you there," she said, and Reid didn't have to ask who she was referring to.

"Hey, if you're talking about the girl—well, girls—who—"

But she cut him off, holding her hand up. "Don't," she said. "No explanation necessary. It's not my business."

Just as he was about to argue that he did owe her an explanation, he heard Indina calling his name, followed by a collective gasp from the crowd. Both he and Brooklyn turned to see Ezra wheeling out a massive cake made to resemble a collection of plumbing tools.

"Time to sing happy birthday and cut the cake," his sister called, motioning for Reid to come to the center of the club.

"Go on," Brooklyn said.

Reid looked from her, back to the cake, then back to her.

She gestured with her head for him to go. "They're waiting for you."

"Promise you won't leave before I get the chance to talk to you again," Reid said. But she didn't answer. Her only response was a smile that didn't quite reach her eyes.

"Reid David, would you come on?" Indina called.

He looked to Brooklyn one last time, silently pleading with her to understand before he started for the main floor where all his family had gathered.

"Reid," he heard Brooklyn call.

He turned back to her.

"Happy birthday," she said.

A somber smile edged up the corner of his mouth. "Thanks," he said. "Thanks for celebrating it with me."

With that, he continued on to the happy faces and birthday cake that awaited him, pasting on a smile of his own. But on the inside, happiness was the last thing he felt.

————

HER EYES PLANTED FIRMLY on her computer screen, Brooklyn kept a laser focus on the database she'd been updating for the past hour. The trailer had been quiet all afternoon, with only the clack of fingers on the keyboard providing any respite from the weighty silence. Occasionally, a heavy piece of construction equipment would rumble, a car horn would blow, or someone would yell out to another worker in the field, but for the most part, those muted sounds faded into the background.

She wished a particular Holmes Construction employee would join his colleagues out in the field, but they were approaching the end of the pay period and Alex had left instructions for Reid to double-check the time-cards. He would be in here until it was time to knock off for the day.

To say it had been awkward from the very moment Reid entered the trailer just after lunch would be the understatement of the century. The tension saturating the air around them was enough to choke on.

Brooklyn had been obsessing over just how today would play out ever since she snuck out of The Hard Court, about twenty minutes after her run-in with Reid Saturday night. She'd prepared as best she could for what she knew would be a strained, uncomfortable encounter. She told herself she would just do what was necessary to make it through this first day back at work, and then figure out the rest later. But an entire year wouldn't have been enough time to prepare for the awkwardness of the brief exchanges she'd had with Reid today.

Saturday night had been a reality check.

More than a reality check, it had been the wake-up call she'd needed to remind her that when it came to Reid Holmes, he was in another league. One she didn't play in. She'd allowed herself to be seduced by the fantasy that they could actually work, but seeing the parade of women glom onto him had put Brooklyn squarely in her place. They were in entirely different hemispheres, and she had always, always, *always* been just fine on her side of the world. Why she thought she could exist in his was beyond her.

But she was back to her normal reality now. She wouldn't allow herself to be put in that position again.

As for her and Reid, Brooklyn still wasn't sure how they would navigate their way back to the friendly co-worker relationship they never should have veered away from in the first place. He'd tried contacting her several times yesterday, sending five text messages before eventually calling. At first, Brooklyn had considered letting his call go to voicemail, but knowing how persistent he was, figured it was easier to just nip it in the bud. She told him she was busy cleaning out the closet in her old bedroom at her parents'—a task she'd been putting off for over a year, which turned out to be the perfect distraction—and that she would talk to him on Monday.

But neither had done much talking today.

She knew it was best they just get everything out in the open so they wouldn't have to walk on eggshells while around each other. More than anything, Brooklyn wanted to assure him she would continue to work on the Dynamo Diane comic for the foundation's kickoff party. The comic had become so much more than just a favor to Reid; it had taken on a life of its own. She was excited to see it through to the finish.

But when it came to anything going on between them *after* work hours, the comic is where their association should stop. That's what she *wanted* to tell him, but something wouldn't allow her to say the words out loud.

The whirl of the printer knocked her out of her daze. She heard Alex's chair roll away from his desk, then felt the trailer vibrate with Reid's footsteps as he walked over to the long folding table that held the printer, scanner, and coffee pot. Brooklyn kept her back to him. She heard his footsteps as he left the printer, but instead of moving away, back toward Alex's desk, it sounded as if they were moving closer toward her. And then stopping. Right in front of her desk.

Her eyes slid shut. She discreetly pulled in a deep breath, searching for calm. If she pretended she didn't know he was standing there, would he eventually walk away?

"Brooklyn."

Guess not.

She released a weary sigh—loud enough for him to hear it this time—and swiveled her chair around. She looked up and nearly flinched at the pain that struck her chest just at the sight of him. Some may consider him rough around the edges, but Reid Holmes was hands down one of the most gorgeous men she'd ever encountered.

"Yes?" she asked.

He shifted from one foot to the other, slapping his solid thigh with the papers he'd brought with him from the printer.

"About Saturday night," he started.

But Brooklyn put both hands up before he could finish. "Whatever you think you need to explain, you don't. It was your birthday party, Reid. There were at least a hundred people there, all clamoring to spend time with you."

"I hadn't talked to half those people in years," he said. "My brothers put a couple of the guys from the crew in charge of invites, and they picked people who they *thought* I'd want there. If I'd known, none of those...those women... would have been invited, Brooklyn."

It's not as if she didn't believe him. She could tell Saturday how uncomfortable he'd seemed as the three women each sidled up to him. But it didn't change the fact that *those* women were the kind he was used to dating.

No matter how long she lived, Brooklyn doubted she'd ever quite get over the sting of witnessing just how right those gorgeous women looked at his side. They fit with him so much more than she ever would.

"I've been thinking about...well...this," she said, gesturing to the space between them. "And maybe we should just stick to being co-workers."

His head jerked back. "What do you mean?"

"I mean exactly what I just said, we're co-workers. That's all."

It pained her to say those words more than he could ever know, but they came from a place of self-preservation. She had a healthy ego. She wasn't over-confident, but she knew her worth. And she would be damned if she allowed anyone to make her doubt herself. It was better to stick with guys in her league, and leave Reid to the Destiny's Child lookalikes from Saturday night.

She pointed to Alex's desk. "Alex will want those time-cards reviewed by the end of the day. You should probably get back to them."

He looked on the verge of speaking, but instead,

exhaled a frustrated breath and pivoted, heading for Alex's desk. Brooklyn's shoulders slumped with relief.

Her relief was short-lived, because a second later, Reid turned and stomped over to her desk. But then he bypassed the desk all together and came around to her chair.

Brooklyn stared up at him. "What are you doing?"

He leaned forward, bracing his palms on the armrests and getting right in her face.

"We are not just co-workers," Reid said. "Me and Donte? We're co-workers. Me and Anthony? Co-workers." He pointed toward the door. "I've worked with some of those guys out there for over ten years, but I've never stretched out on a blanket with them in City Park, or stayed up texting with them until one in the morning. And I sure as hell have never kissed any of them."

"Reid—"

"We're. Not. Just. Co-workers. And you may not think you deserve an explanation for Saturday night, but I think you do." He straightened and stepped away from her chair. Holding his hands out in a plea, he said, "I was put into an awkward position. I couldn't just ignore those women, Brooklyn, but you have to believe me when I tell you that I didn't want anything to do with them. I haven't wanted to even *talk* to another woman since the day you started working for Holmes Construction. Even when I didn't want to like you, I still couldn't stop thinking about you."

Her chest constricted with a bewildering combination of hope and uncertainty. He was asking her to believe in something that, until a few weeks ago, she'd never allowed herself to think was possible.

She *wanted* to believe him. Goodness, did she want to believe every single word he said. She wanted to cast aside all those cautionary flags imbedded in her brain, warning her not to fall any harder for Reid Holmes than she'd already fallen. To push away those notions she'd accepted as truth—that opposites don't attract, and that the shy comics geek could never land the heartthrob.

She wanted to believe all those things could happen. But the potential for heartbreak was too great for Brooklyn to take a chance believing in that fantasy.

Her voice barely a whisper, she muttered, "Let's just get back to work, Reid."

"Brooklyn—"

"We have work to do," she said, putting an end to the discussion. Then she turned her chair back to her computer and pretended the ache in her chest was a consequence of the soup she'd eaten for lunch, and not her heart breaking over what might have been if the world wasn't so damn unfair.

As afternoon meandered into evening, the opportunity to think about the might-have-beens eroded to almost zilch. Alex had called midafternoon with news of a potential contract with a car dealership in Slidell that sought to expand to the south shore of Lake Pontchartrain. He wanted Brooklyn to start running numbers to see if it was feasible for Holmes Construction to bid.

She spent over two hours analyzing timelines of the various jobs currently in progress. Alex might not want to hear it, but unless he worked with several subcontractors, there was no way Holmes Construction could take on a job of that magnitude.

She was reviewing the list of HCC-approved subcontractors when she heard a throat being cleared behind her. Brooklyn startled at the sound.

"I'm sorry," Reid said. "I didn't mean to scare you."

She sucked in a breath before turning her chair around to face him. "What do you need?"

He pointed to the clock on the wall above the door. "For one thing, we both should have been gone about forty-five minutes ago."

Brooklyn glanced at the time on her computer, shocked she hadn't noticed it was going on six p.m.

"I've been so busy trying to figure out how we can make this car dealership thing happen that I didn't even think to look at the time."

"I get it," he said with a nod. He rubbed the back of his head, then brought his hand down to his neck. "Uh, I got a text from Alex a few minutes ago. He needs me to go over to the site on the Westbank for the rest of the week, so I won't be here."

Brooklyn only hoped her expression didn't give away just how deeply that news affected her. Being in this trailer with him all afternoon had been as comfortable as sitting in a pile of red ants, but it was still better than not being around him at all.

She swallowed. "Okay."

Reid shifted from one foot to the other.

"Is there something else?" Brooklyn asked.

"Uh, yeah." He nodded. "About this coming weekend..."

Shit. The Comic Con in Biloxi. How could she have forgotten?

"The whole point of me going was to get ideas for the foundation's kickoff party," he continued. "That still needs to happen, but if you'd rather us not go together, I'll understand."

She was so close to agreeing with him, but her practical side wouldn't allow it.

"That doesn't make any sense, Reid. We can still drive there together."

Just a few days ago Brooklyn had considered cancelling the second room she'd booked. Thank God she hadn't.

"Is eight Saturday morning still a good time to leave?" he asked.

She nodded. "The convention kicks off around noon and there are several early panels I want to make sure I get a good seat for."

"Okay." He stuck his hands in his pockets. "I'll be at your place at a quarter to eight."

She thought that would be the end of it, but instead of leaving, he continued to stand at her desk.

She lifted her hands in question. "Yes?"

"I'm just waiting for you to pack up," he answered. "Like I said, we were supposed to be out of here an hour ago."

There was absolutely no way she could handle him walking her to her car.

"You go," Brooklyn said. "I just have a couple of things I need to finish. Alex will understand that there are exceptions to the work/life balance."

Reid continued to stare at her, a sardonic arch to his brow. She should have expected that reaction. The man walked her to her car for over a week in broad daylight. There was no way he'd leave her to walk alone with dusk quickly settling in around them.

She sighed. "Fine. Give me a few minutes."

His response was a firm nod. Then he hooked a thumb toward the door. "I need to grab a couple of tools that I'll need to bring with me to the other job site. I'll be back in about five minutes."

As she watched him walk out of the trailer, Brooklyn

pondered the dejection she felt at the thought of him being gone for the rest of the week. She should be relishing having the trailer to herself. She could get twice as much work done without Reid here to distract her.

This was a *good* thing. It was a *great* thing. She would be happy about it. Ecstatic. Reid being reassigned to the Westbank site was exactly what she needed.

"Sure," Brooklyn snarked. "Keep telling yourself that."

CHAPTER NINE

REID CLOSED his eyes and leaned his head back as he stood on the balcony of his hotel room, his palms wrapped around the thick metal railing. He welcomed the feel of the sun on his face as the sea breeze blew in from the still warm gulf waters. He opened his eyes and concentrated on the crush of the waves. They kissed the white sand below, foaming against the shoreline.

Colorful umbrellas dotted the beach for as far as he could see. Kids building sandcastles tried their hardest to protect their creations from the rising tide. The occasional whoop of laughter could be heard coming from the group of teens who'd been out there since Reid had arrived on this balcony nearly an hour ago.

Grabbing a nap before they left for the convention would have been the smart thing to do, but he'd proved not to be all that smart these days. He checked his watch. If he went to sleep now he'd probably sleep through the rest of the afternoon. After the hellish night he'd had, he was so damn tired he'd had to drink two Big Gulp-sized cups of coffee over the hour-and-a-half drive out here to Biloxi. But

Reid knew sleep would continue to evade him, just as it had most nights this week. His mind was too busy playing back how he'd royally messed shit up with Brooklyn to get much rest.

He'd held out a slim measure of hope that the situation wasn't as dire as he'd imagined when he left the urgent care job site on Monday, but this morning's awkward car ride pretty much solidified that it was indeed hopeless. Reid wasn't sure which had been the nail in the coffin. Was it those three ex-bedmates barging back into his life like the ghosts from Christmas past, or was it the fact that he hadn't thought to invite Brooklyn to sit at the table with him once she arrived at the party, instead, relegating her to a booth in the back of the club? In the end, it didn't matter. Either was sufficient reason for her to kick him to the curb.

He'd tried more than once to pull her into conversation on their drive over, but her unenthusiastic monotone answers quickly put an end to that. She'd kept her head pointed either straight or toward the passenger side window. After an hour of silence between them, Brooklyn had been the one to bring up the new space and science museum built around the NASA facility just outside of Gulfport, Mississippi. Reid didn't know shit-all about NASA, but he'd glommed on to the opportunity to engage in some small talk.

It hadn't lasted long. Brooklyn had closed up again, mumbling something about missing the shuttle program before turning her attention back to the trees that lined Interstate 10. Silence had occupied the car for the rest of the drive.

He shouldn't have come. He understood that now. He could have easily Googled ideas for the kickoff party and left her to enjoy her weekend alone. He'd arrogantly assumed that, if given the opportunity, he would be able to coax Brooklyn out of her sullen attitude toward him and get things back on track.

"Yeah, you're doing a bang-up job with that," Reid muttered.

With one last look out at the gulf, he turned and headed back into the room, leaving the sliding glass door slightly ajar to let in the warm air. As he pulled out the jeans and New Orleans Saints T-shirt he planned to change into before they left for the convention center, he heard his phone chime with an incoming text. He walked over to the bureau where he'd set his phone and turned it over. His heartbeat quickened at the site of Brooklyn's name.

I'll be ready in a half hour.

She wasn't a smiley face kind of person, so expecting to see one was just stupid on his part. Yet, he wished there was *some*thing to indicate that she was possibly warming up to him. Right now, all he felt was coldness.

No, he never should have come here.

He was her ride, so he couldn't go back to New Orleans without her. Maybe he could claim he wasn't feeling well and just hang out here at the hotel for the next day and a half.

But that would be stupid too. Because he *did* want to be here. He needed to be here. He'd come with the goal of collecting ideas for the kickoff party that he could bring back to his siblings. When he'd told Indina what he had planned this weekend, she'd asked him to look specifically for ideas on how they could promote the party, as well as decorating the ballroom they'd put a down payment on just this past Tuesday.

His brothers and sister were counting on him to get this right. For the first time in his life, Reid had stepped up. He'd put the responsibility solidly on his own shoulders and he refused to shirk away from it. He would not let his family down.

Instead of sequestering himself in this hotel room all weekend, he would go to the conference, but would give Brooklyn as much space as she needed. If she wanted to part ways as soon as they arrived at the convention center, that's what they would do. He had no idea what one did at a comics convention. He might find everything he needed within the first hour and spend the rest of his time in a corner catching up with college football scores on his phone, but he would not ruin this for her.

Reid decided to jump in the shower just because he had a little extra time to kill, but the water felt so damn good he ended up spending way more time in there than he should have. He had to rush to get dressed so he wouldn't be late meeting Brooklyn.

Her room was across the hall and two doors down. Reid had asked her if she'd wanted to switch to the room with the view of the gulf, but she said she would spend most of her free time working on the Dynamo Diane drawings anyway, so the room should go to someone who would be able to truly enjoy the view.

He'd then made the mistake of asking her what she planned to charge for the Dynamo Diane drawings.

It never occurred to him that he *shouldn't* have asked it. He'd meant to bring it up days ago, after Indina emailed him and his brothers the price list for all the expenses regarding the party. Reid still hadn't mentioned anything about Brooklyn's comic to his siblings; he wanted it to be a surprise. And he'd planned to cover her cost out of his own pocket.

That she would get paid for her work hadn't even been

a question. He never expected her to spend all those hours drawing an entire comic book for no pay.

But Brooklyn had taken offense to his inquiry about the price, remarking that if she'd had any intention of charging she would have told him that from the very beginning. Then she'd gone into her hotel room and Reid hadn't heard from her since. That was two hours ago.

He blew out an irritated breath. His ability to put his foot in his mouth these days was worthy of a gold medal.

He grabbed his wallet and phone, and slid both in his pants pocket. He did the same with the small writing pad with the hotel's logo, just in case he needed to take notes. Then he looked around the room to make sure he wasn't forgetting anything he might need.

"Not as if you know what's needed at a comics convention," he muttered. He was so out of his element.

Satisfied that he had everything, Reid opened the door and lost the ability to breathe. Standing just on the other side was one of the hottest fucking sights he'd ever laid eyes on.

"I was just coming to get you," Brooklyn said matter-of-factly, as if she wasn't standing there blowing his mind in real-time.

She wore a deep red bodysuit that clung to her curves like a man holding onto a tree in the middle of a hurricane. The bodice dipped in a deep V between her breasts—those ridiculously gorgeous, luscious, made-for-his-hands-to-squeeze breasts. On her head sat a gold crown shaped like a spear. A matching red cape flowed from her waist, trimmed in shiny gold fabric, what Indina would probably call brocade or some shit like that.

Reid swallowed hard. Then he swallowed again. He was suddenly thirsty as hell.

Brooklyn probably didn't give a rat's ass what he thought about her appearance, but he couldn't *not* say it.

"You look...uh..." *Amazing. Magnificent. Edible.* "You look badass," he finished.

Her lips tipped up in a humble smile. "Thanks." She looked down at her outfit. "I worked on it for months. I would have liked the belt to be a bit more ornate, but I'd already blown my budget by a lot."

She was talking to him again. Not in monosyllables or five-word sentences, but *really* talking to him. Reid was still relishing in the fact that she'd apparently given up her almost totally silent treatment when he registered what she'd just said.

"Wait, you made this yourself?"

She nodded.

"Who are you supposed to be?" he asked, but then answered his own question. "You're Iansan. You're your own freaking warrior goddess! Damn, Brooklyn, what *can't* you do?"

The blush he'd missed so much this past week darkened her cheeks. "It wasn't as hard as you'd think. All it takes is finding a used sewing machine on Craigslist and watching a bunch of YouTube videos."

"That easy, huh?" Reid asked with a skeptical lift of his brow.

"Yeah, okay. So maybe it takes a *little* talent," she said, her lips twisted up in a shy smile.

"Still selling yourself short, huh?" Reid said as he closed the door behind him and stepped into the hallway, reducing the space separating them down to just a few inches. Leaning into her, he said, "I guess I'll just have to remind you how amazing you are every single day for you to finally believe it."

She stared up at him, her expression coated in uncertainty, as if the moment confused her. Then she shook her head and took a step back.

"Uh, so, are you ready?" she asked with obvious unease.

Apparently, he'd read the situation all wrong. Just because she was talking to him again, that didn't mean she was ready to return to the flirtatious teasing that had become a part of their normal, everyday existence.

There were back to taking things slow. He couldn't expect her to just open herself up to him again without his having to work for it.

"Yeah, I guess I'm ready," Reid said. He gestured to his jeans and T-shirt. "Though I now feel a bit underdressed."

"You are," she confirmed with a nod. "But I'm sure you won't be the only one. There's bound to be a few readers who'll be in regular clothes. Maybe," she tacked on before starting for the elevators.

"Wait," Reid said, holding the elevator door open for her. "Should I go out and buy a costume or something?"

"You're fine, Reid. Really. But you have to understand that cons are one of the very few places where cosplayers truly feel as if they can be themselves. So don't be surprised if there are more people in costumes than not."

Yep, definitely out of his element.

When the elevator doors opened to the lobby floor of their hotel, there were several people milling about who were also dressed in costume, but not a single one of them stood out the way Brooklyn did. Reid took notice of how many heads turned as she strode through the lobby in her Iansan costume. She embodied the warrior goddess, her regal head lifted in the air, the elaborate cape flowing behind her.

She was sexy and confident and seemingly oblivious to it all. It was the biggest turn-on.

Of course, there wasn't much about her that wasn't a turn-on for him.

They exited the hotel and headed west toward the convention center. Brooklyn had explained that the hotel attached to the building where the conference was being held had sold out in a matter of minutes. The closer they drew to the event hall, the more Reid felt out of place. Costumed convention-goers joined them on the sidewalk, the swell of people making their way toward the event growing with every yard they traveled. He was tempted to run back to their hotel, grab the shower curtain from his room, tie it around his neck like a cape and call himself the Broke Ass Superhero. It would be better than Loser Guy in T-shirt and Jeans.

The attendant at the gate scanned the ticket code on Brooklyn's phone and they were allowed to enter.

The moment they cleared the atrium, Reid stopped dead in his tracks.

Bright, vibrant colors assaulted him from every angle. Striking poster displays depicting the various heroes and villains from the comics world adorned myriad booths. Thick columns were shrink-wrapped with an assortment of TV show logos. And a huge banner welcoming guests to Biloxi's First Annual Comics Convention hung from the ceiling. The conference had opened to the public less than an hour ago, yet it was already packed with people.

"This is insane. In a good way," Reid quickly added.

"Not what you were expecting?" Brooklyn asked, amusement tinting her voice.

He slowly shook his head as he scanned the massive

space. "I don't know what I was expecting, but this goes far beyond it. How do you even know what to do first?"

"You study the line-up well ahead of time so that you know exactly where all the popular panels will take place," Brooklyn answered. "Which is why I'll be in Exhibit Hall H for the next two hours. You can take the time to look around on your own."

"What's in Exhibit Hall H?"

"A panel discussion on the symbolism found in The Dark Knight movie franchise."

Apparently, his complete and utter horror at the thought of sitting through two hours of that particular discussion was evident on his face, because she patted his arm and said, "Meet me outside of the hall in two hours. Take this time to tour the conference. Hopefully you can find some cool ideas to take back to your sister and brothers."

"You sure?" he asked.

"Reid, if you come in there with me you'll be ready to climb the walls within the first twenty minutes." She pointed to the main floor. "Go."

He acquiesced, setting out in the opposite direction from where she headed. For the next hour, Reid experienced complete sensory overload as he meandered around the convention center. He toured the various booths and snapped no less than a hundred pictures to bring back to Indina. He would let his sister decide what would work for the kickoff party and what wouldn't. Reid knew his limits.

He found his way to the center of the main floor and captured a 360-degree video of the space, then went around to more booths, collecting promotional items from vendors. They would have to get some Dynamo Diane buttons made, and those little cushiony stress balls shaped like a heart were a no-brainer for a foundation whose main purpose was to raise awareness about heart disease.

As he ambled among the crowd filled with Darth Vaders of all shapes and sizes, scantily-clad women as superheroes, and a group of men all dressed as Dorothy from the Wizard of Oz, Reid wondered if he could maybe one day get into this kind of stuff. Brooklyn's comic had been the first one he'd ever read, but since his introduction to Iansan he'd borrowed several of his nephew's Justice League comics.

Maybe, if he showed more interest, Brooklyn would allow him in her world a little more.

His chest ached with his longing to become a part of her world. A mélange of mental images cascaded through his brain, reminding him of the times she'd let him in. Like that afternoon when she'd shared her drawings of Iansan, something she admitted she had not shared with anyone else. And those times he'd been given access to that sweet mouth of hers. Was there anything on this earth as delicious as her kiss? Reid would challenge anyone who tried to make that argument.

An announcement was made over the loud speaker that the next set of panels would be starting in ten minutes. Reid hustled back to Exhibit Hall H, squeezing his way through the packed aisle, apologizing every few seconds to attendees for bumping into their protruding costume components.

When he arrived at the exhibit hall, a collection of people dressed as Batman—both men and women—stood outside the door.

"They're running late," one of the half-dozen Batmans said when Reid pointed to the door.

"Is it okay if I go in there?"

The guy nodded. "Sure. You can come and go as you

please with all of the panels and workshops. Just try to keep the noise down."

Nodding his thanks, Reid cracked open the door to the darkened room and slid just inside. The room was packed, with all eyes on the three men sitting on a raised dais at the front of the room and the photos being flashed across the screen behind them.

Despite the reduced visibility, Reid let his eyes roam over the crowd, hoping to find Brooklyn. His mouth tipped up in a grin when he spotted her mass of naturally kinky curls on the far side of the room. While everyone else watched the stage, Reid watched her. She studied the panelists with rapt attention. He'd never seen her more captivated. It, in turn, captivated him.

The panel came to an end about five minutes later, and the large auditorium was suddenly awash in bright fluorescent lighting. He tracked Brooklyn as she, along with about two dozen others, rushed to the front of the room. Apparently, the panelists had agreed to sign autographs after their talk. He watched as she repeatedly looked from her phone, to the entrance on the opposite side of the room, and then back to the line of people ahead of her. After another five minutes, her shoulders slumped with resignation as she got out of line and started for the door she'd been glancing at while she'd waited.

It was only then that Reid realized she'd been debating whether to stay in line or leave so that she could meet up with him at their designated meeting spot.

Damn. He hated that she'd given up her place in line for him. Yet, at the same time, she'd given up her freaking place in line. *For him.*

It was in that moment that Reid vowed to be the kind of man worthy of her. He knew how much this meant to her.

The fact that she would give up anything for him made him want to do more, to *be* more. He wanted to be the man she deserved.

Reid approached from the opposite end, coming up behind her. "Hey," he said.

She jumped and turned, her brow dipping in confusion at the sight of him. "Hey. What are you doing in here?"

He motioned to where he'd been standing for the past ten minutes. "I slipped in toward the end of the discussion."

"Really?" Her brows arched. "Hmm." She folded her arms across her chest, drawing his attention to his favorite part of her anatomy. "So, what did you think?"

"About?" he asked.

"The panel?"

The panel? He could barely remember his own name right now.

"Uh, it was good," he answered. He was such a damn liar. He didn't have a clue what those guys had talked about. All his attention had been focused on her.

The corners of her mouth turned up in a knowing smile. "So, if I asked you something about what was said—"

"Please don't," Reid said, cutting her off.

She burst out laughing. "If we're being honest, I'm surprised that you've made a full two hours. Maybe there's still hope for my plan to convert you into a blerd."

"Oh." He widened his eyes in mock surprise. "So you've been planning this all along, huh?"

"Is it working?" she asked, a cagey grin tipping up the corners of her lips. Reid couldn't fully describe how amazing it felt to have her smiling at him like this again.

He took a step forward, closing the distance between them.

"You don't have to trick me into doing anything with

you," he said. "All you have to do is ask. I'm here. Ready and willing."

She remained silent, her eyes roaming his face as if she was looking at him for the first time. Reid's chest tightened with anxiety. He knew he stood on shaky ground, and any misstep could tear their tenuous connection apart even more.

When she spoke, the words came out in a whisper. "You want to hear something crazy," she asked. "I'm starting to believe you really mean it."

Reid drew the backs of his fingers along her jaw line, transferring some of the gold dust makeup she wore to his skin.

"What do I have to do to prove to you that I mean every word?"

Another smile slowly drew across her lips, this one more mischievous than the last.

"Let me think on that," she said. "I'm sure I can come up with something."

————

BROOKLYN TRIED to recall that old saying. Something about being doomed to repeat history if your foolish ass didn't bother to learn from it the first time. She was definitely playing the role of the fool in this current scenario.

It wasn't even ancient history she was having a hard time learning from. It was a mere week ago. The memory of how she'd felt watching Reid with his past girlfriends was still fresh in her mind; the stinging rejection still irritating her skin. Yet here she was, ready to tear down all her newly resurrected shields.

She'd spent the last several days steeling herself against

the impact being in such close proximity to him would have on her. She'd anticipated this from the moment she reluctantly agreed that he could still join her at this weekend's comic con. She'd prepared herself because she knew how hard it would be to resist his tempting smile and sexy, light-hearted teasing.

Yet, despite all the safeguards she'd put in place, it had only taken a few hours to fall right back under his spell. As foolish as she knew it to be, Brooklyn couldn't deny that when it came to Reid Holmes, she *wanted* to be under his spell.

It was the antithesis of her normal way of thinking. She usually avoided setting herself up for this kind of heartache at all costs.

What was that other saying? It's better to have loved and lost than never to have loved at all? Yeah, she called bullshit on that one. The way she saw it, if you didn't open yourself up to being hurt or ridiculed, it wouldn't happen. Period.

Which begged the even *more* pressing question of the hour...why was she still contemplating visiting Kurt Bollinger's table?

Her misgivings over the swift one-eighty she'd turned regarding Reid had taken a backseat to her anxiety about meeting one of her favorite comic book illustrators. Mainly because this convention wasn't supposed to be about her simply *meeting* him. It was supposed to be about her taking that next step.

Panic swarmed like a streaming wave of honeybees inside her stomach.

Brooklyn sat at the table in the convention center's huge food court area, pretending she had an appetite. If Reid had been paying any attention at all, he would have noticed she'd been chewing on the same French fry for the past three minutes.

"You know, you could have just told me you weren't hungry," he said.

Ah, guess she wasn't fooling him after all.

She dropped the fry and shoved the food container over to him.

"What's wrong?" Reid asked, grabbing several of the fries and stuffing them in his mouth. "Did a panel get cancelled or something?" he asked, the words garbled.

She shook her head. "No, that's not it." She sucked in a deep breath and slowly released it. After another moment's hesitation, she decided to come clean. "One of my favorite illustrators is here today. When I bought the ticket to attend, it was with the intention of showing him my work."

Reid's eyes widened over the rim of his cup of soda. He swallowed, then asked, "Well, where're the drawings you plan to show him?"

"Back in my hotel room," she admitted. "I chickened out at the last minute and left my portfolio on my bed."

Reid used a napkin to wipe the grease off his fingers, then reached his hand out to her.

"What?" Brooklyn asked.

"Room key."

She shook her head. "No. I'll do it next time. There's another con in Lafayette in the spring."

"Will this illustrator be there?" he asked. Then he shook his head. "You know what? It doesn't even matter. He's here now, and *you're* here now, and you're one of the most talented artists I've ever laid eyes on." He motioned with his fingers. "Give me the key. You sit here and finish these fries. You'll be grateful for the sustenance. I'll run back to the hotel and get your portfolio."

A million voices screamed in her head, warning her not to do this. But after several terrifying moments, she handed him the keycard.

The minute Reid walked away, Brooklyn had to talk herself out of calling him back. Anxiety and adrenaline fought for dominance in her brain, and she wasn't sure which would win the battle.

How many times had she allowed opportunities like this one to pass her by? Too many to count. The fear of being laughed at, of being told she didn't have what it takes, that she should leave comic book writing to the professionals and go back to the construction site; it was all the things that kept her awake at night.

She'd tried to put that horrific online chat room episode behind her, but had never been able to let it go. The taunts haunted her, dictating what she did with her drawings for the past three years.

Here's your chance to move forward. Finally.

Right here, right now. She could put it all behind her. She'd taken a huge step the moment she'd handed Reid the drawing of Dynamo Diane. She'd taken an even bigger step when she shared Iansan with him.

Showing her work to Kurt Bollinger would be more than just a step, it would be an astronomical leap forward. It was one Brooklyn knew she *had* to take if she was ever going to seriously pursue her dream. Even if he called her drawings crap and told her not to quit her day job, at least she would have given herself the opportunity to see what someone who was a master at the craft thought about her work.

Those same thoughts continued to ping pong back and forth in her head until, after what seemed like only five minutes since he'd left, Reid returned with her portfolio.

"Wow. You did that fast," she said.

"I've been gone twenty minutes."

Ah. Time flies when you're obsessing.

"Well, come on," Reid said.

The panic returned. "I don't know about this," she said, gripping the edge of the table. Maybe if she held on tight enough, her fingers would fuse themselves to it and she wouldn't be able to go anywhere.

Pulling the chair he'd been sitting in closer to hers, Reid set the portfolio on the table and turned to her.

"Do you realize how good you are?" he asked. "I know I'm not the best judge. After all, I've only been reading comics for a few weeks. But I know when I see a kickass drawing, and every single drawing I've seen from you is beyond kickass."

His words were exactly what she needed to hear. They washed over her body, bringing her comfort and reassurance.

Her confidence had taken a beating three years ago, but Brooklyn hadn't realized just how much power she'd allowed the words of a random stranger on the Internet to have over her life. This dream she'd held since she was a little girl had been stymied for years, stuck in neutral because some dude-bro who probably lived in his parents' basement had made himself the king of an insignificant message board in one corner of the World Wide Web.

No one knew she was the face behind NOLAComic-Grl28, yet she'd remained hidden all this time, keeping her illustrations to herself for fear of being ridiculed. She could not allow this irrational fear to hold her back any longer. So what if she *was* ridiculed. It wouldn't be the end of the world. It wouldn't even be the end of her dream. One person's opinion—a dozen people's opinions—didn't have to be the end, as long as she kept pushing. She was in control here.

"Okay," Brooklyn said. She released a heavy breath, looked up at Reid and smiled. "Okay. I'll do it."

His answering smile helped mend the fissure that running into the brick wall of reality at his birthday party had rent in her confidence. Maybe it was time she stopped allowing fear to hold her back in *all* aspects of her life.

Reid stood. "Okay, where is this guy?" he asked as he grabbed the portfolio. Holding the flat 11x17 case to his chest, he looked around with purpose.

Brooklyn rolled her eyes. He wouldn't know Kurt Bollinger if the man walked right up to him and drew his most famous character on Reid's forehead. She grabbed the portfolio's handle and pulled it from him, then she put her hand to his chest to halt his movements.

And maybe she should have thought it through before placing her palm on his muscular chest. The effect startled her.

Reid looked down at her hand and then back up at her, and Brooklyn could tell it affected him too.

"I...uh...I'd rather go by myself," she said. "If you're there it'll just make me more nervous."

A trace of disappointment ghosted across his face, but it quickly disappeared. He nodded and said with an earnest expression, "I understand. But try not to be nervous. You've got this."

With a nod and smile, she pulled in a reassuring breath and took his words to heart. She confidently tossed her cape behind her, stuck her head up in the air, and marched toward Illustrator's Row. But with every step she took, that self-assurance began to erode. Her heartbeat quickened. Her breaths grew short. Her grip on the portfolio slacked as her palm became sweaty. When she spotted the line of people waiting in front of Kurt Bollinger's table, Brooklyn's mouth grew as dry as the sandy beaches kissing the shoreline outside of the convention center.

What was she doing? Had she lost her mind?

The man sitting on the other side of that table was one of the most brilliant comic book illustrators in the country. Why did she think she could just walk up to him and show him her work?

Run. That's what she should do. She should kick off these heels she'd been dying to get rid of all day and hightail it out of this crowded convention center.

Brooklyn glanced over her shoulder and caught sight of Reid standing just inside the line delineating the food court, his eyes locked on her. He gave her a brief but encouraging nod. It was what she needed to take the remaining steps that would bring her to the end of the line at Bollinger's table. Brooklyn prayed that no one would get in line behind her. She could deal with the humiliation of one of her favorite artists laughing at her if it was just the two of them. To have witnesses? Witnesses who would actually see her face, and not just an online screen name?

A knot the size of the state of Mississippi formed in her belly.

"Stop it," Brooklyn breathed.

The Captain America standing in front of her turned. "Stop what?" he asked.

"Oh, nothing. I'm sorry." Goodness, could she be any more of an idiot?

The line moved much too slow. It gave her too much time to contemplate backing out. But then, as if even God was tired of her cowardliness, there was an announcement on the loudspeaker, informing convention-goers that the day's signature panel, featuring several actors from an upcoming superhero movie, was about to begin in the main exhibit hall. All but one of the people standing before her vacated the line, and in less than two minutes, Brooklyn found herself face-to-face with Kurt Bollinger, with no one else around to witness her impending humiliation. At least God was also apparently in the mood for answering the prayers of shy comics geeks.

"Well, thank you for sparing my feelings and not racing to hear that panel like everyone else," Kurt said with a light-hearted chuckle.

Brooklyn laughed, not because what he said was particularly funny, but because for a moment she forgot how to speak.

Pull it together, girl!

"I've waited a long time to meet you," she said. "This is way cooler than hearing actors talk."

He smiled.

Good. *Good.* This was going okay.

He picked up a copy of his latest comic—she'd read it twice already—from the pile on his table and, pen poised over it, asked, "Who should I sign it to?"

"I draw comics too," Brooklyn blurted.

Shit.

Shit.

Why couldn't she at least *try* not to be an idiot?

He nodded. "Oh. Good."

Her eyes briefly shut as humiliation filled every corner and crevice of her being. "You can make it out to Brooklyn," she said. "And what I meant to say is that your work has been an inspiration to me for many years."

He gestured to the portfolio she held. "You have some panels in there?"

For a millisecond Brooklyn considered lying. She could say she was holding it for someone else, or better yet, she could just run.

Stop. It.

"Yes," she answered, and with hands that shook only slightly, she laid the portfolio flat on the table and unzipped it. She'd taken out the few Iansan drawings she'd brought with her before they left the hotel, and hoped to God Reid hadn't seen them on the dresser and wrongly assumed that she wanted them in here. A tiny wave of relief crested over her when she flipped the cover open and saw a drawing she'd completed last year—a middle-grade comic based on tiny superheroes who lived in mushroom houses.

Her heart did the Cha Cha Slide in her chest as he lifted one of the panels up and studied it.

"Nice technique," he remarked. "You do a good job with shading." His eyes roamed over the first panel. He pointed to the arm of one of her superheroes. "Proportions can use some work, but that will get refined with time. It took me years to get it right." He flipped through a couple more panels before setting them down and smiling up at her. "You're not ready yet, but you definitely have talent. Keep it up."

How she refrained from bursting clear out of her skin, Brooklyn would never know.

"Thank you," she said, breathless with barely contained excitement. "Thank you so much." She zipped up her portfolio and tucked it underneath her left arm, then grabbed her signed copy of his comic. Sticking her hand out, Brooklyn smiled. "This was such an honor. Enjoy the rest of the con."

She backed away from the table, feeling as if her head was on the verge of exploding following the praise she'd just received. When she turned, she found Reid standing a couple of feet behind her. His arms were crossed over his chest, and the expression on his face could scare a grown man.

He jerked his chin over at Kurt Bollinger's table. "What did he mean by that proportion thing?"

"I thought I asked you to stay back there?" she said, pointing to the food court area.

"I wanted to make sure you were okay." He lifted the portfolio out of her hand and tucked it underneath his arm, his displeased frown still directed just over her shoulder.

Although she usually deplored the knight in shining armor routine, Brooklyn couldn't deny the thought of Reid running to her rescue made her heart skip a few beats. It startled her to think of how much had changed since that first week when she'd considered it silly that he insisted on walking her to her car.

"Thank you, but I'm fine," she said. "I'm *more* than fine. Kurt Bollinger just told me that I have talent." She held her hands to her sides and released a silent scream. She mouthed, "Oh. My. God."

"Yeah, well, he also said you're not ready yet, so I think he's full of shit. Don't listen to him."

"Oh, sure. Because, of course, I would take the advice of someone who just read his first comic two weeks ago over a legend who has been drawing them for decades." Brooklyn rolled her eyes. "I'm not ready. I know this. I want to work on my craft. That's why I want to apply for those fellowships—" she started, but then she stopped herself. Goodness, had she said that out loud?

"Apply for what?" Reid asked.

Shit. Yes, she had.

Brooklyn shook her head. "Nothing. Are you hungry?"

"We just ate," he pointed out. "What fellowships do you want to apply for? Is it for your comics?"

She pitched her head back and stared up at the Teen Titans banner that hung from the ceiling.

"Brooklyn?"

"There are these classes you can take," she started, returning her attention to Reid. "They're usually several weeks long, and almost like a boot camp for writers and illustrators. I'm self-taught, but know that I would benefit so much if I was able to attend one."

"So why haven't you gone?"

"First of all, I just started a new job." It was such a bull-shit excuse Brooklyn almost choked on the words, but as far as excuses went, it worked.

"You don't know Alex. You tell him about this and he'd give you the time off, probably with pay."

Okay, so maybe that excuse wouldn't work anymore. That's what she got for landing the coolest boss in the world.

"It's more complicated than that," she said. She wasn't about to go into the issue with her dad's health problems. She shook her head. "Look, I don't want to talk about it right now. It will mess up my good mood and I don't want anything to ruin what I'm feeling. I want to celebrate!"

A slick grin broke out across Reid's face. He held his hands out. "When it comes to having a good time, you got the right man for the job."

———

"OH, MY GOD." Brooklyn stumbled into her room and pulled Reid in behind her. "I don't know the last time I had that much fun. Wait. I do. Never. I have *never* had that much freaking fun." She released a satisfied sigh as she smiled up at the ceiling. "That club was amazing."

"It was. Although I don't know the last time I had that much fun without drinking," Reid remarked. He followed that with a deep chuckle that reverberated along her hyper-sensitive skin. It had been that way throughout the night, her body responding to every word, every look, from Reid.

She tipped her nose in the air. "I got drunk one time. That was enough for me."

"Let me rephrase that," he said. "I didn't know I *could* have that much fun without drinking. You're teaching me things I didn't know were possible."

An impudent smile curved up one corner of her mouth. "There's a lot more I can teach you."

Wait. Had those brazen words come out of her *mouth?*

"Is that right?" Reid asked, his humor-laced drawl sluicing down her back.

She nodded. Brooklyn had no idea from where this bold, audacious person had emerged, but she was going with it.

He took a step forward. "Why don't you tell me some of the things you can teach me?"

"Tell you?" She arched a brow. "Where's the fun in that?" Her eyes dropped to his lips, and in a raspy voice, she whispered, "I'd rather show you."

Intense heat flared in his eyes. He back her up against the door, capturing her wrists and pinning her arms on either side of her as he swooped down and imprisoned her mouth in a fierce kiss. His tongue plunged inside, demanding full capitulation with every insistent thrust. Brooklyn willingly surrendered as he undulated against her, his hips nudging forward, mimicking the rhythm of his tongue.

Reid drew his hands down her sides, running his palms along her hips, squeezing the same curves she so often tried to hide. He trailed his lips along her jawline, then down her neck to the hollow of her throat. Against her stomach she felt him swell, his thickening length growing harder with each second that ticked by.

"God, Brooklyn, do you have any idea how sexy you are?" he murmured against her skin. His grip moved to her backside. He incased her in his strong hands and squeezed, the action sending a shot of sensation spiraling through her. With amazingly little effort, Reid hefted her up and walked over to the dresser. He set her on top, knocking the empty plastic ice bucket to the floor in the process.

She locked her legs around his waist and clasped her arms around his neck, drawing his face back to hers. Brooklyn devoured his mouth, losing herself in his delicious kiss. Her breasts grew heavy with need, her nipples tightening to the point of pain.

Her skin-tight leotard now felt like a prison. She needed to free herself from the confines of the costume, but there was a voice in the back of her mind warning her not to move too fast.

She mentally shoved that voice in the closet as sensations bombarded her. The feel of his hands and lips and tongue making a playground of her body sent her careening toward the edge of her control. She thrust her hips forward, fireworks exploding within her at the feel of his heavy length colliding with her rapidly warming middle.

The warning came roaring back, imploring her to put a stop to this before they passed the point of no return.

Questions began to assail her, annoying thoughts she didn't want to entertain, but that wouldn't leave her alone. Like how many other women had been privy to his knowledgeable hands, lips, and tongue. Had he treated those women from his party to these same kisses? How many times had they felt his muscular chest abrading their breasts?

She didn't want to know the answers to any of those questions. They meant nothing. Reid was *here* now. He wanted *her*. That's all that mattered.

Until he slipped his hand between her legs and cupped her. Brooklyn fought the natural urge to thrust herself against his fingers. Instead, she reached down and wrapped her hand around his wrist, halting his movements.

"Reid, wait."

He stopped immediately. "What's wrong?"

Don't say it! Don't!

"I don't think we should do this," Brooklyn said.

God, why did she say that?

Reid's shoulders sank with disappointment. "Are you sure?" he asked, the words coming out in heavy pants.

"No." She shook her head. "But I still think we should stop."

He braced his hands on either side of her hips and dropped his head against her shoulder. Brooklyn felt his breath against the curve of her neck.

After heaving a defeated sigh, he raised his head and stared at her, his face blanketed in frustrated confusion. "You mind telling me why you changed your mind all of a sudden?"

"I'm not even sure myself," Brooklyn admitted. "This is just...it's going too fast. Seven days ago I thought I would have to witness you walk out of your party with some other girl on your arm."

"That never would have happened. You should know that by now."

"Should I? You haven't come right out and said that your casual sex days are over. How do I know that's not what's happening right now?"

Hurt slashed across his face and Brooklyn immediately felt like the most horrible person east of the Mississippi.

"I'm sorry," she said. "Forget I said that."

"Yeah, that's not going to happen."

"I didn't mean for it to sound as if I was questioning your motives or anything."

"But that's exactly what you did." He leaned forward, forcing her to lean her head back against mirror. "I know it's asking a lot when I ask you to trust me with your heart, but I'm hoping you'll do it anyway. Just give me a chance, Brooklyn. Are you willing to do that?"

She pulled her bottom lip between her teeth.

"Stop thinking so hard," he said. "This doesn't have to be hard."

"But do you understand why this *is* hard for me, Reid? Do you have *any* idea? It's because guys like you usually ignore girls like me."

"I—"

She shook her head. "No. Let me finish." She let out a shaky breath. "You know all those silly teen movies where the shy, quiet girl has a crush on the star quarterback, and he magically falls in love with her? Those things don't happen in real life. Opposites don't attract. The hot jock doesn't fall for the nerd."

"Is that what you really think?"

"It's what I *know*, Reid. I'm just being realistic here."

"You're wrong," he said. "You're what I want, Brooklyn. You're *all* I want. You want me to prove I'm serious about this? About us?"

"This isn't about you proving anything. Honestly, it's more about me."

"No." He shook his head. "You're not giving me the 'it's not you, it's me' treatment. I'm the king of that line, and I call bullshit every single time I use it. You need me to show you that I'm serious. That's exactly what I'll do."

The determination in his eyes both excited her and sort of frightened her.

Reid closed the short distance between them and placed a swift, but deep kiss on her lips. "Prepare for me to show you just what it means to be Reid Holmes's girl."

CHAPTER TEN

AS HE WATCHED her playing horseshoes with his nephew, Reid fought like hell to ignore the wayward thoughts that had been encamped in his mind for much of the day. One would think if anything could stop the reel of dirty, nasty, filthy images from clicking in his head like a View-Master, it would be the fact that he was surrounded by his entire family. But apparently enjoying barbecue and joking around with his brothers was no match for a libido that was still riding high from what he and Brooklyn had almost done in a Biloxi hotel room last weekend.

Reid stifled a groan. The last thing he needed right now was to have one of his nosy ass family members notice him getting aroused in the middle of a picnic on the New Orleans lakefront.

He counted to ten and thought about Catholic nuns, his shoulders sagging with relief as he finally got his body under control. He tore his attention away from Brooklyn before that thing behind his zipper could get happy again. Instead, he looked over to the patch of browning grass where Griffin and his cousin Eli took practice swings with the new set of

golf clubs Eli had carted in from his SUV. He'd been practicing swings at the adjacent golf course when he noticed
the familiar cars parked in the shared parking lot. His
cousin was such a freaking cliché when it came to the golf-
playing physician.

Mackenna Arnold, his soon-to-be sister-in-law, and the
soon-to-be next mayor of New Orleans if the early polls
were any indication, had suggested they all come down to
the lakefront to put the speedboat she'd won in her divorce
to good use. His dad and Ezra had taken the boat out on
Lake Pontchartrain. Accompanying them were a couple of
his dad's old navy buddies who had surprised him by
coming into town to celebrate the fiftieth anniversary of
their graduation from navy boot camp.

Reid thought he was being an adult by staying behind
and offering to help at the grill, but Harrison was acting like
a territorial ass, not allowing anyone within ten feet of the
barbecue. Instead, Reid had joined the Frisbee match his
niece and a few of her friends were engaged in. He faked an
injury after one of the teens "accidentally" bumped into
him for the third time. He didn't want to cause an embarrassing scene by telling homegirl to back up off him, but he
also wasn't interested in encouraging seventeen-year-old jail
bait either. The only woman he was interested in was the
one wearing a My Little Pony T-shirt with a hot pink streak
in her hair to match.

For the past half hour, he'd sat with his back against the
picnic table, his arms spread out on either side of him, his
eyes trained on Brooklyn. He loved watching her with his
nephew. One would think a ten-year-old and a twenty-six-
year-old wouldn't have much in common. But an obsession
with superheroes brought people together, no matter the
age difference. Reid couldn't hear anything they said, but

their animated faces conveyed the bulk of their conversation. He suspected Athens was developing the same crush on Reid's girl that Reid had developed on Athens's mom back when he was around the kid's age.

Wait. Had he just called Brooklyn his girl?

He had.

And he wasn't hyperventilating.

He liked the thought of her being his girl. He *loved* it. If this was what it felt like to have an actual girlfriend, and not just someone he wanted in his bed for a night, Reid was ready to sign up for life. He never knew he could be this content.

He'd spent the past week at the Westbank job site, but as soon as he clocked off, he hauled ass to Brooklyn's place. They had yet to make it past her living room, and the most outerwear he'd taken off were his work boots, but Reid didn't feel the least bit deprived. They would eventually get fully naked. To be honest, a part of him was enjoying the anticipation. He'd never been made to wait for anything when it came to women. It made the promise of what lay ahead that much more enticing.

For now, satisfaction came in the form of seeing how far Brooklyn would let him go. Last night, his hand made it *inside* her bra. He'd nearly come in his pants the second his fingers closed around her hard nipple.

And why in the *fuck* was he thinking about this right now?

Reid flung his head back and lifted his hips slightly off the bench. He concentrated on the warm sun hitting his face and, once again, fought for control over his own damn body. The battle grew more punishing by the hour.

"Hey, open up the ice chest!"

Popping up at the sound of Indina's voice, Reid hustled

over to where she and Willow were making their way back from the car. They'd had to make a convenience store run after it was discovered that no one had thought to bring ice or plates.

Reid lifted the bag of ice from his sister's hand and teased, "Took y'all long enough. What'd you have to do, make the ice?"

He swiftly dodged the slap he knew would be coming his way and emptied the ice over the bottles of water and cans of soda he'd stacked into the ice chest earlier.

"How much longer on that barbecue?" Indina called out to Harrison as she and Willow began taking the tops off the storage containers filled with dishes that had been made beforehand.

Harrison held up five fingers.

"That means it'll be more like fifteen minutes," Willow said. "Athens will need to eat something soon, but I'm not sure I'll be able to tear him away from his new friend."

"Speaking of this new friend, how long are we going to pretend it isn't a big deal Reid showed up with a girl?" Indina asked, casting a droll look his way.

He was surprised it had taken this long for one of them to bring up the unconventionality of Brooklyn's presence here. Before today, the closest Reid had ever come to bringing a date to a family function was when he would drop by for a plate to take back to his apartment. He'd always asked the woman to stay in the truck.

He should feel like a world-class shit for that, but the truth was, there had never been another girl he'd felt strongly enough about to introduce to his family. It felt right that Brooklyn was the first to hold that honor.

"Yeah, I know it's a big deal," he said now.

"A humongous deal," Indina replied. "So, what's the scoop? Harrison told Ezra that she works for Alex."

His damn brothers gossiped like school girls.

"She's the new site coordinator," Reid confirmed. "She started at HCC about six weeks ago."

"She's cute," Willow said. "Though, I have to admit she doesn't look like your type."

"I don't have a type," he said. Willow and Indina looked at each other and then burst out laughing. "Hey." Reid frowned. "What's up with that?"

"You *so* have a type," his sister replied. "You always have."

"How can I have a 'type' when I've never had an actual girlfriend?"

"Exactly," Indina and Willow said at the same time.

"But one just has to look at some of the shit your friends tag you in on Facebook to know that you've had plenty of girls." Indina's shoulders shook in an exaggerated shiver. "I'm still trying to scrub the pictures I saw from last year's Bayou Classic weekend out of my mind. There are some things I just don't need to know about my baby brother."

Reid rolled his eyes.

"Brooklyn is definitely an improvement," Willow said. "She blew Athens away when she was able to name all the X-Men. Lily doesn't want anything to do with his comics, so he's impressed that a girl would know anything about them."

"You don't know the half of it," Reid said.

He realized now was as good a time as any for the big reveal. He'd finally convinced Brooklyn it was time to share her drawings of Dynamo Diane with his family. With the foundation's kickoff party drawing near, they would need to get started on having the programs printed.

He stood and called for Brooklyn. She said something to Athens, then the two of them jogged over to the table. "Hey," she said, breathless.

"Sorry to stop your fun, but this one here needs to eat a little something," Willow said, setting a plate of carrots and celery sticks in front of Athens. His nephew grimaced, but started eating.

"That's okay. He was kicking my butt anyway," Brooklyn said. She pointed at his nephew. "But I'm challenging you to a rematch after lunch." She turned to Reid. "What's up?"

He gestured with his chin toward Willow and Indina. "Are you ready to let them in on the secret?"

"Oh my God, you're not pregnant are you?" Indina asked.

"No!" Brooklyn and Reid both shouted.

"Seriously, Deenie?" Reid said. He grabbed the oversized backpack he'd brought, unzipped it, and then handed it to Brooklyn. She looked over at him, her lips pressed together in doubt. "Show them," Reid encouraged.

Reid couldn't deny the nerves twisting around in his own belly. The pressure to get this right was overwhelming. He wanted to show his family he could rise to the occasion when they called upon him. He'd left the irresponsible slacker in his twenties.

Brooklyn unzipped the portfolio, but Reid caught her wrist before she could open it.

"Before she shows you what's inside, I should explain that the superhero idea I came up with for the party was inspired by Brooklyn."

She tucked her head down, a flush creeping across her cheeks. "I just wore a shirt. Reid is the one who came up with the idea."

"It was a collaboration," he said. "Anyway, what you're about to see right now is one hundred percent her. It's probably not even necessary for me to point that out. You'll understand once you see it."

"Well, can we finally see it?" Indina said. "Whatever *it* is?"

Brooklyn opened the portfolio and pulled out a plastic-sheathed drawing.

"Meet Dynamo Diane," Reid said.

Willow gasped. She and Indina both stared at the drawing with their mouths agape. Anxiety surged through Reid's bloodstream as he waited for one of them to say *some*thing. It was as if time was suspended as everyone just continued to stare.

Indina looked between Brooklyn and the drawing several times, her eyes wide. She reached for the drawing, then snatched her hand back, as if she was afraid to touch.

"I'm sorry. Can I?" she asked, her voice softened with awe.

"Of course," Brooklyn said.

Indina gently picked up the drawing, handling it as if it was one of the Fabergé eggs that were sometimes on display at the New Orleans Museum of Art. Reid watched her eyes roam the drawing as she studied it with the same wonder he had the first time he laid eyes on it.

"I can't...I can't believe this." Indina's voice caught, and Reid had to clear the emotion from his own throat.

"Remarkable, isn't it?" he asked.

"It looks just like her." Indina looked to Brooklyn. "You drew this?"

Brooklyn nodded and shrugged. "It's a hobby of mine."

"A hobby? Girl, why aren't you doing this for a living? This is amazing!"

"Yeah, we've had this conversation before," Reid said.

"Okay, it's more than a hobby," Brooklyn said, her blush intensifying.

"I just...I'm speechless," Indina said.

"Speechless? Somebody mark the date." They all looked over to find Ezra, his dad, and Dad's navy buddies striding toward them.

Indina held up Brooklyn's illustration. "Would you look at what Reid's girlfriend drew. Tell me this isn't the most amazing thing you've ever seen in your life."

Reid stood back and watched as the others all gathered around the table, marveling at Brooklyn's work. She became more animated with each new drawing she revealed, describing the plan they'd come up with for the keepsake comic book program.

She captivated him. Thoroughly.

Reid was blown away by the ease with which she'd fit in so easily with his family. Chatting with Willow as if they'd been friends for ages, talking comics with Athens, even indulging his dad's obsession with some random show on the History Channel that she'd caught once. She'd charmed the collective pants right off the Holmeses. And that had been *before* they'd seen the drawings.

The introduction of Dynamo Diane had solidified her place in their hearts. Reid was sure if they had to choose between the two of them, his entire family would pick Brooklyn over him.

Now that Indina was over her initial shock, she'd taken off like a rocket in her party planning, using her phone to look up local screen printing shops that could make Dynamo Diane T-shirts, caps, and buttons. Griffin convinced her to take a break only when Harrison announced that the barbecue was finally ready.

Over the meal, Indina rattled off some of the ideas she'd come up with based on what Reid had brought back from last weekend's Comic Con, but an alert on Mackenna's phone soon turned the talk to local politics. Two of her fellow colleagues on the New Orleans City Council had been indicted for taking bribes in what had turned into the biggest political scandal that had hit the city in years.

Funny thing is, that's exactly what Ezra had accused Mackenna of doing for months. Reid couldn't imagine Mack being anything but the honest, stand-up person she'd been for the twenty years since she'd come into their family as Indina's close friend and college roommate, but for some reason Ezra had gotten it in his head that she'd gone rogue. As an investigative reporter, he had made it his mission to expose her.

The only thing his brother had exposed was his ability to get knocked on his ass by love.

"I can't believe Washington and Babin thought they could get away with this," his dad said.

"They're cocky. Always have been. And they think they're untouchable," Mack said.

"I hope they both find themselves under the jail," Indina said. "It'll serve them right for making your life hell while on the council."

"She doesn't have to worry about being on the council anymore, because she's about to become this city's mayor," Ezra said, harkening a cheer from the entire table. "That's why you get the big piece of chicken," his brother said, plopping a grill-marked chicken breast on Mack's plate.

Once they'd all eaten more barbecue than the law should allow, his brothers decided to put the speedboat to the test. Reid took a pass, choosing instead to steal Brooklyn away. It had been too many hours since they'd been alone. He guided her toward the concrete embankment that ran along the shoreline of the lake. When he sensed her attempting to let go of his hand, Reid tightened his hold. He didn't want to let go of her. He needed this connection.

"So, can you ever forgive me for bringing you around my crazy family?" he asked as they made their way toward the Milneburg Lighthouse.

"Forgive you for what?" Brooklyn asked. "Your family is wonderful. Especially Athens. He's adorable. Although, I think he's developing a little crush on me."

"A *little* crush?" Reid asked with a chuckle. "I think the kid's halfway in love with you already."

I know the feeling.

The words were on the tip of his tongue, but Reid knew better than to voice them. He'd learned just how easily she became spooked when things got too heavy.

Besides, he had no idea if love was what he was feeling right now. He'd never come close to the real thing. But if this *wasn't* the real thing, Reid wasn't sure he'd be able to handle truly being in love. It felt as if he'd spontaneously combust from the myriad emotions that constantly crowded his brain.

Brooklyn turned to him, her eyes beaming with excitement. "I did not expect that type of reaction to Dynamo Diane. Your entire family was blown away. Especially your sister."

"I knew they would be," Reid said. "Did you see Indina looking up stuff on her phone? She's going to have Dynamo Diane on everything. I wouldn't be surprised if she shrink-wrapped her car and called it the Dynamobile."

Just as he'd hoped, Brooklyn threw her head back and blessed him with her musical laugh. He wanted to make that laugh his ringtone, but he'd probably spend all day calling his own phone just so he could hear it.

He tightened his grip on her hand as they continued along the lake front. "The best thing about today was the look on my dad's face when he saw that drawing," he said. "I've been worried about him."

Her smile dimmed, and Reid was almost sorry he'd mentioned it. But he wanted her to know how much it meant to see a smile on his dad's face. She was the one who'd put it there. She deserved to know how special that was for his entire family.

"It hasn't been that long since your mom passed," Brooklyn said, her voice so soft Reid could barely hear it over the gentle crush of the waves against the seawall.

"No, not long at all," he answered. He waited a few moments before trusting himself to speak again. "I still have a hard time accepting that she's gone. She spoiled me," Reid continued, a smile tipping up the corner of his mouth. "I was her baby, after all. It pissed Ezra off."

"Can you be a little less cheeky about that?"

"Nope." He laughed, then he sobered. "I just miss her so damn much," Reid said. "I miss having her around to ask for her advice. I even miss her badgering me about having too many pairs of sneakers."

"How many pairs do you have?" Brooklyn asked.

"You don't want to know," Reid said. He huffed out a laugh. "My mom thought more than two pairs was too much. This from a woman who owned at least three dozen church hats that cost well over a hundred bucks a pop."

"Don't you ever tell a black woman anything about her church hats. That's not your business."

"Believe me, I know." He chuckled, then shook his head. "I'd trade every pair of Jordans I own for the chance to see her again. Just one more day with her. That would be enough."

"Oh, Reid." Brooklyn took both his hands and brought them to her lips, pressing a kiss to the backs of his fingers. "I don't want to even imagine what it feels like to lose a parent." She rested her cheek against their clasped hands. "But then, I should probably start preparing myself."

He frowned. "What are you talking about? You're only twenty-six. Your parents can't be that old."

She looked up at him. "Your mom wasn't old." She had a point. "And my parents had me pretty late in life. My dad was almost forty when I was born. But age doesn't matter when you're dealing with a compromised respiratory system."

She got choked up on the last word. Reid remained silent as he patiently waited for her to collect herself.

"You okay?" he asked after several moments passed. She nodded, but he wasn't sure how true that was. "Is this why LeBlanc & Sons closed up shop?"

She pulled in another shuddering breath. "Yeah. It was the primary reason. It was getting too hard for him to continue. If I'd known how bad off he was, I would have insisted he stopped working long before he did."

"How is he doing now?" Reid asked.

"He has his good days and his bad."

He waited for her to continue, but when she didn't, Reid decided not to try to get any more from her. He could sense the difficulty she was having with discussing her dad's condition. Instead, he said the only thing he could say. "I'm sorry you have to go through this. I know the pain of watching a parent slowly deteriorate. I wouldn't wish that on anyone."

Shit. Emotion welled in his throat, making it hard to swallow.

Brooklyn reached for his hand, closing her much smaller palm around it and giving his hand a reassuring squeeze. They stood there staring out at the calm waters of Lake Pontchartrain. Reid watched the waves break gently against the smooth rocks along the shoreline of the tiny peninsula that jutted out into the lake, and tried to remember the last time he'd felt this kind of peace.

He hadn't opened up to anyone about the loss of his mother since the night she died, when Willow showed up at his place to check on him. He'd collapsed into his sister-in-law's arms and cried like a baby. But that was Willow. Reid couldn't imagine sharing these feelings with any of the women he'd been with in the past. He couldn't imagine any of them caring enough about him to want to hear it.

But Brooklyn did. She cared. She offered comfort.

Reid knew in that moment that there was no going back for him. This had to be love. This feeling that being around her evoked, as if his heart would burst clear out of his chest. What could this be if not love?

He couldn't blame her for being unsure if she could fully trust him. With his track record, Reid wouldn't trust a guy like him either. He didn't deserve her yet, but he was getting there. He would eventually prove he was worthy of her love.

———

IT WASN'T PERFECT, but it would do.

Brooklyn dipped the tip of the paintbrush in the purple paint again, then drew it lightly along the canvas, adding a bit of shadow to the curve of the fleur-de-lis.

"Exquisite."

A shudder went through her as the softly whispered word traveled down her spine. She looked back to find Reid just over her shoulder.

"Why are you here and not working on your own painting?"

"I gave up on mine." He gestured to his canvas. "It's a lost cause. Besides, I'd rather watch you paint. You make it look so damn sexy."

She rolled her eyes, but inside his words sparked an erotic charge that shot clear through her body.

"You're such a flirt," Brooklyn said.

"It's working, though. Right?"

She couldn't hold back her smile. She lifted her shoulder in a casual shrug. "Maybe."

Reid's answering grin triggered an abundance of excited tingles all along her skin. He leaned over and pressed a kiss to the part of her collarbone left exposed by the maroon off-the-shoulder sweater she'd bought on a whim this past weekend. She never wore stuff like this, but Reid had her doing things she'd never done before, feeling things she'd never felt before.

She'd been called cute, and a couple of the guys she'd dated in the past—particularly those who were into comics—even thought she was cool. But Reid made her feel sexy. The way he absently trailed his finger along the inside of her arm, the way he brushed his lips against her jaw, or along her neck, or at that spot just behind her ear. He seemed incapable of going more than ten minutes without touching her in some way.

And with just a touch, just a look, he made her feel as if she was everything in the world he could ever want. Never in her wildest dreams did she think a guy like Reid would look at her the way he did, but she wasn't dreaming. This was real.

"I didn't think this through when I booked this Sip and Paint place," Reid said, his lips still too close to her bare shoulder for Brooklyn to think straight. "I'm at a disadvantage."

"What do you mean?"

"I mean that my painting looks like something a second-grader did, while that, on the other hand," he said, gesturing to her canvas, "should be hanging in an art gallery somewhere."

Brooklyn burst out laughing, drawing the attention of half the people in the studio. She gave Reid a playful slap on the arm. "Stop making me laugh," she said. "People will think I'm drunk."

"That's the whole point of places like this, isn't it?" He jutted his chin toward the group of women who were celebrating one of the ladies' 40th birthday, according to their matching T-shirts. The women became rowdier with each champagne cork they popped.

As if on cue, the distinct pop hissed as another bottle was opened and the women let up a roar.

"Maybe I should have read a few online reviews before bringing you here," Reid said. "When I Googled 'best dates for artsy people' this is what came up."

"You Googled for me?" Brooklyn asked, utterly charmed by his effort.

"You're worth Googling for," he said, planting a kiss on the tip of her nose.

She laughed again, but this time she was drowned out by the party-goers.

"Are you finished with your masterpiece?" Reid asked. "I'm ready to cut out early on Tatianya's birthday bash."

"Are you really not going to finish your painting?"

"Nah. But I'm still going to hang it on my wall. I can make a game out of making people guess what it was supposed to be."

A half hour later, they were at a standstill on Interstate 10, waiting for yet another wrecker that had whizzed by on the shoulder twenty minutes ago to clear the last car in what, according to the DOT's Twitter feed, had been a four-car pileup.

"My luck with traffic has been for shit lately," Reid said.

"It's okay," she said. Without thinking, she reached over and put her hand on his thigh. She quickly pulled it away, but Reid clasped her wrist and brought her hand right back. He covered her hand with his, moving it up and down in a lazy caress.

"You should know by now that I want your hands on me every minute of every day."

Her brow arched in amusement. "Every minute?"

"Every fucking minute." He leaned over and buried his nose against her neck. "But it's nothing compared to how much I want *my* hands on *you*."

Brooklyn couldn't adequately describe just how much she wanted that too. Since the night he'd nearly taken her on top of a hotel room dresser in Biloxi, her mind had been filled with visions of what would have happened if she hadn't stopped him. Every time he kissed her, every time his skin made the barest contact with hers, it caused another deluge of erotic images to cascade through her mind.

The traffic finally started to move. Within minutes they were cruising along I-610. Apprehension and anticipation collided in her bloodstream as they passed one exit, then another. Brooklyn contemplated whether she was bold enough to go through with the plan that had popped into her head. When they neared the exit that would take them to Reid's apartment, she quickly reached over and flipped up the blinker.

He glanced over at her with an inquisitive lift to his brow.

"Your place is closer," she said.

The confusion remained on his face for a second before understanding dawned.

"Are you sure?" Reid asked.

Brooklyn nodded. "Yes. God, yes. One hundred percent."

She burst out laughing when he pressed down on the accelerator, swooping into the thankfully empty exit onto St. Bernard Avenue. He sped through two yellow lights, making it to his apartment complex in much less time than it should have taken them.

Reid hopped out of the truck and rounded it, catching her by the waist as he helped her out of the passenger side.

"Tell me now if you need foreplay," he said.

"I don't."

"Thank God." His relief was palpable. "I promise we'll do all that shit eventually. Right now, I just need to be inside you as soon as possible."

His words nearly caused her to orgasm right there in the parking lot.

They raced up to his apartment, kicking off shoes as soon as they cleared the threshold. Brooklyn figured she'd just ruined her new sweater with the way she stretched it out trying to get it over her head, but she didn't give a damn. The only thing that mattered was how quickly she could get naked.

It turned out they were both going for the world record in how fast they could disrobe. Reid had his jeans and polo shirt off in five seconds flat, and it took Brooklyn less than two seconds to determine that the man was perfectly put together.

He should have looked ridiculous standing there in nothing but a pair of socks, but the only ridiculous thing here was how amazingly fine he was. His tight abs were so well-defined they looked as if they'd been carved out of stone. The corded muscle in his solid thighs exuded strength, bunching underneath his dark brown skin, making her hands itch with the need to smooth them over its firmness.

Brooklyn refused to acknowledge the obvious, because his ego was healthy enough, but her knees went weak at the sight of what Reid Holmes had been hiding in his pants all this time. She'd never seen one that big outside of the porn she occasionally—okay, frequently—watched.

Reid pointed past her shoulder. "In the bedroom," he commanded.

She half-walked/half-ran ahead of him, tumbling onto his unmade bed and trying to tamp down her anxiety over what was about to happen. This was a first for her—not the sex, but the sex with someone she'd thought would only be a fantasy for her. Anticipation shot through her veins like liquid fire.

"I've been dying to do this for weeks," Reid said as he joined her on the bed. He shoved his hands underneath her and squeezed her ass hard, while his mouth went on an expedition of her body. He kissed and bit and licked his way around her, starting with her shoulder, then moving to both breasts and down her stomach. He treated the curves she so often tried to hide as if they were the sexiest parts of her body, gently biting that stubborn belly roll that refused to disappear despite the fifty stomach crunches she did twice a week.

"You are so fucking sexy," Reid murmured against her stomach. He started at her bellybutton, dropping light kisses against her skin. Then he traveled down her body, until he reached the spot between her legs. Brooklyn's legs instinctively snapped closed, clamping his head between her thighs.

"Sorry," she yelped as she relaxed her legs.

Reid's response was a low, decadent laugh that reverberated throughout her throbbing sex. He lifted her legs and placed them over his shoulders, then he flattened his tongue against her and pressed deep.

Brooklyn pulled her bottom lip between her teeth, but couldn't hold back the mewl of pleasure that escaped when he used two fingers to spread her open and wrapped his tongue around her clit. Her bottom half lifted off the bed of its own volition, surging toward him, aching for more. More. More. More of everything.

He gave her more.

Brooklyn looked down the length of her body and saw when he sucked two of his fingers in his mouth. A second later, those same two fingers slid into her soaking wet body. He pumped his fingers in rhythm to the pulls on her clit, sucking the nub into his warm mouth. It was an assault on her senses, his knowledgeable tongue and fingers enrobing her in ribbons of hedonistic pleasure. It occurred to her that it would be the first multi-orgasm night of her life only seconds before the first wave hit her. Brooklyn unabashedly lifted her hips up and ground herself into Reid's face. Any embarrassment she may have felt melted away as finding satisfaction took a front row seat.

She collapsed back onto the bed, her jellylike limbs unable to sustain her a second longer.

"Oh my God," Brooklyn blew out on a tired breath. "And we haven't even gotten to the good part, have we?"

"This was my appetizer," Reid said. He swirled his finger around her nipple. "You want to taste it?" he asked before lowering his head and dipping his tongue inside her mouth. Brooklyn tasted herself for the first time, the flavor melding with the flavor of Reid's mouth. It was so erotic she nearly orgasmed again.

After kissing her long and deep, he finally pulled away.

"It's time for the main course." He reached over and opened a drawer on the nightstand, retrieving several condoms. He threw two on the nightstand and then tore open the third packet.

"Three?" Brooklyn asked. "I guess it's going to be a long night, huh?"

"You up for it?" Reid asked.

"I think you're the one who needs to answer that question."

His answering grin was too wickedly sexy to put into words. He rolled the condom on, then reversed their positions, rolling onto his back and pulling her on top of him.

She was attacked by a deluge of self-consciousness as she became aware of how she must look straddling his hips.

"Can we please turn the light off?" Brooklyn asked.

"Fuck no," Reid answered. He clamped his palms on her hips then ran them up the sides of her waist, closing them over her breasts before running them down her stomach. "I want to see every inch of you."

He braced one hand on the mattress and lifted himself up, capturing her nipple between his lips and sucking. His erection pulsed against her ass, teasing her with what was to come.

"Reid." His name came out on a hoarse whisper. "I don't want to rush this, but..." Brooklyn trailed off.

She didn't have to say anymore. Without another word, Reid wrapped his hand around his erection and guided it insider her. Brooklyn sank onto his solid length and held herself steady for several moments, giving her body a chance to get acclimated to his size. When she felt she was ready, she began to ride him the way she had in her dreams, lifting and plunging with long, deep strokes, flattening her palms against his solid chest.

Her head fell back as she concentrated on the unbelievable pleasure coursing through her body. With every delicious slide, she fell a little deeper in love. She knew it was naive, possibly even dangerous, but she didn't care. At this very moment, all she wanted was the very thing she had: Reid Holmes worshipping her imperfect body as if it were flawless.

That's how he made her feel. Perfect. As if she embodied everything he could ever want in a woman.

"Reid." Brooklyn moaned his name as, once again, that pleasurable sensation began to build low in her belly. She pumped faster, reaching for release, craving the exquisite rush that awaited just on the other side. She felt herself tighten around his thick length seconds before the blinding orgasm burst through her body.

Reid clamped his hands on her hips and held her steady as he pumped once, twice, three times, finding his own release within moments of hers.

They lay there for several minutes, their breaths coming out in loud pants. He left the bed only long enough to rid himself of the condom, before diving back under the covers and fitting her against him. Brooklyn found peace in the methodical rise and fall of his muscular chest against her back.

She snuggled more securely in the cocoon he'd created with his arms. As she stared out ahead, her eyes were drawn to the picture on the nightstand. Reid, dressed in khaki slacks and a button down shirt, towered over the much shorter Diane Holmes. She wore a yellow suit with a smart yellow church hat. The love shining in her eyes as she stared up at Reid told the story of how much she loved her son.

"Your mother was such a beautiful woman," Brooklyn said.

"Hmmm," Reid murmured. "Her outside beauty had nothing on the woman she was on the inside," he said. He reached over and set the picture facedown on the bedside table. "I love that picture, but I really need to move it to the living room. One day I'm going to look over and see it while I'm doing what we just did, and that'll be the end of my sex life."

Brooklyn pitched her head back with her laugh. "Probably a good idea to move it," she agreed. She pulled Reid's arm more securely around her middle. He immediately moved his hand to her breast, filling his palm with it.

"Have I told you how much I love your body?" he whispered, pressing a kiss to her damp shoulder as he began to toy with her nipple. His erotic play sent ripples of pleasure cascading through her.

"In both words and action," Brooklyn answered. Her eyes fell closed, renewed desire stirring within her as Reid continued to tease her nipple.

"This feels so surreal," she said.

"What does?"

"This. You. Me. It's hard to believe it's happening. The object of a crush only falls for the person crushing on them in YA novels."

"Okay, first, what's a YA novel? And who's crushing on who?"

She laughed. "YA stands for young adult." She turned so she could face him. "Some people may consider it a guilty pleasure for an adult to read books written for teens, but I don't buy into that. There's enough crap in life that we should find pleasure wherever we can, without guilt."

"Agreed," he said. "And the crush?"

She rolled her eyes. "You're the crush, Reid. You've been my crush since about ten minutes after I first met you."

His cocky grin made her want to take the words back, but there was no denying that she'd moved well beyond infatuation when it came to Reid Holmes. She was wholly in love with him.

"Tell me something," Reid purled as he dipped his head and sucked her nipple into his mouth. "At what point does a crush become the real thing?"

It was as if he was reading her mind. Brooklyn refused to answer. She couldn't, because at that moment he grabbed another condom and lowered her onto her back.

This time he took complete control, directing the pace of their lovemaking in a way designed to make her lose her mind. He would take her to the very edge, then pull back, continuing the maddening rhythm over and over and over again, until Brooklyn thought she would surely die. When she finally came, Reid came along with her, their twin shouts of pleasure resonating in the air.

"God, it's been a long time since I did this," Brooklyn said as she settled back against the pillows.

"I could tell."

She pinched his arm. "Not *that*," she said with a laugh. "Although it has been a long time since I did that too. I mean *this*. Allowing myself to just...just exist for a minute and not worry about the million things I've had to worry about these past months."

"What's been on your mind?" he asked, his thumb slowly caressing her arm.

"Everything. Life has been such a rollercoaster." Brooklyn rested her head against his biceps, amazed at how perfect she seemed to fit. "I haven't had much chance to breathe since we hung up the 'closed for business' sign on LeBlanc & Sons. You'd think being out of work would have led to having *more* downtime, but for the first time in my life I found myself having to look for a job. I knew it was something I'd eventually have to face, but I hadn't been prepared for it to happen this quickly. It's scary."

"I get that," he said. "I'm sort of in that same boat. This is all I've ever done—worked for Alex, I mean. It's a pretty nice safety net."

"Exactly. I counted on that safety. Having that is worth more than gold."

He groaned. "Great, now I'm questioning if I'm making the right decision."

She looked up and was surprised by the torment etched across his features.

"Reid? What is it?"

He blew out a deep breath and looked down into her eyes. "This is weird, you know? This talking after sex thing. I don't think I've ever done this with a woman I've slept with before."

"I can tell," Brooklyn deadpanned. "Because if you *had*, you'd have known better than to bring up previous sex you've had while the woman you're currently having sex with is in your bed."

"Sorry." A chastised grin tipped up one corner of his mouth. Brooklyn had no doubt he'd gotten away with just about everything as a kid because of that grin.

"Back to what we were talking about." She was not about to let him derail the conversation with his sexy smile. "What decision are you questioning?"

He released another of those exhausted sighs. "It's just that lately I've been feeling...I don't know...stuck. Don't get me wrong, I love working for Alex. I'm good at it and I owe my cousin everything for taking a chance on me when most people would have kicked me out the door."

"But?" Brooklyn prompted.

"But...I've been thinking about moving on."

Her eyes widened. That wasn't what she'd expected to hear. "Moving to another construction company?"

"No. Starting my own. Well, not just me. It would be me and Anthony."

Her forehead furrowed as she peered up at him. "It sounds like more than something you've just been *thinking* about."

He nodded. "The app Anthony is building is nearly done. It will be ready for beta testing in the next few months."

"An app? I didn't realize you knew about computers."

"I don't." He went on to explain about the app-based handyman business Anthony had developed. It was genius in both its simplicity and its use of video-telephony technology.

"This sounds amazing, Reid. What are you afraid of?"

He huffed out a humorless laugh. "Everything. I'm

afraid it'll flop. I'm afraid Anthony and I won't be able to cut it. I'm afraid Alex will hate me for leaving."

Brooklyn flattened her palm against his chest, directly over his heart. "Take the advice of someone who has allowed fear to rule her life for far too long. Don't. Don't let fear stop you."

"That's easy to say. Not so easy to do," he replied. "On one hand, it feels as if I've let too much time pass already, yet on the other it feels as if both me and Anthony still have so much growing to do."

"Do you know how old Steve Jobs was when he started Apple Computers?" Brooklyn asked. "Twenty-one. If he could start a company that would eventually revolutionize the entire world at twenty-one, you can surely make this work at age thirty." She pressed a kiss to the center of his chest. "You can do this, Reid."

"You really think so?" he asked.

She cupped his jaw and lifted her head to kiss him again, this time on the lips. "I know so."

CHAPTER ELEVEN

REID ARRIVED at the corner store/barbershop/gas station/hot plate lunch spot not too far from the senior citizen's center Holmes Construction had built a couple of years ago in the St. Roch neighborhood. He spotted Anthony's car parked next to the air pump, noticing the broken hose just to the right of it. He pulled alongside him and climbed out of his truck, chuckling at the grim look on his buddy's face, as if he knew Reid was prepared to give him shit.

Who was he to disappoint?

"You would be the one to get a flat tire at the one joint in town with a broken air pump *and* that doesn't carry Fix-A-Flat," Reid said by way of greeting.

"Just give me the damn thing," Anthony said, jerking the aerosol can from Reid's grasp. "I've got somewhere I need to be." As the tire slowly inflated, Anthony looked up at him. "You busy?"

"Apparently not," Reid deadpanned. "I'm here, ain't I?"

"Let me rephrase that. Are you too busy to follow me to my cousin's place out in the Bywater?" He screwed the rubber cap back onto the tire nozzle, stood and turned to Reid. "Gabriela had a rush of inspiration. She's been huddled up in her house for the past two weeks, working twenty hour days on the app."

"Isn't that what I suggested weeks ago?" Reid said.

"Except I didn't ask her to do it. She just kinda did it on her own. Said a fix to a problem she couldn't figure out popped into her head, and once she found herself in the zone, she couldn't stop. And just like that—" Anthony snapped his finger. "The app is finished."

"Finish?" Reid asked, something akin to panic lighting up his chest. "*Completely* finished? As in you're ready to pull the trigger?"

Anthony slowly nodded, a huge grin stretching across his face.

"Gabriela said that we can start beta testing in a couple of days. That'll give us a few months to work out the kinks. We can launch this thing by Mardi Gras."

Reid quelled the surge of anxiety that threatened to overwhelm him.

"I thought we had at least another six months, but hey, if we're ready to launch, we're ready to launch," he said. "I guess it's time to tell Alex."

"Yeah, I guess so." Anthony shifted from one foot to the other. This time, a tinge of nervousness colored his laugh. "I know I gave you a lot of grief about not being ready, but now that it's finally happening." He shook his head. "This is real."

"Yeah. And? This is what we said we wanted to do." Reid frowned at the apprehensive lines creasing Anthony's forehead. "Don't tell me you're the one getting cold feet now?"

Anthony stuck his hand in his pocket and pulled out a

small velvet box. He opened it, revealing a simple diamond ring. "I went ring shopping today."

Reid's eyes went wide. "Holy shit, man! Congratulations!"

He clamped a hand on Anthony's shoulder and gave it a squeeze, genuinely happy for him. It occurred to him that his immediate reaction to news of one of his friends getting engaged wasn't pity, or relief that it wasn't him. He felt envious. And hopeful.

"You planning to pop the question tonight?" Reid asked.

Anthony shook his head. "Ciara's birthday is in two weeks. I'm taking her to see Johnny Gill at the casino in Bay St. Louis. I'm going to ask her there."

"Congratulations, man," Reid said again. He chuckled. "So that's why you look nervous. For a minute, I thought it was about the app."

"It is about the app," Anthony said, that apprehension creating lines around his mouth. "Is it crazy to try to start a new business when I'm about to ask the woman I love to marry me? We've talked about having kids. How am I supposed to support a family? What if this doesn't work out? We're still a couple of knuckleheads, Reid. What do we know about going off on our own?"

Reid was so stunned he wasn't sure he could speak.

This was it. It was the out he'd been looking for.

For months he'd been vacillating back and forth, trying to come up with his own excuses about why going into business with Anthony was exactly the wrong thing to do. He'd fed himself all the same excuses. He was still too young and irresponsible for this kind of responsibility. What if it failed? Why would he want to leave the safety of working for Alex?

It was time they both stop playing it safe.

"Did you know Steve Jobs was just twenty-one when he founded Apple Computers?" Reid asked.

Anthony looked at him as if he'd just stepped off a spaceship. "Dude, we're no Steve Jobs. He was a genius."

"But could he fit a pipe into a quarter-inch elbow socket in less than ten seconds?" Reid asked. "Look, you know that I haven't been one hundred percent sure about this, but it's not because I think the business will fail. It was fear. That's what you're feeling right now."

"Damn right I'm scared," Anthony said. "There's just so much that can go wrong."

"And even more can and will go right," Reid said. "It's time to stop being scared, man. Alex was younger than us when he laid the foundation for Holmes Construction. And it's not as if we're going into this completely blind—we both know enough about construction to make this work. We can *do* this, Anthony."

He watched as Anthony's expression shifted from doubtful to confident.

"You're right," his friend said.

"I know damn well I'm right," Reid replied. "Come on. I'll follow you to your cousin's so we can check out the app, and then I'll follow you to a tire shop so you can get a new one before they close."

It took less than ten minutes to reach the little wood frame house in the Bywater neighborhood. When Anthony's cousin, Gabriela, answered the door, it was immediately apparent she'd been running on very little sleep. But her bleary eyes shone with excitement the moment she started talking about the app. She walked them through a demonstration, with Anthony going into the hall bathroom while Reid went back outside to his truck, away from wifi so that his phone could run entirely on cellular data. He was able to see the plumbing without a problem.

He returned to the living room. "Both the picture and his voice were clear as a bell," Reid said. He held his phone up. "This is some cool shit."

"You outdid yourself, Gabby," Anthony said, giving his cousin a hug.

"For real," Reid agreed. "It's as if I was right there with him. If there was a real plumbing issue, I wouldn't have had any problem helping him diagnose and fix it. This app is a game-changer."

"When do you think you'll be ready to start beta testing?" Gabriela asked.

"As soon as possible," Anthony said. "There's just one thing we'll need to do before we pull the trigger." He looked over at Reid.

Reid held his hands up. "I emailed Jonathan all our questions. He said he'll get back in touch with me by the end of the week."

"That's not what I was talking about," Anthony said.

"Oh, you mean Alex."

Anthony nodded.

Yes, they needed to finally tell Alex about this new venture. It was the one thing Reid had been dreading from the moment Anthony approached him about this idea. He could no longer avoid it.

"I'll tell him on Monday," Reid said. "I think it's better if I do it on my own."

"You sure about that?"

Reid nodded. "No fear, right?" He and Anthony clasped hands.

Gabriela offered to follow Anthony to the tire place so that she could finally get some fresh air after being huddled in her house for the past week. Reid slipped Anthony a fifty dollar bill and told him to take her out to dinner while they waited for the tire to get fixed.

Seeing that it was still pretty early, he sent Alex a text message, asking if he could come over to the house to talk to him. Better to rip the Band-Aid off instead of fretting over it all weekend.

But before he could pull away from the curb in front of Gabriela's house, his phone rang. It was Brooklyn, asking him to come over to her parents as soon as possible. The fear he heard in her panic-stricken voice caused him to break out into a cold sweat. Before she could tell him the problem, there was a loud thud in the background. She asked him to hurry and disconnected the call.

Reid risked several speeding and red light camera tickets, but the fines would be worth saving those few precious seconds to get to Brooklyn.

She was standing on the sidewalk waiting for him when he pulled in front of her parents' Treme home. Reid had barely put the truck in park before he was out of there, rushing to her. Her distress was tangible.

"I didn't know who else to call," she said. "It's my dad."

Reid followed her into the house and up the stairs.

"I would have called Smitty, but he's out of town. Dad didn't want me calling the ambulance, because the last time they had to come over his insurance didn't cover it and they were stuck with a three thousand dollar bill." She pointed to a door. "He's in here."

"Don't come...back in here," came a voice drenched in fatigue.

"Don't be ridiculous," Brooklyn called as she opened the door. Reid followed her into the narrow bathroom. The man sprawled awkwardly in the bathtub had the weathered skin of someone who'd worked out in the field for most of his life.

"I tried to get him out, but he's too heavy to lift on my own and too weak to give me any help," Brooklyn explained. She shot an agitated frown at her father. "It also doesn't help that he's too busy trying to keep himself covered."

He'd noticed the wet washcloth providing a poor shield over the older man's crotch. Reid understood his indignity. If he had a daughter, he wouldn't want her to see him buck ass naked either.

"Maybe you can catch him under one arm and I can get him by the other?" Brooklyn suggested.

"I don't want you in here," her father said.

"Let me see if I can lift him on my own first," Reid said. She started to object, but Reid stopped her. "Try to see it from his perspective," he whispered.

She rolled her eyes in frustration, but she relented, motioning for him to go ahead.

"Fine." She blew out an agitated breath. "I'll be out in the hallway," She turned to her father. "You do realize I've seen naked men before, right?"

Reid's breath seized in his lungs.

Please don't say you've seen me naked.

Thankfully, she stomped out of the bathroom without revealing anything that would make the impending situation even more awkward than it already was. Reid went over to the bathtub and hooked his arms underneath Warren LeBlanc's armpits. He knew within seconds that this wouldn't work. He was too afraid he would hurt the older man.

"Give me a sec," Reid said. He reached over and grabbed a large bath towel from the towel rack. "Throw this over your lap." Then he approached from the front, pulling him up in a fireman's hold and lifting him out of the tub.

"Whoa, whoa. I've got you," Reid said as he started to slip. "I've got you."

Brooklyn rushed into the bathroom. "What's wrong?"

"Get out!" both Reid and her dad shouted.

She huffed in frustration, but did as they asked.

"So damn...hardheaded," Warren said.

Reid set the man on the closed toilet seat, then went into the hallway. "Towels?" he asked Brooklyn.

She pointed to a door across from the bathroom. Reid grabbed two big towels from the linen closet, and the robe from the hook on the back of the door as he returned to the bathroom.

He started to help the older man dry off, but he gave him a husky, "I've got it," and gingerly toweled himself dry. He was taking way too long, but Reid understood what it meant to let him have that small bit of independence. He patiently waited, patting the water spots on his on shirt with another towel.

"Can I come in now?" Brooklyn asked from the other side of the door.

"No," they both called.

She growled.

Once Warren was done toweling himself dry, Reid handed him the robe and said, "I can help you get dressed if you need me to."

He shook his head. "Let me rest. Just for...a minute."

Reid heard some kind of commotion and another voice seconds before the door burst open.

"What happened? Are you okay?"

There was no doubt the woman who'd just come through the door was Brooklyn's mother. She was an older version of her daughter, with that same smooth, dark brown skin, and those beautiful high cheekbones.

Brooklyn followed her into the bathroom, explaining what happened, and how she called Reid to help her lift her dad from the tub.

Her mom, who introduced herself as Anita LeBlanc, graced Reid with a grateful smile as she edged past him and quickly made her way to her husband.

"Thanks, young man," Warren LeBlanc said. "Now... y'all go so I can get dressed."

"Yes, I've got it from here," Anita said.

Reid could tell Brooklyn was reluctant to leave, but he caught her by the shoulders and nudged her forward, out of the bathroom and into the hallway. "Come on. Let's go downstairs."

She nodded. "Okay. But just one thing first," she said, then she turned, threw herself into his arms, and kissed him like her life depended on it.

———

BROOKLYN ROLLED the unopened can of Dr. Pepper between her palms. She'd grabbed one for herself and Reid once they'd come downstairs, but the thought of consuming anything made her stomach turn. Or maybe it was the cauldron of nerves swirling in her belly that was having that affect.

Unable to stand being in the dark a moment longer, she set the can on the coffee table.

"I should go up there and see if my mom needs help." She started to rise, but Reid clamped his palm on her thigh and forced her to sit back down.

"Your mom said to leave her to it. Don't you think she would have called for us if she needed help?"

Just as she was about to argue, her mother came walking down the stairs. Brooklyn bounced up from the sofa.

"You're still here?" her mother asked, her brows arched in surprise.

"Of course we're still here. How's Dad?"

"He's fine," she answered with an unconcerned wave. "This was my fault. I forgot to put the shower stool back in the tub after I was done with my bath last night. Warren didn't think about it until he was already in the tub."

"When did he have to start using a shower stool?" Brooklyn asked.

"Just this past week, which is why it didn't occur to him to bring it in there. The doctor advised him to start using one to prevent exactly what happened today." She hunched her shoulder. "He just isn't used to it yet."

Brooklyn pitched her head back and drew her palms down her face. "Shit."

Her mother put a hand on her arm. "It's okay, honey. These things are going to happen."

"That's the problem. I'm not ready for any of this."

"It's life, baby. You take it as it comes and learn from it. For example, from now on that bench will be next to the tub at all times."

"Or maybe we can finally add a full bathroom downstairs with a walk-in shower," Brooklyn suggested.

Anita LeBlanc folded her arms over her chest. "You got walk-in shower money?"

Brooklyn rolled her eyes.

"I wouldn't worry about the money," Reid said. "Your daughter has already saved the ass—uh, the behinds of enough people at Holmes Construction that she can get anything she asks for. Just let us know where and you'll have a crew out here on the weekend to start building a new bathroom, ASAP."

Brooklyn knew he couldn't speak for the crew at HCC, but maybe she could work out a deal with Alex. One way or another, she would make sure her father never had to worry about falling in the damn tub again.

Her mother turned to Reid. "Thank you for coming when Brooklyn called. You saved Warren from additional embarrassment."

"He needs to get over it," she said. "There was nothing for him to be embarrassed about."

"I can understand where he's coming from," Reid said. "And it was no problem. Brooklyn knows that I'm always just a phone call away." His gaze caught hers and held. "Whenever and wherever she needs me, I'm there."

Brooklyn's heart melted like butter on a hot roll. She could tell by the way her mother's eyes lit up that she was experiencing the same heart melting. Reid didn't know it, but he'd just garnered himself a new fan.

"Are you staying for dinner?" her mother asked. Brooklyn had to refrain from laughing at the schoolgirl hopefulness she heard in her voice. Reid Holmes had that effect on women. "Warren and I were just going to have some leftovers, but I can cook something."

"No," Brooklyn said. "You don't need to cook. I promise to invite Reid to dinner another time, when things aren't so crazy."

"Yeah, I'm good for tonight," he said. "But I'll take you up on that dinner invitation soon."

"In that case, I'll go and take my own shower," her mother said. "Work was crazy today. Lock up, will you, baby?"

"I will," Brooklyn said.

Her mother kissed her cheek, caught Reid behind his head and pulled his face down so that she could do the same to him, then went back upstairs. Brooklyn picked up her purse and then motioned for Reid to go ahead of her out the front door so she could lock up behind her.

She didn't make it past the first step before her legs gave out. She collapsed onto the top step, dropping her head to her knees and dissolving into convulsive gasps that shook her entire body.

"Hey, hey, it's okay," Reid said, settling beside her and gathering her into his arms.

He rubbed his hands up and down her back as Brooklyn continued her uncontrollable, hiccupping sobs. It was as if all the pent-up anxiety of the last year had finally been released in one rioting deluge of emotion. She'd been paralyzed with fear of what was slowly happening to her dad. Being given this glimpse into what life would be like for him —for all of them—it was just too much to take.

"I'm sorry," she said after she was finally able to get a modicum of control over her emotions.

"What are you apologizing for? You're allowed to break down every now and then, Brooklyn."

She wiped at her eyes and sniffed. "Am I allowed to use your shirt to wipe my nose?" she asked with a hiccupping laugh.

Reid cupped her cheek in his hand and used the hem of his shirt to wipe her face, snotty nose and all. If she hadn't realized she was in love before, Brooklyn definitely knew she was there now.

He lifted her chin and peered into her eyes. "You okay now?"

She started to nod, but then shook her head. "No," she

admitted. "I'm not okay at all. I don't know if I can do this, Reid. I don't know if I can handle watching him go through this."

And just like that, the tears started again. Reid wrapped his arms around her, slipping his fingers in her hair at the nape of her neck and massaging the back of her head. He didn't try to placate her with meaningless platitudes. He just held her while she cried. Brooklyn knew it came from a place of understanding. He'd been here before. That thought made her cry even harder for what he'd gone through when he lost his mother. Having worked on the Dynamo Diane comic these past weeks, she felt a connection to Diane Holmes despite never meeting her.

Brooklyn and Reid sat on the front steps of her parents' house for another twenty minutes. Not a single word had been said between them, but Brooklyn had never felt a stronger connection to anyone. Words weren't needed.

"I think I'm okay to get up," she said.

"You sure?" Reid whispered.

She nodded.

He gave her upper body a light squeeze. "Why don't you leave your car here? I don't want you driving in the state you're in. I'll take you home and then bring you back later to pick it up."

With a nod, Brooklyn allowed him to help her up, and together they walked to his truck.

"Are you hungry?" he asked.

Her first instinct was to tell him no, but now that the stress of the last hour was behind her, she was ravenous. "Yes, but I don't want to go out. What I need right now is my couch and some comfort food." She reached over and grabbed his hand. "And you. Can you spend the night?" she asked in a hoarse whisper.

"For future reference, that's a question you never have to ask."

Brooklyn couldn't put into words how grateful she was for the smile he managed to put on her face.

They made it to her apartment in under fifteen minutes. The moment they entered the door, she took the keys from Reid's hand and set them on the table next to the door, then she wrapped her arms around his neck and pulled him down for a deep, soulful kiss. They continued kissing as they made their way past the living room and down the short hallway toward her bedroom, shedding clothes on the journey, their mouths parting only long enough to pull their shirts over their heads. With only their underwear separating them, Reid wrapped his arms around her and carried her down to the bed.

Unlike the first time, Brooklyn didn't try to fight the feelings of love that overwhelmed her as Reid tenderly worshipped her body. She yielded to the sensual pleasure rioting throughout her bloodstream, craving even more. She wanted everything he had to give her.

When Reid flipped her onto her stomach and lifted her up so he could enter her from behind, Brooklyn clutched the bedding between her fingers and held on for dear life. She rocked back against him, relishing every thrust of the solid muscle plunging deep inside her. He quickened his pace and, before she had a chance to prepare herself for it, a powerful orgasm hit her like a sonic wave, resonating throughout her entire body.

Her limbs liquefied. Brooklyn fell onto the mattress, with Reid following her down, his heavy body imprisoning her on the bed. After pressing a kiss against the back of her neck, he rolled off her and pulled her in close to him, his front against her back. Brooklyn rested her head against his bicep. The firm muscle was quickly becoming her favorite pillow.

"You doing okay?" Reid asked.

A smile instantly angled up her lips. "I am *soooo* much better than just okay." She looked back over her shoulder. "You have no idea how badly I want to make a joke about the way you lay pipe, but I'm sure you've heard all those before."

The entire bed seemed to shake with his laugh. "I've never had anyone make a joke about me laying pipe."

"Yeah right." She twisted around to face him and snuggled against his chest. She couldn't seem to get close enough to him. Reid drew his fingers up and down her arm, his caress gentle, hypnotic.

"I'm serious," he said.

"That's, like, the perfect joke for a plumber. Did your past girlfriends have zero sense of humor?"

"I thought I wasn't supposed to talk about women I've slept with while we're in bed together?"

"Not unless I bring them up," she said.

"Is that a new rule?"

"Yes."

He chuckled, then sighed. "To be honest, none of my past relationships—if you can call them that—were ever deep enough to even discuss professions. I've never wanted to get that close to anyone else. Until you."

Her chest tightened at the implications of his admission. "You realize you don't have to say things like that to me to get laid, right? We've moved past that stage."

That lazy smile looked so sexy on him. "I'm saying it because I mean it."

Brooklyn didn't realize she was holding her breath until she was forced to let air into her lungs. She both anticipated and feared Reid's next words. She knew what she felt, but she wasn't sure she was ready for a profession of love. At least she didn't think she was.

No. She definitely wasn't. Not after the emotional rollercoaster she'd been on today. She couldn't handle hearing those words from him on top of all that.

Reid traced her hairline before taking a lock of her hair and twisting it around his fingers.

"Is everything else okay?" he asked, a trace of caution creeping into his voice.

She didn't have to ask him to clarify his question. She knew exactly what he was asking.

Brooklyn had fought to keep thoughts of what happened today out of her head for as long as possible, but she knew the brief respite she'd found in Reid's arms wouldn't last forever. Reality clawed its unforgiving fingers around her brain, reminding her of the problems waiting just on the other side of that door.

"Does it even matter if it's okay?" She finally asked. "It's like my mom said. This is life. I'm going to have to learn to deal with it." She looked up at him. "Now you see why attending any of those writing programs are impossible."

"Because you don't want to leave your dad," he stated.

"I *can't* leave. Not now. Not when he's like this. I can't leave my mom to deal with this on her own."

He shoved his hand in her hair and massaged her scalp. After several moments passed, he asked, "How often does what happened today happen?"

"This has never happened before. I mean, there have been episodes when he's had trouble walking up the stairs and had to stop for a while to catch his breath. And don't talk about when he tried to cut the grass." Brooklyn rolled her eyes. "Mom has been able to handle it okay, but usually there are others there to help. The guys who worked with dad for years are always just a phone call away. It just so happens that several of them are off on a hunting trip in Mississippi and Smitty is at his daughter's wedding in Jacksonville."

"So this just so happened to be the completely wrong time for something like this to happen," Reid said.

She nodded.

Reid put his hand under her chin and lifted her face. "Your dad's illness shouldn't stop you. This was a one-off," he said. "What are the chances of your mom being in this predicament in the future, especially if it's only for a few weeks?"

"Who knows?" Brooklyn said. "But it doesn't really matter. Even if the chances are small, I don't want her to have to deal with this on her own."

"Don't take this the wrong way, but you weren't able to do anything today," Reid said. She started to speak, but he stopped her, placing his finger over her lips. Brooklyn was tempted to bite that finger. Hard. "I'm not saying that you didn't help. You called me. But you weren't able to help physically. If something like that happens while you're gone, your mom can call me again. Or one of your dad's friends. Or even Alex," he said. "After everything your dad did for him, I know Alex wouldn't hesitate to drop everything and help."

Brooklyn refused to allow his words to affect her, no matter how much those little ribbons of hope tried to snake their way around her psyche. Leaving her family for up to four weeks was out of the question, to say nothing of this brand new job she just started. Even if Alex approved, she couldn't afford it.

Okay, fine, so she had some money in the bank. Enough

to cover her rent and expenses for at least a year. But that's only because her dad had taught her to always be prepared by making sure she had money in the bank. Even though she wouldn't feel a financial pinch, that still didn't mean she could do this.

"I just can't," Brooklyn said. "I've known for a long time that my comics would only be a hobby."

"But it shouldn't be. You're amazing at it."

"I'm also amazing at my job," Brooklyn said. "You can only be the absolute best at one thing, Reid. Once you find out what that is, you should devote everything to it. It's better to be the best at that one thing than to just be good at a bunch of things."

He was silent for several moments before he finally said, "Where'd you hear that crock of bullshit?"

"Excuse me?" Brooklyn said. "It came from my dad. It's what I was raised to believe."

"And that's why you're not going to try for one of those fellowships? Because you think you can only be good at one thing and coming up with flowcharts is the thing you *think* you're better at?"

Brooklyn had never heard a more incredulous voice, but this was her go-to excuse. She'd been using it for years now.

"What is this really about, Brooklyn?" He once again caught her chin between his fingers and lifted her face up to his. "The other night I told you what I was afraid of. What is it you fear that has you so afraid to follow this dream?"

How could he read her so well? How did he know?

"It's because I don't deserve it," she finally answered in a small voice. "I don't deserve to go off and pursue my dream after I purposely put an end to my own father's life-long dream."

Reid's brow creased. "What are you talking about?"

"*I'm* the reason LeBlanc & Sons is no longer in business, Reid. It's because of me," she revealed in a suffocated whisper. The confusion in his eyes begged for her to continue. As much as it pained her to do so, Brooklyn knew she owed him an explanation. "My family's business was much smaller than Holmes Construction, so when it came to the management side, I pretty much did it all. And because I started learning the job when I was so young, by the time I took over for my grandmother, I was...I was phenomenal. I'm not saying that to brag. It's just the truth."

"You don't have to convince me that you're phenomenal at your job," he said.

"The problem is, I was *too* good. I told you my dad's mantra. He believes in giving your all to the one thing you're good at."

"But—"

"So I set out to prove I *wasn't* as good at my job as he thought I was," she continued. "I would intentionally mess up every now and then. Little things like not paying an invoice on time, or inputting the wrong amount of hours on someone's timecard. But that last time—well, let's just say it came back to bite me in the ass."

"What did you do?" Reid asked, his voice solemn now.

She released a fatigued sigh. "We were working as a subcontractor on a house being built in Old Metairie. As usual, I was in charge of getting all the paperwork in proper order. I skimmed the contract before having my dad sign it and didn't realize there was no indemnification clause."

"I may be just a plumber, but I've worked with Alex long enough to know what that does."

"Yeah, it says that we, as the subcontractor aren't liable if the general contractor messes up."

"Let me guess, he messed up."

"Big time," Brooklyn answered with a nod. "He never finished the job, then filed for bankruptcy."

"But LeBlanc & Sons still got paid," Reid said. "The indemnification clause doesn't affect pay."

"No, but the surety bond does," Brooklyn said. "That's the one I knew wasn't there."

"Shit," Reid said.

"When everything fell through, LeBlanc & Sons didn't have a leg to stand on. The legal fees alone would have bankrupt us, so Dad decided to just hang it up."

A heavy silence hung in the air, with nothing to mask the sound of Brooklyn's delicate sniffs.

"Don't take this the wrong way," Reid said after several moments passed, "But the man I saw today wouldn't have been working on a construction site anyway."

"I know that," she answered. "But *he* should have been the one to choose when to retire. I took that choice out of his hands."

"Does it matter?"

"Of course it matters!"

"Brooklyn," Reid started, but she stopped him, mimicking what he'd done to her. With a finger against his lips, she said, "There's nothing to discuss. It's settled. I'm grateful to have the job with Holmes Construction. It may not be what I want to do, but there is an upside." She kissed his nose. "It brought me to you."

There was a cockiness to his reluctant grin that was all Reid. "I guess that's one positive I hadn't considered."

"I consider it way more than just a positive," she said. Cradling his strong jaw in her palm, Brooklyn allowed all her feelings to shine through her eyes. "I thought I was just being a realist when I said that being with a guy like you wasn't in the cards for a girl like me. You've shown me that I wasn't being realistic, I was being foolish."

She took his hand and pressed a kiss to the center of his palm.

"Not only do I deserve someone like you. I'll never settle for anything less ever again."

CHAPTER TWELVE

THESE DAYS REID felt as if he'd taken up residence in his truck, but even getting stuck in traffic couldn't dampen his mood. He felt energized. Useful.

Determined.

After the conversation he'd had with Warren LeBlanc a few minutes ago, his entire perspective had changed. Reid realized he'd been holding himself back, making excuses for his own life, in the same way Brooklyn had been using her dad's health as a way to keep her from fully realizing her own dreams.

It was time they both stop with the excuses.

He'd allow the fear of not being good enough to hold him back for far too long. He'd spent too much of his life flying under the radar, trying not to raise anyone's expectations so that he wouldn't disappoint them when he couldn't rise to the occasion. But he *could* do this. He could do anything he set his mind to. Just as his mother always told him.

But there was one last hurdle Reid had to climb, and it would be his most difficult obstacle yet.

He entered the fenced in area surrounding the piece of land that—if all went according to plan—would be the site of a brand new, state-of-the-art library. Holmes Construction was due to break ground within a week. Unease slithered down Reid's spine. Of all the times to walk away, this seemed like the absolute worst. HCC was experiencing its greatest boon since its inception, and Reid had been on this journey with his cousin almost from the beginning. How could he leave Alex now?

But how could he not?

If ever he was going to take a leap of faith, this would be the moment. After witnessing the demo of the app Anthony's cousin had created, Reid knew there would never be another opportunity like this for him. He had to grab on to it while he could.

Even if it meant having the difficult conversation he was about to have.

He spotted Alex over toward the left side of the property, where a motor grader stood ready to begin the process of leveling the uneven ground.

"What are you doing here?" Alex asked once Reid reached him, a confused frown marring his face. "Everything okay at the other site?"

He nodded. "The last of the drywall was floated just before I left yesterday. Elizabeth and her paint crew started this morning. She said they should be done by Wednesday."

"Good. Good." Alex nodded, then clapped his palms together and grinned. "I signed a three year lease for the office on Magazine Street."

Reid clamped a palm on his cousin's shoulder and brought him in for a one-arm hug. "Congratulations, man. This is a big step."

"One I should have taken years ago," Alex said.

"Renee's already talking about hiring Indina to change the current HCC headquarters into her new 'woman's cave,'" he said. "By the way, I'm going to promote Brooklyn to area coordinator. She's too good to be limited to one job site at a time."

"Yeah. Cool," Reid said with a brief nod.

"You can cut the uninterested act," Alex deadpanned. "You should have known I'd find out about the two of you after you brought her to the picnic you guys had on the Lakefront."

Reid's lack of enthusiasm had nothing to do with trying to hide his relationship with Brooklyn from Alex. He didn't want her using this promotion as yet another excuse not to apply for one of those fellowships. But he couldn't make that decision for her. Brooklyn had to make it for herself.

Alex put both hands up. "I don't care what's going on between the two of you. You're both grown. And I don't have to tell you not to hurt her, so I won't."

"You don't have to," Reid said. He stuffed his hands in his pockets. "I...I don't think I've ever felt this way about anyone. No, I *know* I haven't. I won't hurt her. Just the thought of hurting her makes my stomach hurt."

"Good," Alex said with a nod.

"And she would do an amazing job in whatever position you put her in. She's an amazing person."

"You're not telling me anything I don't already know." Alex folded his arms across his chest. "So, you want to tell me what you're doing here?"

Damn, why couldn't they just end the conversation right here?

Reid pointed to the trailer that looked identical to the one at the urgent care build site. It would serve as Alex's base of operations while on this job. "You mind if we go in there? I need to talk to you about something."

"The furniture hasn't been delivered yet. There's only a couple of folding chairs in there."

"That's fine," Reid said.

Once in the trailer, Alex caught one of the folding chairs and straddled it. Reid took the other. He leaned forward and rested his elbows on his thighs, letting his clasped hands hang between his spread out legs.

"Why are you so serious all of a sudden?" Alex asked, his brow wrinkling with concern. "Nothing going on with Uncle Clark, is it? No. It's Harrison and Willow. They're separating."

"Wait. *What?* Where'd you hear that?"

"Nowhere," Alex said. "That's why I'm asking you."

"No." Reid shook his head. "This has nothing to do with Harrison and Willow. Or with Dad."

Alex slapped a hand to his chest. "You scared me. So, what's going on?"

"It's about...about Holmes Construction," Reid said. "And my working here."

Alex's eyebrows arched. "Care to elaborate?"

Reid dropped his head and massaged the bridged of his nose. When he looked up again, leeriness had replaced the concerned in his cousin's expression.

"Spit it out, Reid."

"Anthony Hernandez and I are planning to start our own business," he said.

Before Alex could ask, Reid went into a spiel about the basic concept of the app, how they'd handled the app development, and how they would *not* be any kind of competition for Holmes Construction. He tried to gauge Alex's reaction, but his expression remained neutral.

"The app is done and we're ready to start beta testing," he finished. When Alex still didn't say anything, Reid threw his hands up. "Look, I don't know how all of this is going to pan out. And I know it may look shitty, me leaving you after all you've done for me, but this is a chance for me to make something happen on my own. I'm thirty years old, Alex. I need to do this."

A noxious mixture of anxiety, uncertainty and dread pooled in the pit of his stomach as Alex just sat there. Just when Reid expected his cousin to throw him off his job site, a small smile gradually lifted one corner of his mouth.

"Congratulations, man!" Alex said. "This sounds like a groundbreaker. Where's Anthony? Why didn't he come with you so I could congratulate you both?"

"Are you fucking serious right now?" Reid asked.

"What?" Genuine confusion creased Alex's forehead.

"Did you not hear what I just said? Anthony and I are taking all that we've learned working for Holmes Construction and going off to start our own business. You should be calling us a couple of ungrateful little shits."

Alex, whose typical expression of amusement rarely went beyond a brief chuckle, burst out laughing. A full, deep belly laugh.

Reid didn't know whether to feel relief or anger. He'd spent months putting this off, dreading Alex's reaction.

"You done?" Reid drawled after his cousin finally stopped laughing.

Alex nodded as he wiped moisture from his eyes. "Can't believe you thought I'd be upset," he said.

"I still can't believe you're *not* upset. You gave me a job right out of high school and, because I'm your cousin, kept me here all these years. Now, I tell you that I'm quitting to start my own business and you're not upset?"

"First of all, I gave you a job right out of high school because you're my cousin, but I kept you on all these years because you're a damn fine plumber. Your ass would have been out of here a long time ago if that wasn't the case.

"Second, you do realize that I didn't start this company out of thin air, right? I worked as an apprentice at a few places, and then I was hired on at LeBlanc & Sons. I worked there for years. And when I told Warren LeBlanc I wanted to start my own business, not only did he give me his blessing, he directed customers my way. And, unlike this app-based thing you're starting, my business *did* compete directly with Warren's for years before I turned to commercial building.

"I'm not going to begrudge you and Anthony for wanting to do the same thing I did, Reid. Everyone has to eventually take that leap, if that's what they really want. *Is* this what you want?" Alex asked.

Reid nodded. "I'm scared as hell I'll mess this up, but it's something I feel I have to do."

"Then do it," Alex said. "You'll regret it forever if you don't. And don't be afraid about messing up. You *will* mess up. It's inevitable. But you just dust yourself off and move on."

"But what if it flops?"

Alex shrugged. "You come back to HCC," he said. "In fact, you and Anthony can both continue to work here while you get the new business off the ground. Just remember to clock out if you're taking one of those video calls. I'm generous, but not generous enough to have you conducting your own business on Holmes Construction's time."

For a moment, shock rendered him speechless. But, to be honest, Reid shouldn't have been surprised at all. Alex had never been anything but fair. And supportive. He should have known his cousin would be behind him, one hundred percent. Yet, the emotion constricting his throat made it hard to swallow.

"Thanks, man," Reid said as they both stood. He pulled him in for a hug. "Knowing I have your blessing makes this a little less scary."

Alex clamped a hand on his shoulder.

"Being scared isn't always a bad thing. Being scared makes you work harder to make sure that you never allow what you fear to become reality." He gave Reid's shoulder a squeeze. "You're going to be okay. You can do this, Reid."

"Thanks," he said. "For everything. I don't know where I'd be if you hadn't taken a chance on me, Alex."

"As if Uncle Clark and Aunt Diane would have let anything happen to you."

"You know what I mean."

"Yeah, I know. But you know I always have your back. And, like I said, the door is always open if you ever need to come back. But I'm hoping you don't."

Reid brought his cousin in for another hug, recognizing that having a family like the one he had was the very definition of being blessed.

———

AS SHE PACED the length of the trailer for the umpteenth time, Brooklyn vaguely acknowledged that she might very well wear a hole in the floor. Too damn bad. If she fell through, she'd just continue pacing on the earth below. She needed an outlet for the rage surging through her veins. If she stopped moving, she would hit something.

Like her desk. Or the wall. She'd hit both already and had the throbbing hand to remind her.

Besides, she didn't want to waste anymore punches on inanimate objects. She would reserve them for the person who deserved them.

She clenched her fists just at the thought of the conversation she'd had with her dad about an hour ago. She'd done her best to maintain her calm as she listened to his labored plea, encouraging her to apply for the fellowship in Chicago. The shock of hearing him mention the fellowship had been so breathtaking that it hadn't occurred to her to even ask how he knew about it. But she didn't have to ask, because there was only one other person she'd told.

Her dad unwittingly confirmed her suspicions when he mentioned Reid coming over earlier today to talk to him about how Brooklyn was wasting her God-given talent. He'd shown her dad pictures that he'd snapped of drawings —*her* drawings—and divulged what she'd told him while they were in bed together.

Hearing her dad apologize for the work ethic he'd instilled in her made Brooklyn want to sob. She never blamed him for holding her back. He'd always done what he thought was right, and she loved him for it. Reid had no right to go to her dad with anything.

Once again, betrayal hit her like a punch in the gut.

Sharing those drawings with him had been one of the hardest things she'd ever done. She'd trusted him. If she'd known he would turn around and use them to try to shame her own father, she would have never laid bare this part of her world to him.

Brooklyn stopped her pacing long enough to pull in a deep, calming breath.

She heard the door open and prepared to let loose, only to find Jarvis entering the trailer.

"Here's a list of supplies needed for cleanup," he said.

Brooklyn took a second to rein in her ire. She didn't want to take any of her anger out on Jarvis. Now that he'd stopped with the cheesy pickup lines, they had become somewhat friends. Mainly because she'd discovered him reading Tolkien on one of his lunch breaks and got him to admit that he was a closet sci-fi/fantasy reader. Brooklyn remembered those days of trying to hide her geekiness from her friends.

She was still hiding in so many ways. And for good reason. Just look what sharing had resulted in.

"Is there anything from this list that's needed immediately?" she asked Jarvis.

He shook his head. "We won't be ready to start the clean-up for another two days, but I wanted to get the list to you ASAP so that you're not scrambling to find the supplies."

"Thanks. I appreciate it."

"Oh." Jarvis snapped his fingers. "Not sure if you heard about it, but there's a talk at Octavia Books with the author of that new sci-fi thriller that's getting all kinds of buzz. I'm planning to go. You interested?"

Her brows rose. "Are you asking me out on a date?"

"Hell no." A look of pure horror flashed across his face. "Reid would kick my ass."

"Ah. Okay," Brooklyn said. "Just making sure."

She shouldn't be surprised that the quest to keep her and Reid's relationship under wraps hadn't worked. She had enough experience with the gossip grapevine on a construction worksite to know keeping it a secret was a foolish endeavor from the very beginning.

"Actually," Jarvis continued, his feet shifting as a reddish tint climbed up his neck. "What I *should* have said is that me and this girl I met are going. But you're welcome to join us if you want to hear him speak."

"I'll let you know," Brooklyn answered, allowing a small smile to ghost across her lips.

It was a relief to know she wouldn't have to worry about shutting down any advances from Jarvis anymore now that he had a new girlfriend. Although, it sounded as if the new girlfriend wasn't as much a factor as not wanting to step into Reid's territory.

And just like that, Brooklyn was mad again.

About five minutes after Jarvis left, the door to the trailer opened again and Reid walked in.

She thought she'd had enough time to calm down. She'd hoped to approach this conversation in a more adult way.

But that wasn't happening.

The minute she laid eyes on him, all the anger that had built up over the course of the past hour came roaring back. Brooklyn marched over to him and shoved his solid chest with both hands.

"How dare you!" she screeched.

The look of utter confusion on his face made her want to shove him again. So she did.

"Ow." Reid took a step back and rubbed his chest. "What's the matter with you? What's going on?"

"You went to my dad?" Brooklyn asked. "You showed him my drawings? You told him about the fellowships?" The befuddlement blanketing his face had her seeing red. "Dammit, Reid! Do you not see anything wrong with that?"

"Uh, no," he said. "I thought I was doing something *right* for a change."

"Right? To violate my privacy like that? To take something that I'd shared with you and broadcast it to the world?"

"The world? It was your dad!"

"And if I'd wanted him to see my work I would have shown it to him years ago! You had *no* right, Reid! None! How would you feel if I went to your family and told them about the learning disorder you've been hiding all these years?"

He took a step back, his face a mask of shock and hurt.

She. Did. Not. Care.

Brooklyn couldn't see past her own hurt and anger to give the briefest consideration for what he was feeling.

"I just wanted him to see how good you are," Reid said. "I figured if your dad knew, he'd encourage you to pursue your comics. Maybe even give you permission to go to one of those programs."

"I'm a grown ass woman! I don't need his permission. And I don't need *you* going behind my back and sharing something that I shared with you in confidence." She slapped her hand to her chest. "I trusted you with this part of me, Reid. Do you know how long I've kept this to myself? Do you have *any* idea how scary this has been for me? I trusted you with it, and you threw that trust away."

"That's not—"

Brooklyn put her hand up. "I don't want to hear it. Keep your excuses to yourself."

Without giving much thought to what she was doing, Brooklyn grabbed her purse and left the trailer. She'd never once walked off the job in the middle of the day, but if she spent another second in that trailer with Reid she would strangle him. And, because she could never see him raising a hand against her, he would probably let her do it without putting up a fight. It was better for the both of them that she left.

Once in her car, Brooklyn automatically started for Tubby & Coo's. It was her go-to spot when she wanted to clear her head. But with every mile that brought her closer to the bookstore, the thought of being holed up in that upstairs room made her start to feel claustrophobic. She needed air. She needed to breathe. She needed some place that would allow her to clear her mind and think without having to interact with anyone or anything.

And just like that, Brooklyn knew exactly where she needed to be.

CHAPTER THIRTEEN

REID SAT in the leather armchair in the quiet second-story room at Tubby & Coo's Mid-City Book Shop, cradling his head in his hands. He'd been so sure he'd find her here, working her frustration out with her markers and sketch-pad. When the owner told him Brooklyn hadn't been here since Saturday afternoon—when Reid himself had been with her—he found himself at a loss. He'd come upstairs anyway, needing to be close to where she found her joy.

As he sat in the chair she usually occupied, Reid swore he could feel her positive energy flowing through his own veins. That small connection was giving him life right now.

But it wasn't enough.

He needed to *see* her. He needed to be in the same space she inhabited. He needed to breathe the same air she was breathing at this very moment.

He needed her. Period.

But he had to give her some time. And some distance. She was upset—understandably so.

Why in the hell hadn't he considered the flaw in his plan

before going to talk to Warren LeBlanc? It wasn't until after Brooklyn had pointed it out that he realized just how many lines he'd crossed by going behind her back and showing her father her Dynamo Diane drawings. He truly thought he was doing the right thing, but he'd been dead wrong.

It wasn't his place to share her illustrations with anyone. She'd told him what the experience with that online bully had done to her self-confidence. He'd witnessed the painstaking steps she'd taken to build it up again—sharing her drawings first with him, then with that Kurt Bollinger guy at the comic con. It was up to her to decide when and with whom to share her talent. He'd had no right to make that decision for her.

He had to find her. He had to beg for her understanding. And for her forgiveness.

Reid knew it was better to hang back and give her space. He'd done enough damage for one day.

But he couldn't stay away. Not knowing how she was doing—if she was still raging mad, or if she was crying her eyes red—it was driving him out of his mind. It killed him to know he'd caused her pain. He had to fix this.

He left his cell number with Candice, the bookstore owner, and asked her to text him if Brooklyn happened to come into the store. Once in his truck, Reid rested his forehead on the steering wheel, trying to think of where she could have gone. He'd swung by both her apartment and her parents' place before coming to the book store, but hadn't seen her car at either. He'd even gone to Pal's Lounge, even though he knew he wouldn't find her there. Brooklyn wasn't the type to drink away her troubles. She *drew* them away.

Reid's head popped up.

He was an idiot. He should have known where to look from the very beginning.

He pulled away from the curb, made the U-turn on North Carrollton and then made a quick left onto Orleans Avenue. Less than ten minutes later, he drove under the canopy of arching oaks that lined the narrow street and parking area in City Park. Reid kept an eye out for her car, his shoulders sinking with relief when he spotted it. He parked two spots down, then jumped out of his truck and started for the place where he knew he would find her.

He caught sight of her hair first. The crown of springy coils with a streak of deep cranberry was bent over her sketchpad as she lay in the grass. He made his way to her, hating to disturb her peace but unable to stay away. She didn't acknowledge his presence, but he could tell when she noticed him because her shoulders tensed. Reid moved a few feet closer, until he stood right over her, his shadow covering half her body.

"You're blocking my sun," she said, not bothering to look up at him.

He started to move, but then he took notice of what she was drawing. He studied her hand's movement as it swiftly glided the pencil across the cream linen paper. This wasn't one of her Iansan illustrations. This one was much darker. The figure in the drawing wore all black, from the mask covering the top half of his menacing face to the fierce boots on his feet.

Was it a villain? Was it him? Had he become the bad guy in her world?

"I'm sorry," Reid opened.

"Then stop blocking my sun," she said.

"I'm talking about going to your dad," he clarified.

He dropped beside her on the grass. Despite the risk of

getting stabbed with the sharp point of her pencil, Reid reached over and stayed her hand. "Can you please just give me a minute to apologize?"

Frustration saturated her heavy sigh. She set the sketchpad on the ground, then turned around and sat up. She stretched her legs out in front of her, crossing her ankles and bracing her arms behind her. The relaxed posed belied the tension radiating off of her.

"Okay," she said. "Have at it. Let me hear your apology."

She wasn't going to make this easy for him. Then again, why should she? He was the one who'd messed up. He deserved every drop of her disdain. It didn't matter that he *thought* he was doing the right thing. What mattered is that he'd crossed the line, and that he'd hurt her in the process.

"I didn't come here to give you a bunch of excuses, even though that's what I'm doing." He shook his head. "I truly thought I was helping, Brooklyn. After meeting your parents and seeing how much they care about you, I just had this feeling that your dad wouldn't want you putting your dreams aside because of him."

"It wasn't your decision to make."

"I know that," Reid said. "I know that now. And if I could change it, I would. I shouldn't have gone to him behind your back. I shouldn't have shown him your drawings without your permission." He dipped his head so he could look her in the eyes. "But you should know that he thinks you're an amazing artist. He was blown away."

A single tear streaked down her cheek and Reid nearly lost it. He wanted to gather her in his arms and beg her forgiveness, but a simple hug wouldn't fix this. He needed to *earn* her forgiveness.

"I was only trying to help you in the same way you've helped me," Reid said.

Her head snapped up and her gaze met his, her teary eyes glistening with confusion.

"It's true," Reid said. "I recognize so many of my own issues in yours. The fear of not being good enough, of lacking confidence in myself. I know you love your dad and you want to help take care of him, but I wonder if you're maybe using your dad's illness as an excuse, because you don't think you're good enough to attend those programs."

"I don't need you psychoanalyzing me," she bit out.

"I'm not," he said. "I was psychoanalyzing myself. Because in trying to figure out why you were so resistant to following your dreams, I recognized that I've been doing the same thing. I've never stepped up to take responsibility for anything in my life because I'm afraid that I'll fail at it. I convinced myself that it's safer to never try.

"But then *you* came along with this incredible talent. You possess this unbelievable gift, yet you've been keeping it to yourself because you've been taught that you can't be good at more than one thing. That's crazy," he said in a fierce whisper. "You're fucking amazing at everything you do."

He reached over and glided his thumb across her dampened cheek, gently caressing her soft skin.

"Neither of us have anything to fear." Reid let several weighty moments stretch before he continued, knowing it might piss her off, but needing to say it anyway. "You have to apply for that fellowship, Brooklyn. Your dad will be fine. Your mom is here to take care of him. His friends are here. *I'm* here," he said. "I'll check on him every single day."

He captured her chin and lifted her face up so he could look her in the eyes.

"Do you know how hard it is for me to push you to do this?" he asked in a hushed voice. "I'm selfish, Brooklyn. Always have been. Maybe it's because I'm the baby of the family and have always been able to get my way." Reid tried to smile, but couldn't quite pull it off. "It's not easy for me to let go of the things I really love, but I'm willing to put my selfishness to the side if it means you get to follow your dream."

Her bottom lip trembled. She pulled it between her teeth, her anguished expression shattering him.

"You just don't get it," she whispered. "It's *my* dream, Reid. *I'm* the one who chooses whether or not I follow it."

She pushed up from the ground and Reid rose along with her. He reached for her hand, but she recoiled.

"No. Not...not yet." She sucked in a breath and released it with a shuddering sigh. Taking a step back, she looked up at him, and said, "I know you meant well, but I just...I need some space."

He hadn't expected immediate forgiveness, but her rejection made it feel as if he'd been knocked in the chest with a heavy duty pipe wrench.

She picked up her sketchpad and the backpack she'd brought with her, and without speaking another word, left him standing underneath the bowing branches of the massive oak tree.

––––––

BROOKLYN ENTERED the house she'd lived in for the first twenty-one years of her life. The mere act of stepping over the threshold usually filled her with a sense of peace, but today it felt different, as if the lid on a jar had been ripped off and the secrets she'd held close had been laid bare. All without her permission.

Thinking back on how many times over the years she'd come close to showing her parents her drawings, yet had decided against it because she just wasn't ready to divulge that part of her life with them, caused her breath to hitch. A dull ache continued to throb within her chest at the thought of Reid so carelessly taking the choice out of her hands.

She set her purse on the end table next to the sofa, then made her way up the stairs, the climb becoming more laborious with every step she took. She walked down the short hallway to her parents' room and noticed the door was slightly opened. She knocked twice on the scarred wood.

"Knock, knock," Brooklyn called.

"Who's there," came her dad's raspy voice.

A nostalgic warmth rushed through her veins. It's how he used to greet her when he'd come home in the evening when she was a little girl.

She walked into the room to find him sitting up in the worn leather recliner he'd started sleeping in when it became too hard for him to breathe while lying down. He patted the arm of the chair.

"Hey, Daddy," Brooklyn said, settling on the chair's wide arm and dropping a kiss on the top of his head. "How's it going?"

"Good. Good," he answered. He then thwarted her plan to ease into the discussion about her illustrations by adding, "I saw those pictures you drew."

"So did I," her mother called from the hallway, seconds before walking into the room. She came over and placed a kiss on Brooklyn's forehead, then gave her shoulder a playful slap. "How come I'm just finding out my daughter is this magnificent artist?"

"I wouldn't say all that," Brooklyn said.

"Oh, please. The pictures Reid showed us are gorgeous. He also told us about the comic book you're drawing for him."

He was quite the damn chatterbox, wasn't he?

"It's for the kickoff party to the foundation his family is starting," Brooklyn explained. "And I wish he hadn't shown you."

The moment she said the words she wished she could take them back. Both her parents looked at her as if she'd slapped them in the face.

"It's not that I'm sorry you now know about my art," she clarified. "I'm just sorry that I wasn't the one to tell you."

"Well, I'm sorry about that too. Why didn't you tell us?" her mother asked. "How long have you been drawing these comic book characters?"

Brooklyn closed her eyes. She'd anticipated their questions and had tried to think of answers that wouldn't come across as her intentionally hiding such an important part of her identity from her parents for all these years. But there were no good answers, because that's exactly what she'd done.

"Since I was about ten years old," Brooklyn finally answered. "And, honestly, I don't know why I never said anything." She moved to the cushioned window seat of the large bay window and pulled her legs up under her. She grabbed one of the throw pillows and cradled it in her lap. "Well, in a way, I *do* know why I never said anything, but it won't make any sense."

"Brooklyn—"

"There's something I need to tell you. Both of you," she said, her eyes darting between her mother and father. She fidgeted with the misshapen fringe that bordered the pillow, twisting the threads around her finger.

"Well, what is it?" her mom asked.

The emotion clogging her throat made it nearly impossible for her to swallow, the weight of the secret she'd been carrying for the past six months bearing down on her very soul. She peered over at her dad's sallow face and had to hold back a sob.

"It was my fault," Brooklyn finally admitted, her voice barely a whisper. "What happened with that final contract, it was my fault."

"What are you talking about?" her father asked.

"Remember when everything fell apart, and I said that I forgot to sign off on the surety bond? I didn't forget. I knew I hadn't signed off on it before the project ever started. I kept putting it off." Brooklyn sucked in a deep breath. It was as if she physically felt the weight of the secret she'd held lifting from her shoulders. "I used to do that all the time," she continued. "I would intentionally let some things slide— things that were usually no big deal.

"But I didn't realize the general contractor had taken the indemnification clause out of the contract," she said. "When he filed for bankruptcy out of the blue, I knew that we didn't have a leg to stand on. LeBlanc & Sons was left holding the bag because of me," she finished on a sob. "I'm sorry."

"But why?" her mother asked.

She hunched her shoulders. "Because I wanted to prove that I wasn't perfect," Brooklyn explained. "All my life I always heard this one thing: find what you're good at and give it one hundred percent. Well, I didn't want to be good at working on construction sites. I wanted *my* thing to be comics," she said. "I thought if I could show you all that I wasn't as good at my job at LeBlanc & Sons, then maybe you would be okay with me eventually leaving the business. I know it was stupid and I am so, so sorry," she said. "I never meant for this to happen."

She dropped her head and studied the paisley design on the worn pillow.

"It's okay."

Brooklyn's head popped up at her father's craggily spoken words.

"What?" she gasped. "How can you say that? You lost your business because of me."

"Brooklyn, do you think your father would have been able to continue working?" her mother asked. "He was already going to close the business. He should have done so a long time ago."

"Still, I took the choice out of your hands."

Her father shook his head. "Don't apologize. And don't blame...yourself."

"But it *is* my fault," she insisted.

"I'm sorry," her father said. "Sorry I put so much...pressure on you."

"No." Brooklyn shook her head. "You weren't putting pressure on me. You were trying to teach me how to have a strong work ethic. You never have to apologize for that."

"What about this fellowship thing?" her dad asked.

She shook her head. "Don't worry. I'm not going."

"Reid said you have several that you're considering," her mother spoke over her. "Do you no longer want to go?"

Brooklyn covered her face with her hands and broke down in tears, her shoulders shaking with her silent sobs. She felt her mother's arms close around her.

"Do you want to go or don't you?" her mother whispered.

"Yes," she muttered through her tears. She dragged her hands down her face, then looked up at both her parents. "I want to go so badly. I want it more than anything I've ever wanted."

"Then you'd better get to work on the applications," her mother said.

"I can't." She shook her head. "I can't leave you to take care of Dad alone."

"No. You're not using your father as an excuse."

"But—"

"No," her mother said more firmly.

"But I just started my job. I can't take four weeks off."

"Have you asked Alex?" her father said. "Ask him. I'll bet you he'll...he'll be happy to let you go to Chicago."

Brooklyn wiped at her eyes. She knew her father was probably telling the truth. In the couple of months she'd worked for Alex Holmes, he'd proven to be one of the most generous men she'd ever met. If she asked, she'd bet all the money in her bank account that Alex would give her the time off with his blessing.

"Even if Alex Holmes doesn't give you the time off, you can't let that stop you." Her mother finally sat down next to her on the window seat. "You only get this one life, baby. You can't let anything stop you from fulfilling your dreams. Send in those applications. If you don't get in, at least you'll know you tried. And if you do?" She shrugged. "You and your new boss will just have to work something out. Or you'll find another job. But that's all that position at Holmes Construction is, Brooklyn. It's a job." Her mother grabbed hold of her hands and held them tight. "What you can do with these; this talent you've been given? *This* is what really matters."

Brooklyn wiped at her eyes again and readily accepted

her mother's warm hug. At this very moment, it was everything she needed.

She walked over to her dad and wrapped her arms around him, holding him a little too tight, but unable to let go for a long, long time. Brooklyn left them with a promise to send off the application for the writing intensive in Chicago tonight, along with an apology for allowing the deadline on so many others to pass her by.

A few minutes later, she walked out of her parents' front door and stopped dead in her tracks.

Reid stood at the base of the steps, his hands in his pockets, contrition etched across his handsome face.

"I'm sorry," he said by way of greeting.

"So am I," Brooklyn answered in reply.

She continued down the steps and walked right up to him, wrapping her arms around his solid frame.

"I'm still upset that you went behind my back," she said. "But I understand why you did it." She looked up at him. "I should have told them about my hopes of becoming an illustrator a long time ago."

"I shouldn't have said anything to your parents without your permission," he said.

"No, you shouldn't have. But your heart was in the right place."

"It's with you, Brooklyn. My heart is one hundred percent with you."

Brooklyn looked up at him and saw nothing but love in his eyes. "I love you," she said.

Reid's eyes slid closed. "Thank God," he said on a shaky breath. "Because I don't know how I would survive if you didn't." He bent his head and captured her lips in the sweetest kiss. "I love you so much. I didn't know a person could feel like this. I never want to *not* feel like this." He pressed another swift kiss to her lips. "You've awakened something in me that I now realize I can't live without."

Brooklyn slid her hand behind his head and pulled his face down to her. "Then don't," she said before sealing her mouth to his.

EPILOGUE

THEY WALKED up the steps of his parents' home, its porch sporting a fresh coat of white paint courtesy of his dad and his Navy buddies. Reid could hear the raucous sounds of his family just on the other side of the door, the sounds of a typical Sunday afternoon.

"Are you ready for this?" Brooklyn asked as she took his hand.

Reid nodded. "I'm ready."

For years he'd lived in fear of his siblings finding out about his learning disorder, but Reid was done with hiding. He'd decided today would be the day he revealed it all, both his dyslexia and his plans to leave Holmes Construction.

When they entered the house, his nephew immediately flew to Brooklyn's side, catching her by the hand and dragging her over to where he'd spread out several comics on the coffee table in the living room. Griffin and Mackenna were hunched over an iPad, while Ezra sat next to them on the sofa, the TV remote in his hand, Saints football on the screen.

Indina came into the living room and clapped her

hands. "Dinner's ready," she called. She turned to Reid. "Hey, when did you get here?"

"Just a minute ago," Reid said. "Before we eat, I need to—"

"Nope. Nah uh. Whatever you need to do can wait until after we eat. I don't want the cornbread getting cold."

Reid rolled his eyes at his sister's bossiness, but welcomed the short reprieve. It wouldn't hurt to get some food in him before he shared his news. The entire family sat elbow-to-elbow around the dining table, with the kids, Brooklyn and Indina having to use chairs from the smaller kitchen table. After his dad said grace, platters filled with baked chicken, mustard greens, candied yams, and cornbread made their way around the table. The chatter followed its usual course, with each of them talking about what they'd been up to the week before and what they had planned for the week ahead.

"You really put your foot in these yams, Willow," Clark Holmes boasted from the head of the table. "Diane would be proud."

"It was one of her favorite recipes," Willow said. "They'll never taste as good as hers, but I'm happy to have gotten close." She looked over at Harrison. "Should we tell them?"

Harrison set his fork down and shrugged his shoulders, a look of resignation clouding his features.

Reid regarded his brother and sister-in-law, a weird feeling settling in his gut.

Willow moved her plate out of the way and folded her hands on the table. "We have something to share."

"You're pregnant!" Indina said.

Reid felt a measure of hope at the smile Willow sent his sister, but it didn't reach her eyes. In fact, her eyes held a sadness that made the hair on the back of Reid's neck stand on end.

"No," Willow said. "We're not pregnant. We—" she looked at Harrison, then back at the rest of them seated at the table. "We've decided to take a break."

Other than Liliana's annoyed huff, the announcement was met with silence.

"Don't everyone speak at once," Harrison deadpanned.

"But what does that even mean?" Indina asked.

"She means they're separating," Lily said. Then she threw down her napkin and excused herself from the table.

"Lily—" Willow called.

"Are you serious?" Indina interrupted. "What in the hell is the matter with the two of you? Can't you get your shit together?"

"It's not forever," Athens said. He looked at his dad. "You promised, it's not forever."

"No, baby, it's not," Willow said.

"Maybe," Harrison interjected.

Willow turned to him and the hurt Reid saw on both their faces was enough to make his stomach turn.

"This is only temporary," Willow stated. "We just feel that maybe a little space will help us to see things more clearly."

"That's the dumbest thing I've ever heard," his sister said.

"Indina." Harrison's voice brooked no further discussion. "We didn't share this news because we wanted opinions, we just wanted you all to know what's going on. Now can we get back to eating Sunday dinner?"

Everyone returned to their plates, but with much less enthusiasm than they had at the beginning of the meal.

Since the mood around the table had taken such an awful turn, Reid decided to put even more gas on the fire.

"And here I thought *my* news would be the thing to put frowns on everyone's faces," he said.

"What news?" Harrison asked.

Reid glanced at Brooklyn, who nodded. He then looked around at the faces of his family members. "I'm leaving Holmes Construction," he finally announced.

Where Willow and Harrison's news was met with silence, his was met with a barrage of questions. But they weren't the questions Reid had anticipated. Instead of being upset, his family was curious. At first, his father thought he was leaving the city altogether. Clark Holmes's broad shoulders wilted in noticeable relief once Reid assured him that wasn't the case.

"Are you going to a competitor?" Indina asked.

"No, it's nothing like that. Actually, I'm going into business with my friend Anthony."

As he explained the gist of the app-based business, the expressions on the faces of the people around the table became more and more impressed. By the time he was done, Ezra had already signed up to become one of their beta testers.

"Damn, that was easier than I thought," Reid joked. Too bad he hadn't gotten to the tough part yet. "There's something else," Reid continued. *This* was the thing he'd been dreading. Everyone looked expectantly at him. "I have a request when it comes to Mom's foundation. I want to make sure one scholarship is set aside for a student with a learning disability. Because, well, *I* have a learning disability, and I know how much harder it is for someone dealing with one to make it through life."

This time there was silence. Complete and total silence.

After several moments passed, his father said, "I wondered how long it would take you to finally tell the rest of the family."

Reid's head whipped around to the head of the table. "You knew?"

"Of course I knew. You told your mother, didn't you?"

"I didn't tell her, but she found out," Reid admitted. "I think she sensed something was up from early on."

"And you think she would keep that from me?"

Reid didn't know what to say. His dad knew all this time, yet he'd kept it a secret, giving Reid the chance to share it in his own time. Damn, he loved that man.

"I think it's a wonderful idea—the scholarship, I mean," Willow said. She came around the table and wrapped Reid up in a hug, holding on extra tight. He needed to hold onto her just as tightly.

"Thanks," he said, pressing a kiss to her temple. "Everything's going to work out," Reid whispered into her ear.

His sister-in-law gave him a sad smile, before announcing that she needed to check on Liliana.

Several hours later, Reid and Brooklyn were back at his apartment. They sat on the sofa, Brooklyn's back nestled against his front. She was like an anchor, keeping him steady and grounded on this chaotic day.

"You're quiet," she said. She looked back over her shoulder. "You're thinking about Harrison and Willow?"

"Yeah." Reid released a weary sigh. "The signs have been there since the summer, but I never thought I'd see the day those two decided to call it quits."

"But they haven't. A separation doesn't automatically lead to divorce. Maybe it'll work out for them."

"God, I hope you're right," Reid said. "Willow has been a part of my life since I was in the sixth grade. I can't imagine this family without her." He tightened his hold, burying his face in the crook of Brooklyn's neck. "Just like I can't imagine my life without you," he said.

"You don't have to." Brooklyn turned and cradled his cheek in her palm. She pressed the other palm to his chest, directly over his heart. "I'm here. And even if I do go to Chicago, or Georgia, or wherever, know that I'll always be right here." She pressed her lips against his. "Always."

ALSO BY FARRAH ROCHON

The Holmes Brothers

Set in New Orleans, the Holmes Brothers series follows the lives of the men of the Holmes family as they find love in one of the world's most romantic cities.

Deliver Me

Release Me

Rescue Me

Chase Me

Trust Me

———

Moments in Maplesville

Visit the sexy, sultry, small southern town of Maplesville in my *Moments in Maplesville* novella series.

A Perfect Holiday Fling (*Callie & Stefan*)

A Little Bit Naughty (*Jada & Mason*)

Just A Little Taste (*Kiera & Trey*)

I Dare You (*Stefanie & Dustin*)

All You Can Handle (*Sonny & Ian*)

Any Way You Want It (*Nyree & Dale*)

Any Time You Need Me (*Aubrey & Sam*)

Visit my BOOKS page to see my entire backlist!

*Turn the page to read an excerpt from **Chase Me**, Indina and Griffin's story!*

CHASE ME

BOOK FOUR IN THE HOLMES BROTHERS SERIES

WHAT WAS SHE THINKING?

The last thing Indina Holmes needs in her life is three days on the open seas with her loving but nosy family. But that's exactly what she's in store for her when her brother guilts her into joining the Holmes family reunion cruise. When she needs a cabin mate at the last minute, her only option is the co-worker she's been sleeping with for the past year. Now, she just has to keep her family from trying to play matchmaker.

WHAT WAS HE THINKING?

For the past eight months, Griffin Sims has pretended to be okay with the co-worker-with-benefits arrangement he's had going with Indina, but he wants more than just her body. He wants a real relationship. Indina's invitation to join her on a cruise is exactly the opportunity Griffin has been looking for to prove to the woman who has been sharing his bed that it's time for her to share her heart.

CHAPTER ONE

Squinting against the sun's vibrant rays peeking annoyingly through the mahogany custom-made blinds, Indina Holmes executed a full body stretch across the silky 1000 thread count sheets. Her previously tense muscles were now loose and languid after the early morning workout she'd just been subjected to in this bed. Thank God for that particular kind of workout. She'd needed it like a man roaming the desert needed water.

It had been dark when she'd arrived nearly an hour ago, but judging by the dawn's insistent intrusion on her post-coital relaxation, it was past time for her to go.

"I don't want to," Indina half groaned, half whined as her eyes focused on the ceiling fan twirling lazily above her.

You can't stay in this bed all day.

Especially not today, when the culmination of countless meetings, hours of field research, and more time at her design desk than Indina wanted to think about, would finally be put forth before the executive committee responsible for several new federal and state buildings that would be built in the city of New Orleans. Her team's performance today would determine if they landed a billion-dollar contract.

And just like that, the tension was back. Too bad she didn't have time to go for another round between the sheets.

Indina sucked in an uneasy breath as she glanced over at the digital clock on the nightstand.

Shit.

If she didn't get out of here soon she would be late for work. She cursed herself for not bringing her work clothes with her when she left her house earlier this morning.

With one last stretch across the king-size bed, Indina

pushed herself up into a sitting position. She could hear the shower's powerful jets coming from just beyond the bathroom door, and cursed herself again. Five minutes in that shower would get rid of the lingering tension in her muscles, with or without the water.

Tossing her legs over the edge of the bed, she walked over to the sitting area and picked up her bra and panties from the chair where she normally dropped them whenever she was here, which had been more often than usual in the past month. Between work and family, her stress levels were at an all-time high. Thank the ever-loving Lord she had a reliable outlet to expend the nervous energy constantly flowing through her bloodstream these days.

Indina slipped her panties on and threaded her arms through the bra's straps, clasping it in the back. Just as she reached for the cotton shirtdress she'd thrown on before coming over, her cell phone rang. She walked back over to where she'd left it on the nightstand, and rolled her eyes when she noticed her brother's name on the screen.

With a sigh, Indina sat on the edge of the bed and swept her thumb across the green button.

"Is there a reason you're calling me before eight a.m.?" she spoke into the phone.

"Good morning to you too," her older brother replied.

She ignored the reprimand in his voice.

"What do you need, Harrison? And there had better be a good reason for you calling me at this time of the morning."

"I need the final head count for the Holmes family reunion cruise. Are you in or are you out? And before you answer that, I want you to think about your newly widowed father and how heartbroken he would be if his only daughter did not participate in this reunion."

She released a disgusted breath. "I hate you so much."

"That was very convincing. It's a good thing I know you don't mean it."

"I mean it," she said.

"Would you just give me the go-ahead to mark you down on the list so I can send the names to the travel agent?" Her brother's harassed voice made her feel marginally better. But only marginally.

Indina massaged the bridge of her nose. She loved her family, but these days she could only take them in small doses. She visited her dad at least once during the week—even more if she could—and tried to make as many Sunday dinners as possible, but that was only a few hours out of her day, and once her brothers started eating, there was very little talking. Could she survive being stuck on a cruise ship with them for three days without going straight-up insane?

And it wasn't limited to her pesky brothers this time around. The entire Holmes clan would be there. Her late Uncle Wesley's three sons, Alexander, Elijah and Tobias, along with their wives and their ever-growing brood of children were all going. And if her boys would be there, Indina knew her Aunt Margo would be there too, along with her husband, Gerald Mitchell.

There would be Holmeses galore. That poor cruise ship had no idea what it was in store for.

"Indina!" Harrison's voice startled her. "Are you coming on the cruise or not? Wait, let me rephrase that. Are you going to break your father's heart or not?"

"Stop it with the guilt trip."

"I'm just saying."

"I've never been on a cruise before," she pointed out. "What if I get seasick?"

"You can wear one of those patches behind your ear.

And if that doesn't work there's medicine you can take," Harrison said. "I'll tell Eli to bring you some."

Great. That's what she got for having a cousin who was a doctor, and who also happened to be married to a doctor.

"You got any more excuses you need me to shoot down before I head to my office?" her brother asked.

"I really do hate you right now," Indina said. She rubbed her temple as she came to terms with the fact that there was no way out of this. "Fine, I'll come on the damn cruise."

"I'd already marked you down as a yes," Harrison replied. "I just called to make sure *you* knew that you were going."

"Asshole," she said.

"I love you too. By the way, I put you in the cabin with Lily and Jasmine."

"Lily and Jasmine?" Indina sat up straight. "You do realize I'm forty-two years old, don't you? Why would I want to room with a couple of teenagers?"

No, make that a teenager and a pre-teen. Her cousin Alex's daughter, Jasmine, was only twelve.

"Because everyone else is paired up and the cabin rates are based on double occupancy," he explained. "If I didn't put you in the girls' room you'd have to pay an upcharge because you're a single."

A single. As if it was some kind of diseased designation she wore on her chest.

"And just why would you think I would be alone?" Indina asked.

"Why wouldn't I?" The incredulousness in his voice made her want to slap him through the phone. "When was the last time you brought anyone around?"

Indina ignored that question. It had been nearly two

years since she'd been in a bring-him-over-to-meet-the-family kind of relationship. That didn't mean her brother had to throw it in her face. Just for that, she would pluck his insensitive ass right between the eyebrows next time she saw him.

"I won't have the cabin for myself," Indina said. "I'm bringing someone."

"Who?" Harrison asked.

"None of your business."

"I need the name for the travel agent."

"I'll text you the name later. Now leave me alone. I need to get going."

The shower stopped the minute she disconnected the call. Moments later, the bathroom door opened and Griffin Sims walked out, wiping his face with a plush cranberry-colored towel. There was another towel wrapped around his waist, hanging low on his hips. His chiseled dark brown chest glistened with specks of moisture. Indina tracked a water droplet that traveled down his torso to the smattering of curly hair that trailed from his belly button to below the towel.

She pulled her bottom lip between her teeth and damn near whimpered.

Griffin stopped short when he spotted her.

"You're still here?"

"I'm sorry," Indina said, rising from where she'd sat on the edge of his bed. "I got a phone call that I had to take just as I started getting dressed."

"No need to apologize. It's just that you're usually gone by the time I get out of the shower."

Her eyes roamed over his muscular back and shoulders as he walked over to the dresser. She didn't know where he found the time to go to the gym, but she appreciated the way he took care of his body.

"Are you still nervous about today?" Griffin asked.

He turned to her, holding the pair of heather gray boxer briefs he'd retrieved from the dresser. He dropped the towel and Indina couldn't hold back the whimper this time.

She had explored the heavy weight between his legs with her tongue just an hour ago, yet her mouth still watered at the sight of it. She just stood there and marveled at his beauty as he pulled the briefs up his well-toned legs.

"Indina," Griffin called.

She blinked several times. "Wait. What?"

A knowing grin curled up the side of his mouth. "I asked if you were still nervous about today?"

"A little, but at least I'm no longer tense."

"Happy I could help with that," he said. His deep chuckle reverberated along her nerve endings, straight down to that spot between her legs he'd pleasured this morning.

Over the last eight months, she'd relied on Griffin for that particular kind of pleasurable help on a regular basis. They'd met a little over a year ago, when Indina decided to move away from residential interior design and concentrate on the more lucrative industrial sector. She began freelancing with the structural engineering firm where Griffin worked after one of the owners sought her out.

Griffin was the lead engineer on the very first project she worked on with Sykes-Wilcox. The physical attraction had been there from the moment she walked into a conference room and saw him braced over a set of blueprints, his shirtsleeves rolled up on his strong arms. Indina decided not to act on that attraction until several months later, after she learned through the office grapevine that Griffin was divorced and not necessarily looking for a relationship.

She knew all about that. Not the being divorced part, but being burnt out on relationships?

Hell yes, she knew about that.

But there were only so many *Top Ten Self-Pleasuring Tips* articles a girl could be expected to read. And she'd read them. *All* of them. She needed the real deal. The way Indina saw it she and Griffin were in the perfect position to provide each other with some much needed sexual relief.

She could still remember how her fingers had trembled as she'd typed the text, asking Griffin if he was up for a little casual, no-strings-attached sex. She wasn't sure how she would have handled working with him if he had turned down her bold invitation to meet her at the Bourbon Orleans Hotel in the French Quarter.

He'd arrived at the hotel even before she did, and with that one afternoon, they'd embarked upon a coworkers with benefits arrangement that never failed to leave her body satisfied and her mind free of relationship drama.

Her phone beeped. It was a text from Harrison with the travel agent's name and phone number, and a reminder to send the name of the person who would be sharing her cabin.

Indina looked over at Griffin. He'd just put on a gingham blue dress shirt, but hadn't bothered to button it up yet. Her mouth watered again at the expanse of exposed skin.

He looked up from the neckties he'd been contemplating.

"Everything okay?" he asked.

Indina nodded and decided not to ask the question that had been on the tip of her tongue. Hadn't she just acknowledged that what she and Griffin had going was perfect? Why would she jeopardize it by asking him to come with her on this damn cruise?

She slipped her dress over her head, then picked up her wristlet and keys from where she'd dropped them on the dresser.

In a real relationship this is where they would kiss each other goodbye. But this wasn't a real relationship. It wasn't how she and Griffin rolled.

And that was just fine with her.

"See you in a few hours," Indina said, gripping the handle on the bedroom door. "I'll lock the front door on my way out."

———

Read Indina and Griffin's story! Pick up your copy of Chase Me.

ABOUT THE AUTHOR

A native of south Louisiana, Farrah Rochon officially began her writing career while waiting in between classes in the student lounge at Xavier University of Louisiana. After earning her Bachelors of Science degree and a Masters of Arts from Southeastern Louisiana University, Farrah decided to pursue her lifelong dream of becoming a published novelist. She was named *Shades of Romance Magazine*'s Best New Author of 2007. Her debut novel garnered rave reviews, earning Farrah several SORMAG Readers' Choice Awards. *I'll Catch You*, the second book in her New York Sabers series for Harlequin Kimani, was a 2012 RITA ® Award finalist. Yours Forever, the third book in her Bayou Dreams series, is a 2015 RITA® Award finalist.

When she is not writing in her favorite coffee shop, Farrah spends most of her time reading her favorite romance novels or seeing as many Broadway shows as possible. An admitted sports fanatic, Farrah feeds her addiction to football by watching New Orleans Saints games on Sunday afternoons.

Connect with me online:

www.farrahrochon.com
farrah@farrahrochon.com

31347442R00190

Made in the USA
Columbia, SC
02 November 2018